IT TAKES A THIEF

IT TAKES A THIEF

SLOANE STEELE

W RLDWIDE

TORONTO • NEW YORK • LONDON
AMSTERDAM • PARIS • SYDNEY • HAMBURG
STOCKHOLM • ATHENS • TOKYO • MILAN
MADRID • WARSAW • BUDAPEST • AUCKLAND

To all the fans of *Leverage* who have been writing fanfic and
wanting more bad guys who make the best good guys.

WORLDWIDE™

Recycling programs
for this product may
not exist in your area.

ISBN-13: 978-1-335-53004-2

It Takes a Thief

First published in 2021 by Carina Press, an imprint of Harlequin
Enterprises ULC. This edition published in 2021 with revised text.

Copyright © 2021 by Shannyn Schroeder
Copyright © 2021 by Shannyn Schroeder, revised text edition

For questions and comments about the quality of this book,
please contact us at CustomerService@Harlequin.com.

Harlequin Enterprises ULC
22 Adelaide St. West, 40th Floor
Toronto, Ontario M5H 4E3, Canada
www.ReaderService.com

Printed in U.S.A.

IT TAKES A THIEF

ONE

December

JARED WAVED AT the doorman as he made his way to the elevator. He spent enough time here that no one expected him to sign in. When Mia first moved in, they stopped him every time, worried that he was an overbearing lover. The thought still made him cringe. Explaining that they were cousins gave him a pass to go up to her apartment without question.

When the door swung open, Mia looked surprised to see him. "What are you doing here?"

"Happy birthday." He bent and kissed her cheek. "Did you think I would let you spend your thirtieth alone?"

"Who says I plan to be alone?"

He glanced around the empty room, taking note of the open bottle of wine on the table and single glass beside it, and raised an eyebrow. The woman had lived barely above hermit status for years. She worked, spent time with her mother, and came home to a tastefully and artfully decorated condo. Alone. She'd been gun-shy ever since her engagement ended in a very public humiliation. Her face was free of makeup and she had her thick black hair tied back. She wouldn't let a new man see her bedtime routine, even though she still looked regal. Mia was like her mother in that way.

She huffed. "Fine. So I'm alone. I have things to do. Plans to make."

He took off his coat and hung it on the rack. Then he turned and handed Mia a wrapped gift.

"You know you didn't have to get me anything."

"Until you find some guy that will spoil you, I reserve the right. Everyone should have a gift on their birthday."

She tugged at the ribbon and slid her finger under the tape.

"Hey, you know you don't have to save the paper, right?"

"Leave me alone."

It was the same exchange they had every year, at her birthday and at Christmas. Mia was meticulous in her approach to everything. Jared preferred to dive in.

Moments later, she held up the thin diamond bracelet. "It's beautiful. Thank you."

She placed it back in the box and went to the liquor cabinet. After she handed him a glass, they settled on the couch in front of the marble fireplace where a fire burned.

He picked up the open bottle and poured himself some white wine. "Are you slumming today? Since when you do you drink regular wine? No vintage Dom for your birthday?"

"There is nothing regular about Domaine Leflaive, thank you very much."

"So what has you so busy you're not celebrating with a party?"

She sniffed. "As if. That's the last thing I would do."

He set his glass on the table without drinking any. "I

thought things had gotten better for you. You've been making the society circuit again."

Their fathers' crimes had taken a toll on Mia and he wished he could do something to repair the damage done. Both her mother and his felt like pariahs in the society they'd been a part of long before they'd gotten married. In his personal life, he hadn't taken a hit, mostly because he was a man. Professionally, however, his dreams had been crushed.

"I've been to functions and other than the occasional whisper by the same catty trolls I've dealt with my whole life, it has been better. But no big celebrations with me in the spotlight."

"Other than sitting around in your pajamas and drinking alone, what are you doing?" He picked up his glass and drank the wine, even though he'd prefer whiskey.

She reached across the table and flipped open a file folder. He knew immediately what it was. The faces of men they'd grown up around, men who were their fathers' confidants and friends. "You're really doing this?"

Years ago Mia had come to him with a plan to get back at the men who'd gotten rich with their fathers by bilking innocent people out of their life savings. She couldn't go after her own father or his because they'd fled the country. But she wanted to do something proactive.

"Did you think I was kidding? You should know better."

"I do. Part of me hoped it was a whim you'd plan out and never act on."

She laughed. "I would never waste my time. And

now that I'm thirty, I have the funds to put everything in play."

Their mothers were smart women. They'd made their husbands sign prenups, which protected the Washington family fortune. Mia's and Jared's inheritances were safe from the federal government. Their mothers also made sure the money wouldn't be wasted on immature whims, so they had to wait until their thirtieth birthdays to access the money.

"Let me help."

"It's dangerous. If I get caught, I don't want you going down with me."

That had always been her argument every time they discussed this. "Then we won't get caught. Wait until my birthday. I'll be able to foot half the bill for the plan."

"I've already waited five years."

"Then six more months won't matter." He was well aware of how long it had been. He'd just graduated law school and all of his plans and dreams had been sucked into the black hole of his father's dirty deeds. Who the hell would hire the spawn of a criminal? "It'll give us time to find the right people to carry this out."

She sipped her wine and studied him. His offer intrigued her, but Mia was not someone who liked to give up control.

"I can be very useful. I have connections you'll need and have no idea how to get." Once his law career had gone down the drain, he'd taken all the tools his father had instilled in him, and he'd learned to play in all the gray areas of the world. And he was damn good at it.

He'd embraced their fathers' teachings about business and people. While Mia had bucked against the lessons in manipulation, he'd made a career from it.

"I don't want to use people who know us, who we are. Word will spread and our anonymity will be lost."

"*You* should know better," he said, throwing her own words back at her. "The players I know on the dark web never reveal their identities. It's a given that we all use aliases."

She sipped more wine. "All right, then. Let's talk about who we'll need. A thief, obviously."

"A hacker, someone who can get past security systems." Immediately he thought of Data. He'd used her services many times over the last few years. Efficient and relatively cheap. "I have someone I can reach out to when the time is right."

Mia crossed the room and returned with a small notebook and pen. She made a few notes. "I've been looking for a forger, but I haven't found anyone I like."

It figured she would start with the forger. Art was her area of comfort.

He chuckled. "You don't have to like them."

"I'm aware. I meant I don't like the quality of their work in conjunction with their attitudes. It's as if making a forgery isn't enough. They want to make it *better*."

"I'll put some feelers out for a thief while you continue to hunt for a forger." He leaned back on the couch and drank the rest of his wine.

She paused in taking notes, tapping her pen on the pad. "What about selling the artwork once we have it?"

"I can definitely find buyers."

Her jaw muscle pulsed. It was a small twitch, but he

knew his cousin. He leaned forward, resting his elbows on his knees. "Is there a problem?"

"It suddenly feels like you're taking over. I've spent years gathering information and planning this, and now you walk in and want to handle all of the active pieces."

He sighed and shook his head slightly. "We each have a skill set. You've utilized yours masterminding this plan. Let me use mine to help you carry it out."

She didn't seem convinced. He reached over and laid a hand over hers. "This is my legacy, too."

Sometimes it seemed like she forgot he shared the same guilt she felt.

"Fine. But I make all final decisions. This is what I have so far." Spreading the images from the folder across the coffee table, she ticked off the list of twelve— men who not only aided and abetted their fathers, but who also got rich off the same scheme.

"How do you see this working?" he asked.

"I'm still developing the list of artwork they have. We'll only get one shot, so I want to choose the piece from each of them that will hurt. I'll commission a forgery. Then the thief goes in, swaps the forgery for the original and we sell the original."

"And then?"

"We use the money to make some reparations for what they did. We might not be able to repay every family, but we can make a difference."

He smiled. That was the cousin he knew—all cold steel on the outside but a soft, mushy center. "And how do you decide who gets the money?"

"I haven't figured that piece out yet. I have a list of names, people who came forward and publicly criticized our fathers for what they did. That is one way you can help. They can't know it's coming from us and you can dig around and see who needs the most help. Prioritize who needs what."

Jared nodded and considered who he could have do background checks on the victims. He picked up Mia's notebook and saw a list on the inside cover. It took a minute, but he recognized the lessons. Their fathers had said these mantras as if they were motivational quotes:

1. Spending money to get the best is worth it 99% of the time.
2. Endearing yourself to others makes it easier to manipulate them.
3. Loyalty to the right people is vital to success.

He'd assumed that Mia had never paid attention to the rules for business. She'd been an art history major after all. She preferred the pretty things in life over the gritty side of making money.

He pointed at the list. "Why have this here?"

"Because I plan to use their life lessons against them." She splayed her hands across the photos. "I'm going to teach all of them—including our fathers—Mama's lesson: actions carry consequences."

Karma might be a bitch, but it had nothing on Mia. This summer was going to be interesting.

Green: I know it's the holidays, but are you available?

Data: I'm always available for you.

As soon as she hit send, she cringed.

Green: Interesting. I hadn't realized we'd arrived at that point in our relationship.

Data: I'm available for WORK. You know what I meant.

Green: Hmm... I think it might've been a Freudian slip.

Data: And I think your ego is too big. What kind of job?

Green: I'll send you photos. I need you to dig up some dirt.

Data: Ooooo... Blackmail. Intriguing.

Green: I said nothing about blackmail.

Data: It was in the subtext. I read between the lines.

Green: It's all right for you to read between the lines but I'm not allowed?

Data: Glad we're clear. :)

She waited for the link to pop up and scanned the information he sent.

Data: What's your timeline?

Green: Soon. But given the holidays, I can wait the week.

Data: Got it. I'll let you know when I have info.

Audrey closed her laptop with a smile. Things usually quieted down for her over the holidays. She was grateful to have anything pop up, and the fact that Mr. Green had a job was all the better. The man always paid well, and at this point, she needed every penny she could get. After shoving her computer in her bag, she bundled up against the cold for her walk to the bus stop.

Before leaving the apartment, she glanced at her bedroom door. She'd been living here with Misty for almost three months, but over the last couple of weeks, she'd had the feeling that her room wasn't secure. Misty said she hadn't stepped foot in the room since Audrey moved in, but her roommate often had guests. The sleazy kind she brought home from her job at the strip club.

Her equipment was all she had of value and most of Misty's "dates" wouldn't have a clue what to do with any of it; she just didn't want creepy guys touching her stuff, so until she came up with a better lock, she carried her laptop with her. She patted her pocket to double-check that her present for Gram was still there. This was their first Christmas apart. Not really apart, but not living together. Three months ago she'd made the painful decision to sell everything she had and pour every penny into getting Gram the care she needed.

Audrey couldn't take care of her anymore.

The assisted living facility cost more than Audrey made, but Gram deserved the best care possible. So here she was on Christmas Eve trekking on the bus in twenty-degree weather to share Christmas with Gram.

The dark sky made it feel closer to midnight than din-nertime.

Horizons looked like any other residence on the out-side. Kind of stately but bland. Inside, they at least put in some effort to be festive. They had a Christmas tree in the corner of the lobby as well as a menorah on the reception desk. Audrey signed in without chatting with the receptionist and went straight to Gram's room.

Room. That was funny. Gram actually had more of an apartment than she did. Gram's place had a small kitchen as well as a living room—bedroom combo. Gram answered the door.

"Audrey? What are you doing here?"

"Hi, Gram. How are you? I thought we'd spend Christmas Eve together like we do every year."

"I don't know that I'm done being mad at you for sticking me here," Gram said as she walked away from the door.

Audrey took it as an invitation. She unwrapped her scarf and laid her jacket and bag on a side table near the door. Pulling the gift out, she said, "I brought you a gift."

"Pfft. Hope you weren't counting on anything. I'm like a prisoner here. I couldn't go shopping." She settled in her recliner facing the TV.

"They told me they do trips to the mall." In all like-lihood, Gram had probably forgotten. That had been happening more and more. "Here."

She accepted the small package and peeled at the paper. It wasn't much, but Audrey had chosen a box of Gram's favorite chocolates, ones Gram typically only indulged in for special occasions. The doctor had said that small reminders might help prompt her memory.

"What's this?" She studied the box for a minute and then practically threw it at the table beside her. "I hate chocolate. Makes me sick."

"No, it doesn't, Gram. Remember? These are the ones filled with booze. They're your favorite."

She sniffed, a look of irritation on her face. "I never drink."

Audrey sighed and sat on the edge of the loveseat. So much for holidays with family. They fell into silence, except for the blaring of the TV showing reruns of *General Hospital*. Audrey longed to talk with Gram like they used to do.

Gram suddenly turned and looked at her. "Tina? What the hell are you doing here? I told you to stay away."

"Gram, it's me, Audrey."

Gram rose and jabbed a finger at her. "Don't you lie to me. Get out!"

Audrey's throat closed. This was why she'd been forced to bring Gram here. There had been more days of confusion than reality. Audrey missed Gram.

"Have a good Christmas," she said quietly as she picked up her jacket and bag and left.

On the bus ride back home, she swallowed tears. She'd believed she'd have more time with Gram. Being alone had never really bothered Audrey, but losing Gram was unfathomable.

She let herself into the apartment and stepped over three pairs of sky-high heels that Misty typically tossed when she walked through the door. A smudged mirror sat on the coffee table, alerting her to the fact that partying had been happening in her absence. Misty must've celebrated the holiday before going in to work.

She went straight to her bedroom. Burying herself in work was just the antidote for her abysmal thoughts. Mr. Green had given her a job, so that was where she would focus her energy. Spending the night digging into someone else's misery made her feel better about her own circumstances.

It didn't take long at all. Seven hours later, she had a dossier of dirt for her client. With it being almost three in the morning, she debated whether she should send it now or wait. It was officially Christmas, so would it be rude to interrupt his holiday? No, he was the kind of guy who worked around the clock. She didn't know how she knew that, but she did.

Data: I have a Christmas present for you.

She immediately rethought the message because the dude might not even be Christian. If he was Jewish would he be offended that she'd made the assumption? She sent the link to the file and set her laptop on the bed next to her with the intention of logging off for the night. But a message immediately bleeped at her.

Green: You work fast. I appreciate that.

Data: Don't you sleep?

Green: Of course. Do you?

Data: Sometimes

Green: Alone?

Audrey snickered. Where the hell did this guy get off asking if she slept alone?

Data: Sometimes. You?

Green: Sleeping? Always.

Hmm... Mr. Green was letting her know he was a player. She shouldn't care, but this was the most personal they'd ever gotten.

Data: Kind of a sad comment on your life. Not only do you always sleep alone but you're working on Christmas Eve.

Green: The same can be said of you.

Data: I'm just fulfilling the stereotypical image of a hacker sitting alone in a dark room playing with my gadgets.

Green: Oh, to be one of those gadgets.

She burst out laughing and she couldn't stop.

Misty suddenly pounded on her door but didn't wait for a response before swinging it open. "Are you okay?"

Audrey gulped air and swiped at the tears on her cheeks. "I'm fine."

"Damn, girl. You're always so quiet that when I heard the noise, I thought you were having a seizure." Misty placed a hand over her heart as if to calm it. She must've just gotten home from work. Although the baby pink hoodie and sweatpants might appear to be workout clothes, Audrey knew that was Misty's to-and-from-work outfit.

"I'm fine. Just laughing over something that probably shouldn't even be that funny."

"Okay." She turned, her overly teased and sprayed red hair looking like a cloud around her head.

"Thanks for checking on me." *It's good to know that if I die in this crappy room someone would notice.* Her computer bleeped again.

Green: I'm sorry. Did I offend you?

Data: Not at all. I was laughing so hard my roommate felt the need to check on me.

Green: That's good then. Have an excellent evening.

Data: It's closer to morning.

Green: Not for people like us.

A few minutes later, she received notification of payment. If Mr. Green kept her busy like this, paying for Gram's care wouldn't be too bad. She opened the payment email. Mr. Green included a note in the memo.

Get yourself a nice new gadget and think of me.

While there was no new gadget in her budget, thoughts of him would be hard to ignore.

TWO

June

Green: new job

Data: send the details

Green: has to be f2f

Data: not how I work

Green: I'm aware. I'll make this worth your while

Data: How do you know what will be worth my time?

Green: Even if you don't like the terms, I know you want to meet me :)

JARED STARED AT his screen and hoped she'd come back with the answer he wanted. In all honesty, he wasn't one hundred percent sure she was a *she*, but every conversation they'd had led him to believe so. Regardless of gender, Data was the best, most discreet local hacker he'd worked with. As far as he knew, she never bragged online about her accomplishments. For her, it was always about the money. Months ago, when he and Mia started planning, Data had been his first thought, no matter what Mia said about crossing lines between their real lives and the lives they needed to project to the people they hired.

For him, it wasn't quite so straightforward because he lived in the space between the lines.

He tapped a pen while waiting for an answer. Data either had an affinity for cash or was desperate. She was always hungry for work, like a squirrel gathering nuts for a winter that would never end. She never turned down a job. Then again, he'd never asked her to cross this line. This job was one hundred percent illegal. There was no doubt, she wouldn't just be crossing the line; it would barely be a dot in her rearview.

If she accepted, she would be a good fit. Someone who was desperate was someone they could control. And they needed to control the narrative they spun as well as the outcome of every job.

His computer bleeped again.

Data: You're full of yourself Green. Didn't we discuss the size of your ego months ago?

Green: This particular job comes with a price tag that will more than double the highest paying job you've done for me

If nothing else drew her out, that should. People could rarely turn down obscene amounts of money.

Data: time and place?

He loved being right about people. He named a coffee shop near his downtown office to meet her at in two hours. Long enough that she would be able to reach the location from pretty much anywhere in the city, but soon enough that she wouldn't get cold feet.

His office door swung open without notification from the receptionist. Mia stormed across the room. *It must be bad for her to come to my office.*

"What's wrong?"

She tossed her small purse on the chair across from his desk. "I knew I shouldn't have trusted you to find the people we need."

He couldn't imagine what had her rattled. He rose and closed his door. "You shouldn't be here," he said in a low voice. "Not about this."

"It's not unheard of for me to visit. And what I'm discussing isn't far from the status quo for you." She waved a hand. "At the rate things are going, our plan will never get off the ground anyway. Five years of planning. Gone."

Her nostrils flared and her hazel eyes blazed. Irritation radiated from her five-foot-nothing frame. Her glossed pink lips pursed in an unmovable line. Any other woman would've been screaming at this point, but not Mia.

"What are you talking about?"

"The thief you said would be the perfect addition to our little *team* has been arrested." She said the word *team* as if it might make her gag.

"What?" His brain scrambled. Nikki had a stellar reputation. She didn't get caught. No matter how many people knew she was guilty, she simply didn't get caught.

"Drunk and disorderly."

Jared released a pent-up breath. "So what?"

"We agreed everyone had to fly under the radar. Avoid drawing attention. This is far worse than drawing attention."

"I told you she was a little rough around the edges. But we'd be hard-pressed to find someone better. She was probably blowing off some steam." He pulled the chair out to get Mia to sit. When she took the offered seat, he went back behind his desk. "I have our hacker. I'm meeting her in a couple of hours."

"No, you're not."

"Yes, I am. I just made plans."

"You need to go to the fifth precinct and bail out Nikki. Make it go away. Bring her to the apartment and make sure she understands the severity of our terms. We're too close to start over."

"What about my meeting?"

"I'll take it."

He laughed. Mia was incredibly intelligent. She could read every person in a room. But she knew very little about computers or hacking.

"It's a meeting. You said she knows what she's doing. What's to stop her from blowing up our whole operation because she knows who you are?"

"We've never met. To her, I'm Mr. Green, a man with deep pockets." He left out the part of his relationship with the hacker that included flirtation.

"It's better for me to go anyway. I'll be objective in a way you might not be." She released a slow breath as she calmed down. "How bad is this other thing going to be?"

"I have no idea. What do you expect me to do?"

"You have a law degree. You have connections. Obviously, you can't meet with her in any official capacity. Hire someone to go bail her out." She rose from her chair. "Make sure you get her under control. We've come too far."

He didn't need the reminder.

"What do I need to know for this meeting?" she asked with her purse in hand.

"Give her the terms and the timeline. Ask what equipment she needs. If she agrees, give her this phone." He pulled the burner from his desk. "Tell her we'll text with the address to meet us when we have her setup ready."

"Simple enough."

Then she swept out of the room. He loved Mia. She'd been his best friend most of his life. No one knew him better and there was no one he trusted more, but sometimes she pissed him off.

He made some calls to get Nikki out. She'd been charged but refused to give her name. On his way to the police station, he got the call from the bail bondsman letting him know Nikki would be out within the hour.

Jared watched the clock. Maybe if he could wrap things up with Nikki quickly enough, he could make his meeting with Data. Around the corner from the station, he had his driver stop and idle. He handled a few emails while he waited.

When he finally got the text saying they were headed out, the driver stepped from the car and waited by the back door to open it. Gary, the bail bondsman, pointed at the car. Nikki slid her sunglasses down on her nose, stared right at him through the darkened windows, and flipped him off. The driver opened the door and whatever Gary said to her worked. She strutted across the sidewalk as if she didn't have a care in the world.

At the door, she bent over and peered in.

"Get in," he said.

"Why?"

"We had an arrangement. You were supposed to keep your nose clean."

She snorted. "My nose is clean. My liver, on the other hand, might be a little messed up."

"This isn't a game."

"That's where you're wrong. Everything is a game. It's all in how you play it." She saluted Gary before climbing in.

The driver shut the door and got back behind the wheel. "Where to?"

"Just drive." Jared closed the privacy glass before turning his attention to Nikki.

She sprawled all over the opposite seat, ripped jeans and dirty white T-shirt clinging to her thin frame. She'd removed her sunglasses to reveal dark makeup smudges around her eyes. Her usual bronze complexion appeared pallid. Her long black hair was piled messily on top of her head. He stared at her until she broke.

"Look, I'm sorry. I went out with some friends. Things got rowdy. I might have taken out some anger on a trash can."

What the hell? The property damage was to a trash can? "What exactly did you do to it?"

She snickered. "I threw it through a plate glass window."

Jared didn't even want to know. Property damage was easily taken care of. The right dollar figure kept people quiet. He'd get the charges dropped. He only hoped Mia's meeting with Data was going better than this.

He propped his ankle on his opposite knee and picked at imaginary lint, as if the upcoming conversation didn't matter to him. "You have an important decision to make here, Nikki. Do you or don't you want to work for me?"

"The money's good. But I can make that anywhere."

He shot her a look that called her bluff. They both knew no one was paying what he was.

"But you don't make all the terms," she continued. "From what you've told me, I'm expected to put my life and my freedom in the hands of strangers. I don't like that. I work alone."

They'd been around and around on this. Mia insisted each player not have contact with the others. It made sense. If one person was picked up and questioned—which in his mind was a long shot since no one would even be aware they'd been robbed—that person couldn't give up any information on the other players.

On the other hand, they wouldn't be able to function as a team, which was what Jared had tried to get Mia to understand. It was hard to put trust in people you didn't know. She wanted them to rely on each other sight unseen.

Knowing he'd have to face Mia's wrath later, he offered a compromise. "How about you meet my partner and the person who will get you into the house? Those

are the only people who have an impact on your job."
At least it kept the forger separate. And as long as no
one used real names, they'd be fine.

"I suppose I could live with that."

"In the meantime, you'll move in to the apartment
we've set up as a base of operations and stay out of
trouble." He wouldn't have to make such demands of
the other players, but Nikki was a wild card. However,
knowing she was the best made it worth dealing with
her.

"So in order to participate in your illegal job, you
expect me to be an angel."

"Something like that."

"What if I have other jobs?"

"As long as you're in our employ, you don't."

"Then you better open your piggy bank. Good be-
havior is gonna cost extra."

AUDREY STARED AT her screen far longer than she should
have. She hated that Mr. Green had guessed right about
her desire to know more about him. She'd done a number of jobs for him over the last few years. He'd even
referred other clients to her. She didn't know who he
was or exactly what he did, except cause trouble to gain
an advantage. Never anything truly evil or dirty. Nothing to raise a red flag for the need to turn him down.
At least nothing she knew of.

Every time he reached out with a job, their conversation floated into the realm of flirtation. It was safe for
Audrey, though, because she never met clients. Ever.

But he tempted her.

Added to that temptation was a payout that would

take care of her grandmother's assisted living facility for months. She'd finally have some breathing room. She glanced around at the shithole room she sublet. She and Misty rarely crossed paths, which suited Audrey just fine. The walls were paper-thin and yellowed from Misty's cigarette smoking. More often than not, the outside hallway was littered with passed-out junkies and drunks. But it was cheap.

Maybe she could even get her own place. One without roaches.

After securely locking up her room with a keyed padlock and a combination lock, she struck out on her two-train-and-one-bus ride to get to the meeting with Mr. Green. Her stomach fluttered the nearer she got. Maybe it was the crowd on public transportation or the summer heat. Maybe it was doing something she knew was stupid.

Or maybe it was finally satisfying her curiosity.

No other client made her wonder. Alone in her dingy room, sending out DDOS hacks to what she imagined was some rival corporation, she found herself wanting to know more about him. He never just sent directions and money. He…chatted. Like he was intrigued by what she did for a living. He was as curious as she was.

By the time she got to her stop, the afternoon sun sat low in the sky, beating on her face as she hiked the last block to the coffee shop. Commuters jostled against her and no matter where she walked, she was going against the flow.

This was why she hardly left her apartment.

She pushed through the door and let her eyes adjust to the dimmer lighting. A quick glance around let her know that Mr. Green probably wasn't there yet. No single dude sat by himself. At the counter, she paid cash for a bottle of water and then took a seat in the corner, which afforded her a safe view of the entire place.

She sipped her water and picked at the label as she studied each person who came through the door. No Mr. Green. She'd arrived a little early, so she tried not to get anxious, but it was no use. Just as she prepared to get up, a short woman in a designer dress—at least Audrey assumed it was designer since it looked like it fell from the pages of a magazine—stepped up to her table.

The woman held a cup of coffee with her hand covering the name and she slid chic sunglasses off her face. Shockingly bright hazel eyes stared at her.

"You can have this table. I'm done," Audrey said.

"I believe you're the person I'm here to meet."

A million thoughts flew through Audrey's mind. Mr. Green wasn't a mister? Had she totally misread all communication and mistaken it for flirting? Was she really that far gone? Or had this Ms. Green been flirting with her? If so, how did it make her feel?

As the questions rapid-fired through her brain, the woman simply said, "I work with Mr. Green."

"Oh," Audrey managed and sank back into her chair. Disappointment stabbed at her. She'd wanted to meet him. *If he wasn't going to show, why demand a face-to-face?*

The woman sat down and crossed her legs. She had perfect posture, like that of a dancer, as she studied Audrey. "Data, is it?"

Her voice held the quality of a rich person—not an accent exactly, more like the pitch of someone who spoke like everyone else was beneath her. She reminded

Audrey of Whitley Gilbert from *A Different World* without the Southern belle twang.

Audrey didn't like her. "Yes. And you are?"

One corner of the woman's mouth twitched. "I suppose you could call me Ms. Green."

"Kind of formal."

"Well, in our business, informality can lead to trouble."

Our business? Audrey didn't believe for a moment that this woman had ever gotten her hands dirty doing anything.

Ms. Green blinked a couple of times and released a soft sigh. "Mr. Green sends his apologies. Something urgent required his attention, and he didn't want to reschedule this meeting. We're on a tight timeline."

"What exactly does this job entail?"

"Bypassing a security system."

She thought of the price tag Mr. Green quoted. "I don't break into banks or government facilities."

"A private residence."

"For what?"

"We're interested in some artwork."

Audrey's curiosity was piqued. She would be able to flex hacking muscles she hadn't used in a while. And make bank doing so.

"I assume by the look on your face, we have an agreement." Ms. Green slid a blank piece of paper across the table. "Write down a list of equipment you'll need. Make sure it's complete."

"Anything?" She knew she could probably make this happen with the stuff in her room, but if they were buying… "When the job is done, I get to keep the equipment."

Ms. Green gave her a stony look.

Hmm...the woman didn't like being challenged.

"Possibly. If not, you'll receive a duplicate for your services."

Audrey scribbled her dream on that tiny piece of paper. Every item she'd ever ogled at the store, the best of everything, right down to the cables. When she slid the sheet back, Ms. Green didn't even blink. Either she had bottomless pockets or she had no clue what it would cost. Not Audrey's problem.

"You said you had a tight timeline. How much time do I have?"

"Unless you've requested something we can't get our hands on, which is highly unlikely, we should have everything in place within two days. The job will transpire in less than three weeks." She set a phone on the table. "We'll text you the address. Needless to say, no one else should have that address or know anything about the work you're hired to do."

"Not a problem." She dropped the phone in her bag.

They sat and stared at each other. Ms. Green made no move to leave. The shop was becoming more crowded and Audrey wanted to bolt, but part of her didn't want to give this woman the satisfaction.

"Seriously?" Ms. Green huffed. "We'll leave at the same time."

Audrey rose and waited for her companion to join her. She stood at least four or five inches taller. For such a small thing, Ms. Green acted as though she were six feet tall. As Ms. Green tossed her cup in the trash, Audrey saw that her name started with an "M," but she couldn't see the remaining letters. Melanie, Margaret,

Madeleine, Michelle, Molly…none of the names coming to Audrey seemed to fit this woman.

When they reached the sidewalk outside, Ms. Green
turned to her again. "One more thing. No other jobs for
the duration of our project."

"But—"

"But nothing. We are paying you handsomely for
your undivided attention."

Again with the we. *Maybe Ms. Green is actually
Mrs. Green.*

A sleek black car pulled up to the curb and a driver
got out and opened the door. Ms. Green stepped to the
car and added, "We'll be in touch."

Audrey watched the car pull away and thought about
her trek back across the city. With the money she was
promised for this job, she could call an Uber. But that
would require a credit card. And giving a stranger her
address.

At least as she turned the corner for her hike back to
the bus stop, a cool lake breeze washed over her.

The Greens' offer could change her life. The only
real question was whether she could suck it up and deal
with Ms. Green. What if Mr. Green was as pretentious?
She couldn't imagine that based on the back-and-forth
they'd shared, but she'd keep her reservations to herself.

Stepping onto the cramped bus, Audrey decided it
didn't matter what Mr. Green was like. As long as the
biggest risk she had to take was a virtual break-in, she'd
do their job and take their money. She'd done worse
for a whole lot less, so how could she go wrong with a
fat payday and a bonus of top-of-the-line equipment?

THREE

AFTER THE FIFTH trip into the apartment carrying boxes of tech equipment, Jared was beginning to hate Mia's plan. Normally he would have paid for a rush delivery and some burly guys with a hand truck would have carried this into the apartment. Mia, however, insisted that the fewer people who could place them at this location the better.

Nikki lay nearly upside down in front of the TV, her legs hanging on the back of the couch, a bag of chips on her chest. She'd offered no help in carrying in the equipment.

As he unboxed the devices, he thought about Data. He'd finally get to meet her. She was brilliant, but when he'd asked Mia what she looked like, his cousin wasn't very forthcoming.

Mia strode through the door a few minutes later. She took in the sight of Nikki and shot Jared a look. "Why is she here?" she asked in hushed tones.

"You said you wanted her to stay out of trouble. If she's here, we can keep an eye on her."

"I thought our other friend was coming today."

"Should be here soon."

Mia darted another look at Nikki.

Jared sighed. "Nikki has a right to know who she's

trusting on this. She won't work with people she hasn't met."

"It's a mistake."

"It'll be fine. Trust me."

The doorbell rang and Mia strode to the intercom. "Hello?"

"It's me."

Mia rolled her eyes at him while she pressed the button to let Data up. He crossed the room, murmured to her to be nice and waited at the door for Data. She stepped off the elevator with wide eyes. Without even a look in his direction, she turned in a circle, taking in her surroundings. She wore a drab brown, stained T-shirt and threadbare jeans. The denim was ripped in a few places, obviously from wear, not because some designer charged hundreds of dollars for pre-made tears.

"Data?"

She spun quickly and their gazes locked. He wasn't quite sure what he'd expected. He'd imagined someone more like Nikki, a confident woman who believed she could rule the world and who walked with a swagger. This woman seemed in awe or shock, unsure of her next move. Not the snarky woman who routinely called him out for his ego while flirting.

Then she threw her shoulders back and extended a hand. "Mr. Green?"

"Yes. You can call me Jay." He hadn't thought about being addressed as Mr. Green in person, so he used the nickname he'd used in college. They really needed to simplify this name thing or by the time they actually got to work, he might need a cheat sheet to remember who he was. He took her hand, which was soft but strong. No mousy handshake for her.

He took in her face: eyes that would be a brilliant sapphire blue if not for the shadows beneath them, full pink lips, and fringes of dark brown hair falling from under the cap she wore. If she was wearing makeup, he couldn't tell. Everything about her from head to toe was plain by design. He bet she had no problem disappearing into a crowd.

"Come inside. I was just unboxing your equipment. I figured you'd want to create your own setup."

"That would be great."

As they stepped through the door, he grabbed the lock box and said, "Your cell phone?"

She looked up at him, confused. He pointed in the box where three other cell phones lay. Another of Mia's precautions.

Data dug in her pocket and pulled out the burner phone they'd given her and set it in the box.

"Your personal phone as well. To be safe."

She riffled through her ancient messenger bag and pulled out a phone not much different from the one she'd already handed over. With a raised brow, she asked, "I assume it's okay for me to keep my laptop?"

Mia obviously hadn't considered that. The box he held was too small.

"I told you we would provide everything you need," Mia said from behind him.

"Where I go, my computer goes," Data shot back. Slinging the bag on her shoulder again, she pointed to the boxes. "Do you really think I'd need my personal computer to record anything that goes on here when you're supplying me with state-of-the-art equipment?"

There was the woman he knew. He turned his laugh into a cough, hoping Mia wouldn't get angrier. She didn't like to be wrong.

"Regardless, I would feel better if you put your items in one of the bedrooms for now." Mia nodded in the direction for Data to move. Then she tapped his arm. "May I speak to you for a moment?"

She waited for Data to shuffle away and then led him to the opposite wall. "This is not a good idea. I told you we need to be able to control what happens here."

"You also said you wanted the best. The best in any industry isn't likely to be meek and cower under one of your looks."

The muscle in Mia's jaw pulsed.

"Remember when I told you not to invest in the new casino because something shady was going on there?" He waited for Mia to nod. "Data found the information I needed to shut that down. Information no else could access."

Mia's mouth slipped open.

AUDREY HAD NO idea what to think. She knew Green— Jay—had money, but she'd also assumed he was a middleman when he'd hired her. The jobs had been too diverse for them all to be for his benefit. Or so she thought. Maybe he was some tycoon who had a hand in everything. He had CEO written all over him.

Even with the knowledge that he had money, she still hadn't expected this. Their conversations had made her think they were similar. He, however, had never led a life like hers. He wasn't new money. He was legacy money. It unsettled her. She suddenly felt more like an employee than a colleague, and she didn't like it.

She walked down the hallway where Ms. Green indicated. The carpet under her feet squished softly, like walking on a pillow. She pushed a door open and found the bathroom. White, silver, and gray gleaming surfaces filled the space. If not for the towel balled up on the floor and the makeup scattered on the counter, it would look like a magazine spread. For a brief second, she considered inspecting the makeup to see if it was Ms. Green's. As swanky as this apartment was, Audrey didn't think Ms. Green lived here. So if the makeup was hers, she'd just spent the night. Audrey inched forward.

No, this makeup couldn't belong to Ms. Green. Audrey didn't know much about makeup but this was the wrong shade for Ms. Green. How many women did Mr. Green entertain here?

She backed out and turned across the hall where she saw two other doors. She pushed the first one open.

"That one's mine."

The sharp, quiet voice behind her startled her, but at least she didn't jump. Audrey looked over her shoulder. The woman who had been on the couch had silently followed her. Creepy.

Audrey moved to the next door. This room was fully furnished but held no signs of use. The woman continued to follow her. Audrey set her bag on the dresser and turned.

"I'm Nikki." The woman looked her up and down. "You must be… Data?"

Audrey nodded and studied her face. The makeup could be hers. "Who are you?"

"I just said Nikki."

Great, now she thinks I'm stupid. Will I ever remember to think before blurting out a half-assed comment or question? The bad habit often made very poor first impressions. "I got that. I meant, are you working for them, too?"

"Oh, yeah. I'm your thief." She said it proudly, as if she'd just announced she was a rocket scientist. "You're the hacker, right?"

Audrey didn't like people she didn't know having information about her. She nodded. "You live here... or just spending the night?"

Nikki wobbled her head. "Living here. For now. Jay thinks I get into too much trouble, so I'm a prisoner."

"What?" It came out almost as a screech.

Nikki laughed. "Not really. I more or less come and go as I please. He wants to keep tabs on me since he had to bail me out."

What have I gotten myself into? The place was nice, though, so if she had to be a prisoner, she could think of much worse places. Like her own apartment. She moved back toward the living room. The Greens were still in a heated discussion. She stared for a moment. They looked like a couple in an argument. Irritation struck her again.

"Are they always like this?" she whispered.

"At least half the time I see them together, yeah." Nikki brushed past her and flopped back on the couch.

Ms. Green's harsh whisper carried across the room. "Still. She looks like a junkie who needs a fix."

"Screw you," Audrey blasted as she walked up to them and forced her way into their conversation. She held out her arms, palms up. "Look, no track marks. You want to check between my toes, too? Or would you prefer I piss in a cup?"

The woman said nothing. She simply arched an eyebrow at Jay.

Audrey looked back and forth between them. "I'm clean. One hundred percent." Turning to Ms. Green, she added, "Not all of us can afford your hoity-toity beauty products. Some of us work for a living."

Jay sighed behind her. "Give us a minute."

Audrey had no idea who he was talking to until he pushed past her and grabbed his girl's arm and propelled her toward the door, handing her a phone from the box on the way. "I'll handle things here."

"You better," Ms. Green said. Then she slipped out the door.

Jay came back to where Audrey waited. From the corner of her eye, she saw Nikki leaning on the back of the couch, giving this scene more attention than the TV on the wall.

Figuring she was about to lose this gig before it even started, she continued her rant.

"Look," she started with her hands up. "I don't know what game you're playing. Flirting with me every time we talk. Maybe you were thinking about slumming it, but it was douchey."

His eyes flashed for a second. "Conversations go both ways. If you didn't want to talk, you could've shut it down any time you wanted."

Therein lay the problem. She hadn't wanted to shut

it down. She enjoyed their banter. But she couldn't afford to think about that now. "That was before I knew you were involved. I don't know what your girlfriend's problem is, unless she found out how you talk to other women, but I'm not going to put up with someone looking down on me and calling me a junkie."

"What? She's *not* my girlfriend."

She hadn't clocked a ring on the woman's hand, so not wife, and the total look of horror on his face almost made Audrey laugh. Of everything she'd said, that was the one thing he homed in on? Definitely defining boundaries.

"You sure about that, sport?" Nikki asked. "The way you two fight…when you see that in a movie, you know they're hitting the sheets in a few minutes."

Audrey could've sworn he turned green.

"She's my partner. My purely platonic partner. That's all." He took a deep breath and scrubbed a hand over his face. While he didn't say the words, his eyes held an apology for the misunderstanding. Something else simmered there, drawing Audrey out. Too bad she sucked at reading people.

"I don't know," Nikki continued, "I feel the sexual tension in the air."

Audrey swallowed. She was feeling it now, too, except it had nothing to do with Ms. Green and everything to do with the man standing in front of her.

Then he blinked, breaking whatever spell he'd been weaving. "We've been planning this job for a long time. She's worried about being successful. For everything to work, we need a functioning team."

Audrey rolled her eyes and Nikki snorted.

"What?" he asked, looking back and forth between Audrey and Nikki.

"You think your *partner* views us as a team?" Audrey asked.

"She will. Why don't you set up the equipment the way you want and we'll start fresh tomorrow?"

So, not fired.

Audrey looked over to where the boxes of equipment stood. She wanted to play with everything. Was it worth putting up with someone who assumed she was an addict?

Walking to the massive L-shaped desk, she tossed her hat on a chair, letting her hair fall to her shoulders. "Fine. But if she insults me again, I'm out."

Nikki laughed. "Good luck with that. I don't think she knows how to talk to people without insulting them."

"She's not that bad," he said. He stood next to Audrey, offering her a soft smile.

When he looked into her eyes like he was right now, she imagined the guy she'd flirted with for months. This was the man who treated her like she was important, not the help.

Then she got a whiff of his cologne. Even that smelled expensive. Like they could charge for sniffs. She glanced at him standing there in his suit, shirt sleeves rolled to the elbow, and then glanced down at the stained shirt she'd worn for her shift at the Grind. So she wasn't glamorous. She also didn't look like a junkie. Ms. Green had probably never even seen an addict up close and personal. They came from different worlds. Audrey was used to it. At least she was when she expected it. Being around Jay was definitely throwing her off her game.

"Just keep her away from me and we'll be fine."

"Take everything for a spin and let me know if you need anything." He motioned for her to sit in the leather chair he wheeled over.

She sank down. Wow. It felt good, like a cushion to cradle all of her curves. Much better than her lumpy mattress or the creaky old chair in her room.

He pushed the chair toward the desk. Near her ear, he said, "I'm glad you took the job. I'm sorry I missed our initial meeting."

The quiet tone sent a shiver down her spine. She glanced over to the couch. Nikki's attention had returned to the action movie she'd been watching.

"See you tomorrow," he said and headed to the door.

"What about my phones?"

"The box isn't locked. You can take them back." He winked and slipped out.

"What the hell is going on?" she asked aloud.

Nikki threw an elbow over the back of the couch. "They're weird. She's paranoid. Afraid we're going to record her and out her to the criminal underworld or something." She jumped up. "I'm going to order pizza. You want some?"

"I don't have any cash on me right now." Or ever.

"It's on Jay."

"In that case, I'd love some."

As Nikki got on her phone to order, Audrey finished unboxing the equipment. By the time the pizza arrived, she had the computer hooked up and running. She even mirrored the monitor to the big TV on the wall.

"How did you get internet access?" Nikki asked.

"I tapped a neighbor's."

"Oooh… I think I'm going to like you. Can you get me premium channels?"

With a smile, Audrey said, "Maybe."

"Thank God. I've rented every disk in the damn box to play on my game console. I need some variety. The Greens are strongly opposed to having too much running through this place that would tie us together. Can't log on to my accounts and they don't want me opening new ones."

"I have an easy work-around for that. I'll get you access that will hide who you are."

"I think this is gonna be the start of a beautiful friendship."

They sat on the couch and shared a pizza. It was a weird kind of comfort. Nikki didn't look like a thief. Not that Audrey had an expectation for what a thief should look like. She was pretty but kind of sloppy, and she had a general don't-give-a-fuck attitude.

Nikki chatted about nothing important, but she seemed so open. A thief should be more secretive.

Looking across at Audrey, she suddenly asked, "Did he really flirt with you?"

"I thought so. But online, who knows?" Audrey lifted a shoulder. It was totally within the realm of possibility that she had no idea what flirting was anymore. She couldn't remember the last time a guy hit on her.

"I know. No man is going to defend his actions like that unless he was guilty. Plus, you add in the way he keeps looking at you? Yeah, that sexual tension wasn't about him and his partner."

Audrey sucked in a breath. She'd assumed Nikki hadn't paid any attention to what happened between her and Jay. Unsurprisingly, the thief was sneaky. She had Audrey openly talking about her personal life without too much effort. She really needed to get out more, maybe make some friends, so she wouldn't be tempted to cave so quickly in the workplace. "It doesn't really matter now, though, does it? We have a job to do. No time for flirting."

Maybe if she kept repeating that to herself, she'd believe it.

FOUR

JARED HAD A long conversation with Mia over dinner later that night. He knew she was worried, but she needed to chill a little when dealing with people. He also spent quite a bit of time thinking about Data. She was older than he'd imagined. He hadn't pictured jailbait because no way would he have intentionally flirted with a kid, but he figured she would be younger, like fresh out of college. Maybe it was her eagerness to work. Maybe he'd assumed a good hacker had to be young to be familiar with the latest tech, but she had to be near his age.

She was striking, and something in her face made her look experienced, a wariness in her eyes. Experience mattered, and it made her that much more appealing.

When he got back to the apartment the next day, he let himself in and called out, "Nikki, I'm here." He set the coffee and donuts he'd brought on the table. The computer was set up on the desk. "How long was Data here last night?"

"Until we polished off a pizza," Nikki said from behind him. "Good. You brought breakfast."

He turned around as she flipped open the donut box, her bare ass in the air. "Lord, Nikki, put some clothes on." He spun back.

"I am wearing clothes. I normally sleep naked. I put on a thong and T-shirt for you."

Waving a hand in the air, he said, "Could you put on some pants?"

She huffed. "Fine."

While she was out of the room, hopefully covering herself, he made his way around the desk to see what Data had done. "Did she say what time she was coming back?"

Upon her return, Nikki crammed half a glazed donut in her mouth. "Nope."

He'd been up since before five to wrap up some projects with clients. It was after nine thirty. Surely she should be here by now. He texted, Where are you? We have stuff to go over.

Work.

Work? This was supposed to be her only job. He and Mia were paying well to avoid these kinds of conflicts. We said no other jobs.

It took so long for her to answer he thought she wasn't going to.

I thought you meant JOBS. This is my regular bill-paying gig.

"Did Data happen to mention where she worked?"

Nikki was on her second or third donut. "She didn't say, but she was wearing a T-shirt from the Grind yesterday. It doesn't take a genius to figure out it was a uniform."

He let Nikki's sarcasm roll off.

Come straight to the apartment when you get off.

That's the plan. I should be there by noon.

Why the hell was she working at a coffee shop? Assuming he wasn't her only client, she could be raking in plenty of cash. Even if she had a cover job, why not in her preferred field? The puzzle of Data just kept expanding.

"When are you going to fill me in on the job? I'm getting kind of antsy sitting around here every day with nothing to do," Nikki complained.

"It hasn't even been three days. We'll be going over the entire plan later today."

"Good. Will your partner be here for the briefing?"

This woman was such a smart-ass, it was a wonder she'd never been caught. "Yes, she will. Any other questions?"

"I have plenty more. How long have you had the hots for Data?"

"Yesterday was the first time we met."

"That doesn't answer the question. You've had some kind of relationship before now."

Jared began to see the brilliance of Mia's plan of not letting anyone meet each other. "Prior to now, I utilized Data's talents for a number of business matters."

"Uh-huh." She drew the syllable out in a way that called him a liar.

Why was he even attempting to answer her questions satisfactorily? She was just trying to get under his skin. He didn't know how to answer her questions anyway.

Whenever he communicated with Data there was some flirtation, but it had been safe because they were never supposed to meet. Now that he'd met her, he wanted to continue the fun banter they shared. Part of him had hoped he wouldn't be attracted to her in person, because Mia would hate knowing that he was drawn to Data in anything other than a business relationship.

But he liked Data even more. Even though he knew it would complicate things.

Since he had a couple of hours until Data would be back, he texted Mia to let her know so he wouldn't have to listen to her bitch. Then he sent money to Data's usual account. She couldn't be making that much at a coffee shop. Five thousand should be enough for a deposit on three weeks of her time.

Handling clients came next. A normal week had him running sixty to seventy hours for clients. He needed to clear part of his schedule to have time to be here to keep an eye on Nikki and make sure Data accessed everything they would need. While he was pretty tech savvy, he wasn't a hacker. He did, however, know what they would need.

The hours passed quickly while he dealt with clients. The biggest situation he had going right now was brokering a deal between two tech companies. One wanted to swallow the other and as usual, the loser wouldn't go down without a fight. It was his job to show him how futile the fight would be. Sometimes that involved a little underhandedness, but he didn't think he'd need to explore those avenues this time. He hoped to have both players settled by tomorrow.

At noon, Mia entered the apartment carrying bags

of food for lunch. His cousin might not like the people he'd hired, but she was always the consummate host. She glanced around as if to take note of the lack of Data's presence. Before she could comment, the bell rang.

He met Data at the door. He didn't want another scene between Data and Mia. For some inexplicable reason, he was protective of Data. "I've sent five grand to your usual account. You need to quit the job."

"I need that job."

"No, you don't. You'll make plenty from us. You at least have to take a leave of absence while we're doing this. It's not negotiable." He couldn't understand why she was working a menial job that didn't even utilize her skills, but now was not the time to ask.

"Is this *her* doing?"

"It's an expectation we have of all of you. We're under a tight deadline. We need your undivided attention." He looked closely at her face. She looked even more exhausted than she had yesterday. "What time did you start today?"

"Four a.m."

"Are you going to be able to focus?"

She crossed her arms. "What time did you get up for your day of world domination?"

"Four thirty, but I'm not the one walking around with dark circles under my eyes from lack of sleep."

"I'm fine. I'll make sure to apply some makeup tomorrow to look more presentable."

He sighed and shook his head. "That's not what I meant. I don't have a problem with the way you look." *Just the opposite. I want to spend far too much time looking at you.* "I'm concerned that you're not taking care of yourself."

"I'm good. I take care of myself just fine." She pointed to the apartment behind him. "Let's do this."

Great. Now he'd pissed her off. He needed to take a page from his own book and relax when it came to these players. They'd chosen people who work alone and now they were expecting an instantaneous team, but it would take a little time. Hopefully not too much. He'd have to put his attraction aside because Data no longer seemed all that interested.

In the kitchen, Mia had a full spread of food. Three kinds of salad, cold cuts, cheeses, a dessert tray. "Help yourself," she said as she walked to the couch carrying a cup of coffee.

While Mia might see it as a sign of weakness to eat in front of Data and Nikki, he dove in. As usual, Nikki piled a plate high with food. He had no idea how she managed to eat so much. Data made a simple sandwich and wrapped it in a napkin.

Sitting on the floor with her legs crossed, Nikki took a bite of sandwich and said, "Shoot. Give us the deets."

Mia inhaled slowly. "As you know, we've hired you to steal a painting. Data, your job will be to bypass the security system to get Nikki in and out."

"That's it? All the buildup for that?" Nikki sounded disappointed.

"What were you hoping for?" Mia asked.

"I don't know. Something more spectacular than *steal a painting.*"

JAY BRUSHED HIS hands together and then tapped on the keyboard. Audrey watched his fingers fly over the keys. She knew it was weird, but she always found it sexy when a man could type without chicken pecking. Admittedly, her standards were pretty low.

Focus. He's the boss. Plus, he just got done telling me that I look like crap. She pushed down her obnoxious inner voice and forced her attention to the TV.

"It is a little more than that," he said. On the screen, an image of a huge house—a mansion really. "This is the house. Not only will you steal a painting, but you'll replace it with a forgery."

Nikki sat up straighter. "Well, that's a little more interesting. Why?"

"So the owner doesn't realize he's been robbed."

Nikki's whole face frowned. "Where's the fun in that? When I get one over on someone, I want him to know. I want to push his nose in my superiority."

"This isn't about proving your superiority," Ms. Green said.

And she would know all about a superiority complex.

"Then what?" Nikki continued.

"Money. Pure and simple."

Audrey listened to what the woman said, but she wasn't buying it. The Greens were not like her and Nikki. They didn't need money. They looked like they stepped off the set of a nighttime soap opera. There was more to the situation than they were letting on.

"Who's doing the forgery?" Nikki asked.

Audrey didn't much care. She knew next to nothing about art. She wouldn't be able to tell a fake from the original.

"Not your concern," Mia said. "We'll be providing that."

"And we're supposed to trust that this forger is good enough that no one will be able to tell?"

"I'll make sure of it," Mia said confidently.

The woman was so confident that Audrey wondered if she was the forger.

"Not to sound like a bitch, or anything, but I've stolen plenty of things in my life. Why do I need you?"

"We have access to clientele who are interested in this particular painting." Jay rose with a smile and crossed the room.

Audrey could imagine him in a boardroom owning everything. He commanded attention. She couldn't take her eyes off him. He wasn't a huge guy, maybe five-ten and fit, but not physically imposing. It was the way he carried himself, as if he could do whatever he wanted and no one would question him. And if they did, he wouldn't care.

He continued, "Masterpieces are rarely stolen. When they are, they're usually found and returned quickly. Part of the reason is that it's hard to fence a priceless work of art."

"Or you could just ransom it instead of fencing it."

"Ransom?" Audrey asked.

"You steal a painting and as soon as they discover it's missing you call and demand a ransom for the safe return." Nikki chuckled. "I've done it with the same Dali three times."

Dali? So much for masterpieces not being stolen. Audrey had no reason to doubt Nikki. She'd come across the woman's name in passing, although they didn't travel or work in the same circles. Where Audrey flew under the radar, Nikki liked to let everyone know how fabulous she was.

"What makes this different? As far as fencing it," Audrey asked.

"Me. I have access to the right people," Jay said.

When his dark eyes met hers, she saw a spark of excitement.

"People who won't care that it's stolen," Nikki said. "You sound like you have a plan, but we get paid up front." She flipped a thumb toward Audrey.

Audrey felt an odd kinship with Nikki, like they were in this together. Which in a way they were, separate from the Greens.

"Yes," Ms. Green said. "In addition to the deposit up front, you get paid as soon as you deliver the painting."

"What happens if you can't sell it?" Audrey asked.

"Shh," Nikki blurted. "Not our problem."

Jay chuckled. "She's right. It's not your concern. I know I'll be able to sell it."

The man acted as if he had no worries in the world. As if nothing could go wrong. But like Nikki said, it wasn't their problem. Getting Nikki in and out was her only concern. That and a fat paycheck.

"What kind of alarm system do they have?"

Irritation flashed across Ms. Green's face.

What the hell did I do now? This is what she hired me for.

"They just did an upgrade, so we're not entirely sure. I have the specs on what they had. Same company, and as far as I know, same equipment."

So she wasn't pissed at Audrey. She was upset at her

own failings. Audrey got a little sick enjoyment from Ms. Green's misery.

Jay was back at the computer. On the screen, photos of the keypad and a few of the sensors from the house showed.

"If you have an inside man, why not have them do this? It'd be cleaner," Nikki said.

"We don't have someone inside," Ms. Green said.

Audrey locked gazes with Nikki. Without an inside man, one of the Greens had to have been there to take photos.

"Can you get me in?" Audrey asked. "A quick sweep will tell me what we're dealing with."

"It'd be too risky. Getting one of you in so close to when we plan to make the trade isn't worth it." Ms. Green tapped her perfectly rounded manicured nails on the desk. She shared a look with Jay, then turned back to Audrey. "What exactly would you need to see besides what we've provided?"

"In a perfect world, I'd like to access the network. But seeing as I don't live in a perfect world, I can make do with knowing the number of cameras, system type, and provider."

"Some of that we know," Jay said. "No new cameras have been installed. There are six exterior cameras. Motion detectors on the main floor. Keypad by the front and back doors as well as in the master bedroom."

"Where is the painting?" Nikki asked.

"At the landing of the front stairs," Ms. Green told them. "It hangs so when you stand in the foyer, it draws your attention."

Foy-ay. Not foy-er. People with money, man. Always sounding fancy.

Nikki stood and rolled her hand at Jay. "Go back to the layout." Pictures flashed on the screen. "So I can go in through the window in the den, run up the stairs, and grab the painting. In and out the same way. Easy-peasy."

"Not so easy," Ms. Green continued. "The motion sensors on the main floor extend into the den. And we're not sure if there is a trigger on the painting itself."

Jay pointed at Nikki and Ms. Green. "Why don't you two start looking at the prints and decide best point of entry? I'll work with Data on the specs we do have, and see what we can figure out about the system."

Ms. Green showed Nikki what looked like a blue-print. Audrey scooted her chair toward the desk. She did her best to tune out the conversation across the room as well as the scent of Jay's cologne. Time to work.

"If you give me the specs you have, I'll see what I can come up with. I also need the address. I might be able to do a work-around in case you can't get the information I want."

He slid his chair away so she could move in front of the keyboard. He left a sheet of paper beside the computer with the security company's name. Below it, he scribbled the address. She started with a basic search of the address and the owner.

"No way. Randall Scott? That's who we're stealing from?" He was a well-known builder in the Chicago area.

Nikki spun from where she pored over the print. "The douchebag developer?" She snickered. "This just got way better."

Randall Scott had a reputation for being a sexist pig. He'd been sued by a number of female employees for sexual harassment and discrimination. Of course, nothing ever happened to the man. Audrey's opinion of the Greens went up a few notches.

"The owner of the painting doesn't matter," Jay said.

"Maybe to some of us it does," Audrey shot back.

"Why should it?"

"Because if he was some poor schmuck and this was literally his only possession worth anything? I'd want to know why him. Why not any of the tons of pompous, rich assholes in the city." She tried not to look at Ms. Green when she said it.

"Well, then. I'm glad you approve of our mark."

"But it's not up to you to approve or ask for explanations," Ms. Green added. "We're paying you for a job. The rest doesn't matter."

Audrey withheld a growl and returned her attention to the simplest of tasks—a Google search of both Scott and Frontier Security. It never ceased to amaze her how many people allowed their names and quotes to be used as testimonials on websites. Then she looked to see what the latest upgrades were being offered.

She was working slower than usual, but she couldn't figure out why. Maybe it was the distraction of having other people around. Maybe it was Jay watching her every move.

"This isn't going to work," she announced and shot out of her chair.

"What are you talking about?" Jay asked.

Without answering, she left the room, Nikki and Ms. Green staring. Audrey went to her bag that she'd left in the bedroom again, away from prying eyes, to grab her noise-canceling headphones. Then she returned to the desk without bothering to explain herself to anyone. They wanted her to work; she needed to do it her way. Talking her way through it wasn't her method.

Plugging the headphones into the computer, she opened a music streaming app and blasted her favorite playlist. Caught up in her own head, she could finally focus. She spent time copying down information on the specs of the security system and notes on possible bypasses. She had ideas, but that was all they were. She needed specifics on what the Scott house had.

When she finally pushed away from the desk and looked around, she was alone. Removing her headphones, she stood and stretched. In the kitchen, she grabbed a couple bottles of water and considered if anyone would notice if she took leftovers from lunch.

The front door behind her opened. "Data?" Nikki called.

She straightened and closed the fridge.

Holding up a bag, Nikki said, "I got dinner. Hope you like Chinese."

"You brought me dinner?"

"Everyone's gotta eat. I figure you're starving since you were working all afternoon without a break."

"I didn't even realize everyone had left."

Nikki set the bag on the counter and pulled out containers. "Did you figure it out?"

"How to get you in? Hell, no. I don't have enough information. But I have ideas." Audrey took a container of rice and dumped it on a paper plate. She added some beef and broccoli—mostly beef. "Do you trust them?"

Nikki didn't ask for clarification. "Of course not."

She didn't know why, but it made Audrey feel a little better. "But you trust me enough to get you in and out?"

"Not yet." She shoved a forkful of food in her mouth. "But we're alike. We work alone and do what we have to do. The Greens? This isn't their world."

Audrey had the same feeling.

"One more question before we plop down and watch TV. What's your real name?" Nikki asked.

"Why?"

"Because I can't look at you and keep calling you the robot from *Star Trek*."

Audrey laughed. "Actually, the name comes from *The Goonies*. The kid with the booby traps." Gram bought a VHS tape of the movie when Audrey was little and she'd fallen in love with the kids on a treasure hunt. She set her plate down and weighed her options. She'd never given her real name to a client before. But Nikki wasn't a client; she was more like a colleague. After this job, they probably wouldn't see each other again, so did it matter? "Audrey."

Nikki winked at her. "Cool beans."

"Cool beans? Really?" She paused and then said, "Tell me about the Dali."

A smirk broke across Nikki's face. "The first time I took it, it was on a dare. Jay is right—you can't fence a masterpiece. I stole it and couldn't do anything with it. I was young and stupid. I didn't want to keep it. I didn't even have my own place to hang it on a wall. So I called the owner and ransomed it. They slapped that cash down like it was nothing. It had been so easy that in those early years of being on my own, I did it two other times when I was strapped for cash."

"Didn't they figure it out? Beef up security? Something?"

"After the first time, they did add an alarm, but nothing complicated. Plus, desperation makes people do stupid shit. I wouldn't have cared what they had."

"But they still just paid?" Audrey couldn't wrap her head around it.

"Sure. It was easier than something happening to their precious art. Way easier than convincing the insurance company they didn't screw up. The third time, they paid triple what I asked for and just said, 'Don't ever come back.' So I didn't."

Audrey burst into laughter at Nikki's brazenness. She would never have the guts to pull that off once, let alone three times. Again, Audrey wondered at the lack of secrecy. She never spoke to anyone about the jobs she did. She'd never consider doling out details to anyone who asked. It was like attorney-client privilege or doctor-patient confidentiality. She might not be bound by law, but she was by her own code.

As they fell into silence, instead of going to the couch to watch TV, Nikki returned to the table where the drawings of Scott's house sat. For all her flippancy, the woman continued to study them. Audrey joined her and they discussed their options. Nikki was right. They were in this together.

FIVE

JARED FOLLOWED MIA to her condo. He hadn't seen her this riled up since the day she realized their fathers were guilty of running a massive Ponzi scheme. That day—the same one their dear old dads left the country—changed her. She swore revenge for what they'd done to the family.

They both parked and as soon as they got inside, Mia collapsed on her couch. At least as much as she ever collapsed. He doubted his cousin knew how to collapse. Or flop. Or do anything that wasn't elegant and graceful.

"What did you need to talk about that you couldn't say at the apartment?" he asked.

"I'm starting to have doubts."

"About?"

"The hacker. She doesn't seem all that committed. Really, what we're paying her, and she's still working at some coffee shop?"

"You're still working at the Art Institute—even after getting your inheritance, which would allow you to quit and just be a socialite. And I'm still taking on clients."

"Something's not right about her situation."

"Do you think she knows who we are? Or that she's one of Dad's lackeys?" He couldn't imagine it. Their fathers were excellent con men, but to have a hacker he'd been working with be part of a long con? He didn't see it.

"I don't think she has anything to do with our fathers. But she is a hacker. If she's as good as we expect her to be, how hard would it be for her to figure out who we are?"

"We haven't given her anything to go on. I suppose if she wanted to know, she'd dig. But to what end? As you said, we're already paying her plenty. She has no real reason to care who we are." He unbuttoned his jacket and sat on the other end of the couch. "Mostly, I think she's a brilliant hacker who needs money for something. Otherwise, why keep the coffee job?"

"Are you sure the thing she needs money for isn't drugs?"

"What is your fixation on drugs? Every interaction I've had with her, she's been clear-headed. I doubt someone who spends a good amount of time high would be able to find the information she does. It takes a certain level of focus to do such things."

"I guess I'll have to take your word for it. Every time I see her, she's shifty."

He thought about how tired she looked the two times he'd seen her. Something was weighing on her. "I'll keep a close eye on both her and Nikki. Will that make you feel better?"

"As long as you aren't watching from her bed." Mia always saw through him.

He laughed. "I like her."

"You said you didn't know her."

"I said we had a business relationship."

"There is no flirting in business."

"You're not participating in the right kind of business then."

She rolled her eyes and stood. Sliding her hand behind the painting on the wall above the pristine white marble fireplace, she pulled out a file folder. He didn't need to ask what was in it. It was the scaled-down version of her list.

After pouring a tumbler of scotch for each of them, she laid the folder open on the table. "I would give almost anything to see his face when he realizes he has a forged painting."

"We could always take Nikki's route."

"No. Insurance would pay him if it was stolen. The plan is good." She tapped the picture of Randall Scott. "He needs to suffer public embarrassment. They all do. And with any luck, they can apply enough pressure to get our fathers back in the States."

Jared seriously doubted that hopeful part of her plan. Their fathers were too selfish to worry about their friends.

"You don't have to give me that look," she continued. "I know they probably won't come back. I'm thinking about letting them know it was us. After the fact. When the painting has been sold and there's no trace of us."

"You mean you'd tip them off to tell Scott? That will ruin your whole public embarrassment."

She sipped her scotch with a slight shake of her head. "I mean after they try to sell."

"That could be years."

"Maybe. Maybe not."

"I don't remember you being quite this vindictive when you were younger."

"I had no reason. They broke the law and left our mothers looking like fools. Outcasts in what was rightfully our mothers' world. A world they fought to be a part of. They destroyed lives of so many hardworking people who believed their lies. I wish I could find a way to reach out and destroy them."

"Remind me to never get on your bad side." Pointing at the list, he said, "You should tuck those back in your hiding place. Thanks for the drink. Don't worry about the team. I think we have the right people. Find a forger yet?"

"Working on it."

"Will they have enough time to produce it before we need it?"

She rolled her eyes. "If they're good. Do you have a buyer?"

Jared set his empty glass on the table and rose. "I'm waiting until we have it in hand. If things go sideways, there would be people in the world who could connect it back to me."

As he walked past on his way out, he kissed the top of her head. Mia had a long history of rubbing people the wrong way. She had a hard time connecting. She'd barely had contact with Data, and the two women were at odds. In their few brief meetings, they'd managed to figure out how to bring out the worst in each other.

Keeping a closer eye on Data wouldn't be a hardship. Her humor, wit and intelligence created quite a pleasant package.

THE FOLLOWING MORNING Audrey went into the coffee shop to talk to her boss. Part of her felt bad for lying when she asked for a leave of absence. Diane knew some of what Audrey had been dealing with, with her grandma, so the lie rolled off easily enough when she said she needed a few weeks to handle Gram's care.

While the Greens were, in fact, paying her plenty of money to allow her to be able to quit the minimum wage job, she didn't trust them. Even with the nice advance Mr. Green sent her way.

This job was also her cover as a normal person. She'd set up a trust for Gram and all of her hacking money went there. The job at the coffee shop gave her a way to pay taxes and bills like a regular person. And it wasn't tied to anything tech related. She was good, but she was sure that like most hackers, her voice or style would show in all her work. She preferred to keep all that work underground instead of risking a tech job that would trace to her.

If she could keep the job at the Grind, it would give her peace of mind. Of course, she told Diane she totally understood if her position couldn't be saved, but to keep her in mind. Diane said she could juggle the schedule for a couple of weeks at most.

She allowed Diane to hug her tightly, even though she would prefer not to engage. When Diane told her to keep in touch, she nodded solemnly.

Walking away from the Grind was weird because that had been her only source of human interaction for years. Other than working here, Audrey didn't like people. Not in real life anyway.

And now look at me. I'm heading off to meet Nikki again. Another person.

She just hoped the Greens weren't going to be

around. She preferred to work without someone watching her every move. She rang the bell at the apartment. She couldn't believe their base of operations was in a high-end downtown building. Whatever the Greens were paying in rent here for a month would cover the cost of her room for a year. Nikki finally buzzed her in.

Audrey briefly wondered what she would have to do to be "forced" to live here like Nikki. It didn't seem like much of a punishment. Nikki opened the door, bleary eyed. Her black hair stuck out all over and she wore a skimpy T-shirt and underwear. The woman had no boundaries.

"Hey," she mumbled. "Shower."

Then she disappeared into the bathroom. Audrey made a pot of coffee and looked at the blueprints. Ms. Green had the cameras marked on the property as well as where the entry keypads were. Part of the problem was with the new upgrades. If Scott had opted for being able to use the cameras and system remotely, he could tap an app on his phone and look in his house.

Audrey began running down ideas: clone his phone to block the app, hack the security company, cut the power. All of it seemed far too risky.

She pulled up a satellite view of the neighborhood and then checked to see what internet and cable service providers were in the area.

When Nikki finally emerged from the bathroom, Audrey asked, "Do you have access to a car?"

"I can get one. Why?"

"I'm thinking a field trip. Go to Scott's house and try to get them to switch cable companies. Those dudes are hard selling all the time. It would get me in the door and get a quick peek around."

"My dad always said to watch out for the quiet ones."

"What's that supposed to mean?"

"You sat here for hours yesterday not saying a word to anyone. Today you're in here talking about doing exactly what Ms. Green doesn't want." She gave Audrey a wicked grin. "I'm in."

She hadn't thought about what Ms. Green did or didn't want. This made the most sense. Audrey could go in, look around, and know what her options were.

"Okay. Let's go. What do we need?"

They compiled a list of what they'd need: clothes for Audrey, a nametag, a business card, order forms for the cable company and a portfolio to hold them. Audrey began printing what she'd need while Nikki went to get a car.

"Now I just need a uniform," Audrey said when Nikki got back.

"I think I might have one. Come on."

Nikki drove to a storage facility. At the gate, she punched in a code and drove to a unit.

"Please tell me you're not going to randomly choose a unit to break into."

"Of course not. This is mine." She got out of the car and led her inside one of the temperature-controlled units. She unlocked the rolling door.

Inside was wall to wall stuff. While Nikki went straight to a rack of clothes, Audrey took a minute to be nosy. Propped on a shelf on the far wall was a painting. A very famous-looking painting. "Oh my God. Is that a Banksy?"

Without a glace back, Nikki answered, "Yep."

"You have a Banksy—genuine Banksy—just sitting in a storage unit?"

Nikki lifted a shoulder. "Like Jay said, masterpieces are hard to fence."

Audrey continued to stare at the painting and suddenly was smacked in the head with clothes.

"I think those will fit you enough and make you look like you are a cable guy. I thought I had a hat, but I can't find it. We'll have to stop on the way."

"Do I really need a hat?"

"Cameras, babe. A hat will obscure your face."

And this was why she worked behind a computer and not out where she would have to interact with the world.

By lunchtime, they had procured a cap and were rolling down Lake Shore Drive toward the north suburbs.

Nikki parked down the block and Audrey headed to the Scotts' house, ball cap strategically covering most of her face and avoiding the cameras. She walked up the long driveway and swallowed her awe at the house. It was more impressive in person. The side yard was bigger than any she'd ever seen, a four-car garage stood farther back, and she knew more land continued out back even though she couldn't see the yard. The front of the house had flowers and bushes and a perfectly manicured bright green lawn. She climbed the concrete steps and rang the bell. Keeping her head ducked, she glanced at the expansive bay window beside the front porch.

A slew of scenarios ran through her head. When a pretty blonde open the door, Audrey was surprised. She hadn't thought Scott's young trophy wife would answer her own door.

"Hi, I'm from Avox Cable. I'd love to tell you about the specials we have going on right now."

"I don't have time. I'm on my way out."

Audrey looked her up and down. The woman wore a cute white tennis outfit with a gym bag slung over one shoulder.

"Can I ask who your current provider is?"

"I really don't know. My husband handles all of that. I don't watch much TV."

Crap. She was losing her window of opportunity. "Can I leave some information about our specials and you can have him call us?"

"Sure," the woman said with a heavy sigh.

Audrey flipped open her portfolio and all of her forms and papers shot out into the house all over the floor. "Oh, my gosh. I am so sorry." She bent and began picking up papers, scooting closer in the doorway as she did.

Mrs. Scott bent and picked up a few pages. Audrey crawled across the floor. "I am so sorry."

"Connie," Mrs. Scott called. A moment later a maid came from the other room. "Connie, when this young woman retrieves her papers, please take the information she has and put it on Mr. Scott's desk. I'm late for my lesson." Then she walked out.

Connie bent down and helped to gather the papers. As Audrey straightened the pages, she looked at the keypad. When she stood, she glanced around to find the sensors for the motion detector. She accepted the pile Connie handed her.

"I'm really sorry about this. This is my first day out on my own." Looking at the papers, she asked, "Can

I set this down for a minute to reorganize? I'm such a mess and I can't afford to lose this job."

Connie nodded and led her to a side table in the foyer. Audrey shuffled the papers, taking a cable flyer out and setting it aside. Without looking at the pages, she stacked them with care, as if the order mattered, while she shifted her gaze around the room. From her spot, she couldn't see the painting. She saw no sensors pointed toward the stairs.

She turned and handed Connie the flyer. "I'm sorry. Thank you for being so patient." As she hustled out the door, she called, "Have a good day."

Head down, she walked back to the car, where Nikki sat playing on her phone. When Audrey climbed in, she said, "How'd it go?"

"I think I have the information we need."

"No one suspected anything?"

"Nope. Mrs. Scott was on her way out for a tennis lesson. When I spilled my papers all over the floor, she couldn't leave fast enough. She left the maid to watch me clean it up."

As they pulled away, Audrey's phone lit up with texts from Jay wondering where she was. She responded to let him know she and Nikki were together. They hit a drive-thru on the way back to the apartment but didn't talk. Nikki had the radio turned up loud and that was enough to let Audrey know conversation wasn't needed.

Jay was already in the apartment when they got there, messing with her computer. Okay, so it wasn't hers yet, since they bought it, but still. It was her domain. She hadn't quite figured out exactly what his role was, but it wasn't hacker.

"What are you doing?"

"Checking what you accomplished yesterday."

"A lot of information gathering."

He looked up from the desk and scanned her body. "What were you two doing?"

"Recon," Nikki answered.

"What?"

Audrey set their food on the table. "Don't get your panties in a bunch. I went in as a cable salesperson. I got as far as the foyer." She made sure to pronounce it *foy-ay*. "From what I could see, no motion sensors are directed at the painting. I couldn't see the painting, so obviously I couldn't see if there was a trip wire behind it. But I did get the new model of the alarm."

He sat quietly listening to everything she said. She couldn't read his face. Nikki had been sure they'd be pissed that she and Nikki had gone, but he didn't look mad. He looked almost…impressed.

"And where were you this morning?" Nikki asked.

"Working."

Audrey sat at the table but turned to face him. "So we aren't allowed to continue working, but you are? Doesn't seem quite fair."

"My job not only affords you, but it also gives me the names of people who might want to buy this particular painting."

"What exactly do you do?" Nikki asked.

He leaned back in the desk chair, and Audrey didn't think he was going to answer.

"I negotiate things."

"Like?" Nikki prodded.

"Whatever my clients need."

"You're a fixer," Audrey said. Suddenly pieces were falling into place. The variety of jobs he'd hired her to do, the amount of money he was willing to spend. But this job, stealing a painting and replacing it with a forgery, didn't sound like a fixer job. So while some things made more sense, this job made less.

FIXER. HE HATED that word. It oversimplified everything he did and it carried a connotation of someone who only accomplished negotiations through illegal means, like a con man. While he wasn't averse to dabbling on the dark side, he didn't see himself as a criminal. He wasn't like his father.

"You could say that." He pasted on his best smile, hiding his irritation. If Data knew how much the difference in terms bothered him, she might make use of it.

Data studied him as if checking to see if she could spot a lie. He almost wished she had turned out to be a man. Then he wouldn't be attracted to her.

His answer seemed to satisfy their curiosity enough to stop them asking questions. He sat back and watched them eat their lunch. He didn't need to be here, but he'd told Mia he'd keep an eye on them. When Mia found out about their little field trip this morning, she'd be pissed, but he couldn't help but be impressed by their initiative.

He must've zoned out while thinking about the team and their plans because he suddenly found Data standing in front of him waiting. His gaze met hers.

"You're in my way. I have things to do."

He slid over, pulling the other chair to where he'd been. She slid past, careful to not let any part of her touch him. She took off the cap she wore and sailed it across the room at Nikki.

"Thanks for that."

Nikki picked it up and twirled it on her finger. "I'll add it to my collection."

"You collect ball caps?"

"Costumes. You never know when you'll need to be someone else."

Jared watched the interaction with the realization that the women were becoming friends and wondered how that might develop into a problem later.

Data tapped away on the keyboard. He watched as her fingers flew over the keys. Then the monitor had his attention. Since Nikki was lounging and watching TV, Data hadn't bothered using the big screen. She was downloading specs for an alarm. Then she switched over to familiar-looking forums. The place they had met.

"Do you have to do that?" she asked without looking at him.

"What?"

"Stare at me."

"I'm fascinated by your work. You should know that by now. Plus, you're pretty."

Her cheeks grew pink, but she didn't say anything.

"What are you looking for?"

"A shortcut. If this system has a back door, someone will know about it." Now she did glance over her shoulder. "I assume you're willing to pay if someone has the information?"

"If they're reasonable, yes."

She chuckled. "I have a feeling your idea of reasonable and mine are completely different, so we'll be fine."

She opened a chat box and talked with her dark web friends.

"You're doing it again," she said from between clenched teeth.

"Get used to it. I like to watch."

"Sorry, that's not my kink," she said with a straight face.

He didn't know if she was joking or if she meant to imply she had a different kink.

Before he could ask, she reached over and pulled on her headphones. She pursed her lips and he was pretty sure she was holding back a smile. He wondered what she listened to. Was it classical music? White noise? No, she was a hard rock girl.

He took out his phone to take care of some texts and emails so she couldn't tell him he was being creepy. But she was fascinating. Just like yesterday, she fell into her own rhythm, her own world, and the rest of them ceased to exist.

After a while, Nikki became restless and went for a run. Jared moved through the apartment. Although Nikki lived there, she left few signs of her presence. Some clothes thrown haphazardly across one bedroom. Nothing personal. He knew she traveled a lot, going wherever her next job took her. But to his knowledge, Chicago was her home base. What did her real home look like?

A glance at Data had him wondering the same thing. *Who is she outside these walls?*

Suddenly she slid back from the desk with a loud clap and threw her arms in the air. "Yes!"

He returned to the chair beside her and studied the screen. A long list of meaningless code.

She stood and tossed her headphones next to the keyboard. She shimmied and danced to the music still blaring from the headphones. Joan Jett?

"What?" he asked.

"I got it. I have the way in."

The look on her face was sheer joy. A victor in battle. She held both hands up, palms facing him. "Hello? High five?"

He dropped his phone and raised his hands to meet hers. Her excitement was contagious and he couldn't help but smile. Tugging her arm, he said, "Now tell me what you have."

She pulled back. "Can't just let me enjoy the moment, huh? Always on my back to check my work."

He took a breath. "I'm not checking up. I'm genuinely interested. I want to know how you do what you do."

"If I give you all my trade secrets, I lose my edge, devalue my contributions, and make myself replaceable."

"Not likely."

Her cheeks flushed pink again and she ducked her head. "Well, no one single person had a way in, but based on a few conversations I've found, I think I can overload the system and force a reboot. If I can make that happen, Nikki has time to get in."

He nodded. Sounded good. "Enough time to get the painting and get back out, too?"

"Sheesh," she said with an eye roll. "Give me time. I've only been at this a couple of days."

For the next hour, they worked side by side, bouncing ideas and trying to figure out how they could do a test run.

Then Nikki strode back in. "Here." She tossed a package at Data.

"Oreos," she said reverently. "How'd you know?"

"You dumped like five wrappers from individual packs out of your sweatshirt when you changed. I figured as hard as you're working, you deserve a reward. And if you're going to indulge, I say go all the way," she said, pointing at the full package of cookies. Then she smiled at him and winked. "Don't you agree, Jay?"

Nikki's constant teasing was tough to get used to. He hadn't grown up with siblings, just Mia, and she wasn't the poking-fun type.

"About a trial run. Why not have the same system installed here? Then I can play with it and learn the ins and outs," Data said.

"That's not feasible." He'd considered the same thing, but they couldn't afford to buy every system they might encounter. Of course, Data and Nikki weren't yet aware that there would be other jobs. Jared and Mia wanted to see how successful they would be on this first one.

"How risky would it be to do it on Scott's house?" Nikki asked. "Like in the middle of the night."

"The system might send a signal to the monitoring company," Data said.

"Let's do this old school. Make a list of questions. I'll call the alarm company." He held up his burner phone.

SIX

AUDREY MADE A list of questions, some of which she had no idea how Jay would ask without sounding like a thief trying to hack the system. He got on the phone with yet another phony name. Smooth as melted chocolate, he spoke like the man she suspected him to be: someone rich enough to need a top-notch security system. She wondered what kind he had on his house.

Her phone buzzed in her pocket. Her phone, not the one Ms. Green had given her. The only person who ever called her phone was the assisted living facility. She ducked into the spare bedroom to answer. "Hello?"

"Ms. Abbott?"

"Yes."

"This is Mrs. Merriweather at Horizons."

"What's wrong? Is my grandma okay?"

"She is, but she's had a very bad day. Is there any way you could visit? Seeing a familiar face might help."

Familiar. Sure. At this point it was hit or miss if Gram recognized her at all. She peeked through the door and saw Jay still on the phone. "Yeah. I'll be there soon."

She stuffed her things in her bag. In the living room, she told Nikki she had to go take care of something and left without saying anything to Jay. Knowing him, he'd probably try to tell her she wasn't allowed to leave. She ran to the corner and hopped on a bus. If she timed it right, she could be back here within a couple hours.

The sun was lowering, but the air remained warm. Inside Horizons, the air felt slightly cool and stale, like being in a hospital. At the front desk, she signed in. Rather than ask for Mrs. Merriweather, Audrey went straight to Gram's room.

She knocked.

When Gram opened the door, she looked at Audrey blankly. It was one of those days.

"Hi, Gram. How are you today?"

"I'm fine. How many times are you people going to ask me that?" She turned and walked into the apartment, leaving the door open for Audrey to follow. She wore her favorite light blue tracksuit. On good days, she sometimes walked around the park with a group of residents. On bad days, she still dressed like it was a possibility.

As she neared the living room, she turned back to Audrey. "Audrey?"

"Yeah, Gram."

"When did you get here?"

"Just now."

"Come in and tell me what's going on in your life."

Audrey made her way into the room, taking note of the magazines and newspapers on the floor. A quick glance at the kitchen let her know that at least someone had been by to make sure dishes were clean. "How are you feeling?"

"I'm fine. I want to hear about you." Gram eased into a recliner that had seen better days. It was one of the few items they'd kept from their place. A small piece of home. Then she studied Audrey as she always did. "You look so much like her. I can't get over it."

Being told she looked like her mother was far from the worst thing Gram could've said. Some days, Gram thought she was Tina and yelled and threatened her to make her stay away. Audrey didn't have many fond memories of her mother. Tina was an addict who never had the desire or ability to get clean. She also hadn't had the desire or ability to care for Audrey. Men, however, she always had a fresh desire for.

"Tell me about your boyfriend. What's his name again? Michael?"

Audrey smiled. Sometimes she made up stories to tell Gram about her life. As far as Ruth Abbott knew, Audrey was a successful computer engineer who left a trail of broken hearts as she looked for the perfect man. With a wave of her hand, she said, "Oh, I broke up with him. He wanted me to scale back on my career for him."

"Pssh," Gram said, giving Audrey a shove with her bony hand. "There are plenty of fish in the sea."

"Actually, I've already met someone else." As long as she was playing out a fantasy, she might as well have fun. "His name is Jay and he's loaded. Wears fancy suits every day. Has a driver take him around the city."

"Really? What's he do for a living?"

"He's in some kind of business."

"Does *he* value your career?"

Audrey swallowed a laugh. "Yes. He's not only supportive of my career, he's downright fascinated by it."

"Sounds like a keeper." Gram leaned closer. "Is he good in bed?"

"Gram!"

"Well, you have to think about those things."

Audrey shook her head. "We're not there yet."

Gram turned her attention to the TV. "This is getting good," she said as she pointed to the soap opera she had on.

They watched in silence for a few minutes. Then Gram looked at her. "Who let you in here?"

She stood. Every time she lost Gram like this, it broke her heart a little more. "I'm sorry. I was just leaving."

As she made her way back down the hallway, Mrs. Merriweather called to her. "Do you have a few minutes to talk?"

"Sure." Audrey followed the woman to her office. "What's up?"

"I'm assuming you saw your grandmother?"

"Yeah. For a while, she was herself. We had a whole conversation before I lost her again."

"I'm sorry to say it's been happening a lot more lately. I think it's time to think about transitioning her to the full-time care wing."

Crap. She'd thought she had more time.

"We do have an available bed. But I'm afraid it won't stay available for long."

"And if I don't take it?"

The woman's whole face pinched, as if she couldn't imagine why Audrey wouldn't jump on the offer. "That would be your choice. However, if your grandmother gets worse, and we don't have a bed available, you'll need to make other arrangements."

Audrey had hoped that at some point her life would

move beyond rock and hard place. Even for a little while. "How much for her to move over?"

She knew it would cost more than the little apartment Gram currently lived in because they had around-the-clock care in the other wing, but she wasn't quite prepared for the contract Mrs. Merriweather slid in front of her. The advance Jay had given her for quitting her job would cover most of the month.

"Can I pay for part of it now and the rest in a couple of weeks?"

"A down payment would hold her spot and the rent you've paid on the apartment would be shifted over." At least she had the capacity to look at Audrey with sympathy.

Audrey moved money into Gram's trust and did an electronic payment that left her with approximately a hundred bucks in her personal account. So much for her own rent.

She walked around for a while instead of jumping back on a bus. She needed a plan. The Greens didn't want her working, but she wasn't sure if she could wait for this job to be done. She'd lived on less than a hundred bucks before. And if she ate at the apartment with Nikki, she'd save more.

It took longer than she planned to get back to the apartment. When she rang the bell, she tried to mentally prepare herself for Jay's irritation, but she couldn't muster the energy. Someone buzzed her up without asking who was there, so it was probably Nikki. The door stood open.

Audrey walked in and looked around. No Jay. Maybe something was going her way for a change. She dropped her bag next to the couch and moved to the desk. Jay had left her list of questions with answers scribbled everywhere. She tried to read them, but her mind kept going back to Gram.

"Jay's pissed."

"So what else is new?" Audrey mumbled.

"Where'd you disappear to?"

"I had to take care of something."

"You okay?"

She didn't bother with a lie. The only person in her life who really knew her was fading fast. "No."

Staring at the notes Jay left, she willed them to make sense. She had no idea how long she stood there not moving. Images of Gram getting worse assaulted her. Thoughts of bills piling up and her not being able to pay for Horizons scared the crap out of her.

Then Nikki was standing beside her with a glass of whiskey. "Drink up."

She wasn't much of a drinker. Being the child of an addict had that effect. Plus, alcohol was expensive. She swallowed the amber liquid and coughed as it burned its way down her throat.

Nikki refilled Audrey's glass and drank straight from the bottle of Glenfiddich. "We'll both get drunk, you'll spill your guts to feel better, and neither of us will remember it tomorrow."

It made no sense, but Audrey didn't care. She slugged back the whiskey again and held out her glass. "Sounds like a plan."

Audrey had no idea why she agreed. Maybe it was Nikki's seemingly carefree attitude. Maybe it was knowing Gram was getting worse. In that moment, though, she felt incredibly alone and Nikki offered a reprieve.

After the third shot, Nikki turned the TV on and booted up a video game. "Let's kill something."

"Is that supposed to help?"

"It can't hurt."

"I didn't peg you as someone who'd use gaming to de-stress." Audrey picked up a controller.

Nikki chuckled. "It's sure as hell not my first choice for relaxation. I mean, really, it's not like it could top thieving. But since I'm here…"

Audrey slammed another shot and created a character profile for the game. They played in silence for a while.

After the first round of killing, Nikki said, "You're not drunk enough."

"Why do I gotta be drunk?"

"You're not talking yet."

"I don't need to talk." She'd never been much of a talker. Growing up, she'd never wanted to burden Gram with silly adolescent feelings or thoughts. She'd been an outcast in school. She hadn't cared about grades, so people thought she was dumb. The only things she had talked about had been gaming and coding. Even though Gram didn't understand anything about video games or computers, she'd listen to Audrey talk about each new thing she'd learned. Gram always supported her, no matter what.

After two more shots, Nikki asked, "Ready to spill?"

"No need."

Nikki poured another. "Look. I need your head in the game. And not this one," she added, pointing to the screen. "If you're distracted by personal issues, my ass is in trouble. So what is it? Man problems?"

Audrey downed the whiskey and closed her eyes. "My grandma has dementia."

She choked on the words. Words she'd never spoken aloud. She always said Gram was sick or old or simply needed help.

"That sucks." Nikki refilled the glass.

"She needs more care. Gonna cost more." Was that her slurring? "I don't have anyone but Gram."

"Damn."

Another shot.

And another.

The graphics on the TV began to blur. She no longer cared how her on-screen character performed. Thoughts of Gram not recognizing her anymore swirled in her head. Her eyes filled and she blinked hard.

"Give me that." She snatched the whiskey from Nikki and drank straight from the bottle. It would be nice to forget everything for a while.

AUDREY FELT LIKE crap when she woke up the next morning. Most of her night was a blur. She and Nikki had talked and played video games and eaten. They'd drunk. A lot. Then she'd puked at least as much.

She rolled to the edge of the bed in the spare room. If she hadn't been so drunk, she might've enjoyed the spacious, perfectly comfortable queen-size mattress. A soft knock sounded.

"You awake?" Nikki called.

"Barely." God, she sounded like she'd swallowed a frog.

Nikki pushed through the door with a glass of water and coffee. She set them both on the dresser. "Take the pills, drink up and jump in the shower. Jay already called. He'll be here soon."

"Doesn't he have anything better to do than check up on us?"

"Hell if I know. Maybe it's because he has a thing for you."

"Huh?" Audrey vaguely remembered Nikki saying that last night. She lifted her shirt and sniffed.

"You can borrow something of mine. It'd be better than going back home and missing your lover boy."

Audrey snorted. She picked up the pills and studied them.

"Just aspirin," Nikki said.

Audrey looked at Nikki as she downed the pills. The woman didn't look hungover at all. How was that possible?

"Get moving," Nikki added before she left.

Audrey drank the coffee, which was too strong and bitter for her liking but better than nothing. She took the cup to the bathroom. One look in the mirror let her know she didn't have to worry about Jay trying to be her lover. At least not today.

She found a new toothbrush under the sink and brushed her teeth twice to get rid of the fuzzy feeling. Then she stepped into a shower that was damn near magical. No groaning pipes. Real water pressure. Super-powered jets. Yeah, jets, as in more than one. There was even a built-in bench. It took all of her willpower to not settle in to stay. The hot shower helped and her head no longer thumped.

After squeezing the excess water from her hair, she wrapped a towel around her body and went to borrow Nikki's clothes. She made it two steps out of the bathroom and almost crashed into Jay's chest.

Pulling up short knocked her off balance, and warm, strong hands steadied her. His tan fingers pressed into the flesh of her arms.

"What are you doing?" he asked quietly.

Swallowing hard, she said, "Going to Nikki's room to borrow clothes. I fell asleep here last night."

Although he released her arms, she felt his chuckle more than heard it. "Based on the empty bottle of my whiskey, I'd say there was more than sleeping going on."

Damn. I'm going to kill Nikki. She had to know it was his. "I thought it was Nikki's." Although she should've known. It tasted expensive. She shifted to move around him. "If you'll excuse me."

But he didn't move. He stood there, doing his staring thing. "What's wrong?"

"I'm hungover."

"It's more than that. Where did you disappear to yesterday?"

"I had to take care of something." She realized he probably thought she had another job, so she added, "Something personal."

"Anything I can help with?"

No. The last thing I need is more help. I had enough of that with Nikki last night. "I have it handled. Where's Nikki?"

"I don't know."

"She must've gone for a run. She's weird like that."

Again, she angled around him. This time he let her go. "I'll be out in a minute."

In Nikki's room, she saw a pile of clothes on the bed, seemingly left for her. She put them on and checked her reflection. Jay was a little too perceptive. She couldn't afford to have all these people up in her business. At the same time, she couldn't afford to piss him off and get fired. She'd have to make herself indispensable so he'd keep her working.

She schooled her face—all business, no flirting—and went to meet her boss, determined to prove her worth.

Jared waited in the living room, pacing. Catching Data in nothing more than a towel caused him to lose all thought.

As he cleaned up the empty bottle and glasses they left on the table, his unsettled feeling about Nikki and Data becoming friends grew. Mia's concern had him considering how together they could possibly work against him and Mia. He hadn't thought about Nikki corrupting Data. He didn't even know where the thought had come from. He didn't know her all that well, but he didn't think getting drunk on a bottle of whiskey was the norm for her. For Nikki, on the other hand, it was just another night.

The front door opened and Nikki came in carrying food. She set a bag on the corner of the table beside the drawing of Scott's house and opened a box of dough-nuts to offer him one. "The greasy breakfast sandwich is for Data, but you can have a doughnut."

"Very generous of you since I paid for it." He took a

chocolate frosted. This was the second time Nikki had brought specific food for Data. The woman appeared to have a soft underbelly when it came to their hacker.

She smirked. "I told you that keeping me here would cost extra. Say the word and I'll leave."

He knew better than to fall for that. She might land herself somewhere she couldn't get back from in time for this job. "I can afford a few doughnuts."

"Be nice. She had a rough night," she said as she closed the box.

"I think that's on you."

"Before I got her drunk." She glanced over her shoulder. "Maybe you forget, but some people have lives outside your little caper here."

He shoved the rest of his doughnut in his mouth. He *had* forgotten that they had lives away from here. The people they'd chosen for this job were picked because of their seemingly isolated lives. No discernible family or obligations. Loners. That was what made them perfect.

Obviously, he'd missed something with Data.

She came from the bedroom wearing a concert T-shirt that was too small for her. It stretched across her chest, inviting a whole host of inappropriate thoughts to cross his mind. Her hair curled against her shoulders in soft waves, leaving wet patches on the shirt. The shorts clung to her like a second skin, so looking at her legs didn't help clear his head. Forcing his gaze to her face, he looked for evidence of Nikki's warning. But Data had shut down.

Nikki tossed a sandwich at her. "Trust me. It'll help."

"Let's get this show on the road," Data said to him.

"I read your notes last night, but I have questions."
Sliding into the chair at the desk, she was all business.

It wasn't the same energy she'd had for the last few
days. More than just the hangover. Something was off,
but she wouldn't tell him if he asked, so he plowed
ahead. If she wanted to work, they'd work. Maybe that
was her method for clearing her head.

As she sank her teeth into the sandwich, she opened
a spreadsheet and began inputting the information they
had on the alarm system. She asked questions as she
typed without looking up at him at all. Every time he
didn't have an answer, she responded with a huff.

He needed to break her out of this funk. Although
she was working, they weren't actually making any
progress, and her dreary attitude cast a pall on the whole
apartment. He wouldn't say she had a normally sunny
disposition, but her energy had a way of zinging through
the air.

Since he had nothing else in his arsenal, he leaned his
chin in his hand and stared at her. To her credit, she let
him sit like that for at least ten minutes before breaking.

"You're staring again."

"You're still fascinating to watch."

She rolled her eyes. "If this is fascinating, maybe
you should sit with your assistant on a daily basis to
get your groove on."

"Who said I had an assistant?"

"You look like you would." Her fingers stopped,
poised over the keys, and she glanced at him as if to
check for a lie.

Dropping his hand from his chin, he leaned closer.
"I do have a receptionist who polices my office door. I

don't want people to think they can just stroll in. But I could never let a personal assistant run my life. I enjoy being in control far too much."

"Semantics." Her lips separated with the intake of her breath and for a moment, they were frozen in time. Whatever attraction existed between them was suddenly supercharged. Her mouth was close enough to taste.

And he wanted to.

The phone buzzing in his pocket broke the spell and he pushed away to answer it. The corner of her mouth twitched and a gleam in her crystal blue but bloodshot eyes was one of victory. The same as she'd had when she figured out how to break into Scott's house.

This was definitely going to be an interesting couple of weeks.

SEVEN

Mia

MIA HAD BURNED through three different artists and none of them could forge the Gavin Mathis painting she wanted from Randall Scott's house. It was modern art for Pete's sake. It wasn't like she expected them to imitate Monet or Rembrandt. But today, she had a good feeling about the artist she was going to see.

London George had no degree in art but had worked in five different galleries without ever having her own show. As luck would have it, Jared heard through his contacts that she'd done some forging of documents on the side to make ends meet. Even better was that no one Mia knew in the art world had ever heard of her. She would be the perfect addition. With any luck, she could work fast since they only had a couple of weeks.

Mia rang the bell on the seedy-looking building. The warehouse had been converted to co-op space for artists and musicians, but no amount of renovation would change the neighborhood. When the buzzer sounded allowing her entrance, she was met with noise from behind the doors leading to each loft. Some people rented space by the day, some by the month.

She knocked on the metal door to 1C and waited, trying to ignore the heavy metal music pounding in the other lofts. The door in front of her swung open and a tall, thin woman wearing a paint-splattered apron said, "Can I help you?"

"I'm looking for London George."

"You must be Ms. Green?"

Mia despised the silly name Jared used, but at least no one suspected her real name. She extended a hand. "Yes, may I come in?"

London took her hand and then stepped back. Mia took in the space. The walls must've been well insulated because the noise that was clear in the hallway was only a dull roar in here. Canvases were stacked in one corner and shelves held a variety of paints.

"You were pretty cryptic on the phone when we spoke. What exactly would you like to commission?"

"A replica of a Gavin Mathis painting."

London snorted.

"Is that a problem?"

"I'm not sure I would even call it art."

"I take it you're not a fan?"

"Hardly. He's one of many privileged white men whose art is deemed extraordinary even though it exhibits little thought or imagination." As she spoke she waved a paintbrush in the air to punctuate her points.

Mia didn't have the patience for another pompous artist. They all thought they were better than everything and everyone. "We might not be a good fit."

"Wait." London threw her hands up. "I can do the replica. I don't have to like the artist to copy his work. Which painting?"

"*Space Endeavor.*"

London scrolled on her phone and made another face. Then she turned the screen to Mia. "This one?"

Mia nodded.

"How soon would you need it?"

Mia smiled. "How quickly could you have it done?"

"That would depend on how exact it needs to be. If you're looking for something to hang in your living room for people to look at, I could have it done in a couple of days." She stepped closer. "But if you want something a little closer to the original, say, good enough that it would be hard to tell the difference, I'll need at least a week. Assuming the price is right."

From all accounts that she'd heard, Mia thought London was going to be mousy, but she didn't appear to be a pushover. And she was smart. "You have your week. Make it perfect and there will be a bonus in it for you."

London's eyes lit up. "Let's talk numbers."

Mia handed her a slip of paper and the burner phone Jared had given her. "I'll be in touch on that phone only."

"Okay," London said, drawing out the word laden with suspicion. She eyed the paper with the dollar amount. "Canvas stretched on wood to match. If you want a decorative frame, you supply it."

"No extra frame needed." She had no idea how to match what the Scotts had. Nikki would just have to swap them out. "I've also heard you're a bit of an expert in documents."

London's gaze darted around the room, almost as if she thought someone might be watching. "Where did you hear that?"

"Not important. What is important is whether you can create papers to show provenance."

London stepped closer. "You want me to forge documents?"

Her voice was low but not full of surprise, so Mia knew she was in the right place. "Call it what you will."

"I call it making sure a painting that I've created has proper ownership papers."

"Yes, that."

"When you arranged this meeting there was no mention of papers."

"I wasn't sure if I'd want them. I wanted to meet you first and decide." She glanced around the room again. "I decided I like you."

"Okay," London repeated.

Mia set five hundred dollars on the table. "That should be enough to get you started. Send me an account number for a wire transfer for the rest of the deposit. The remainder will be paid on delivery."

"Okay."

Mia was beginning to wonder if the artist knew any other way to communicate agreement. No questions. No discussions. She only hoped they had a clear understanding.

"I'll be in touch," she said. "I'll let myself out."

Once back on the street, she called Jared.

"Hello?"

"I have our artist. Your information panned out. How is everything there?"

"Good, I think. It seems as though Nikki and Data are becoming friends. They got drunk together last night."

"I told you letting them know each other would be a problem. What if they complete the work and don't give us what we want?" Damn. She hated being on a phone and having to be careful of her word choice.

"I think you're looking at this all wrong. If they bond, we can have a team. We won't have to assemble new players next time. They'll be comfortable and things will move faster."

Mia wasn't so sure. Team members were like family. There was nothing to stop them from turning on each other. Friendship removed the practicality and business from the relationship.

To Mia, that spelled trouble.

EIGHT

"WHAT EXACTLY IS your plan for overriding the security system?" Jared asked.

Data sighed, clearly irritated that he'd interrupted her again. "It's a multi-step process. First, I need to access the system remotely and infect it with malware. Then I keep going until it's overloaded and forces a reboot. When it reboots, Nikki goes in."

The plan didn't sound any different than it had when she'd mentioned it before. "How does she get out?"

"I trip the alarm."

"What?" he and Nikki both asked simultaneously.

Data smirked. "Trust me. I'll already have sent the Scotts information letting them know that we're upgrading the network system and if some features don't work correctly, their system will reboot. Ask for their patience as we work hard to improve the safety and security of their home."

"What if they call the security company?"

"Or the cops?" Nikki added.

"I plan to trip it earlier in the day when the good Scotts are home. They'll look around and see nothing wrong. I'll call from the security company, ask for their password, and they'll give it to me. They'll think nothing of it happening again later that night. And I'll have the bonus of knowing the password if I need it to get Nikki out. All will be back to normal by the following day."

"You really think Scott is dumb enough to fall for a fake email?"

"Most people do. Especially when I don't ask them to click on anything. It won't raise red flags as a phishing scam. It'll work."

"How will you gain access?" Jared thought it all seemed too simple. They'd hired an expert hacker, provided top-of-the-line equipment, and it sounded like she planned to do what a random teenager could do from his bedroom.

"I'm going to tap into the other devices in the house. That way the security system isn't breached until I want it to be."

"If you have access, why not just disable the alarm?"

"I don't have enough time to wade through the code I found to try to find the root access. If I could go back to the house as an alarm tech, I could have everything I need in under five minutes."

"Too risky."

"But better for me," Nikki called from the couch.

Jared spun to look at her. "How do you normally get in and out of a place? You work alone."

"I hire someone to give me a code. I *normally* spend months casing a job and figuring out the best way in and out. A few weeks is a rush job."

He knew they should've started sooner. Lesson learned. Given the timeline and the number of people they planned to hit, they would have to start the next job immediately. Maybe even before this one happened.

Could they take the chance that everything would be successful and their team would be intact?

"How much time would you need, knowing that you're not planning alone?"

"What difference does it make? You said we have to go with this in two weeks."

"I'm thinking of future endeavors." He knew he'd said too much, but Mia tended to be shortsighted when it came to how things worked on a team. Of course, she'd never wanted a team.

"You have more jobs planned?" Data asked.

"Possibly."

"That means he and the ice queen already have a schedule plotted out," Nikki said.

"Answer the question," he prompted.

"If it's another one like this, I could do it inside a month, assuming I have Data over there getting through the electronics. I personally like to scope out the place, though. I don't like going in blind."

He pointed to the prints and photos on the table. "You're not blind."

She waved a hand dismissively. "That's better than nothing, but trust me, I'm blind. I can't plan for what I might encounter."

"Then why do it?" Data asked.

"It'll be fun." Nikki smiled and then turned back to the TV show she was watching.

"She's crazy," Data mumbled and concentrated on the keyboard and screen in front of her.

"She likes the thrill. It's why she does what she does."

Data lifted her face. "Have you known her long?"

"Just by reputation."

"Then how do you know why she does it?"

"I'm good at reading people."

"Hmph."

"I'll admit, you're a tougher read. You keep your guard up more than Nikki. I think she doesn't give a fuck. But you, why do you do it?"

"It's a job."

"Have you ever thought about going legit?"

"I've done hacktivism and some white hat stuff. But black pays better." She swept her arm out to the area surrounding them.

He didn't consider anything here excessive. If she did, it gave him a little more insight into who she was. Her going rate had always been competitive. Maybe she didn't get enough work. It would explain her need to work at the coffee shop.

"I guess I can't argue that."

"Why do you do it?" she shot back.

"Karma."

She spun her chair to fully face him. "You think you can make up for screwing up in a past life by stealing in this one? I don't think you understand how this works."

"It's complicated. But I'm righting some wrongs in this life."

"Forward-thinking man." She tapped her forehead. "I get it. Securing your place in luxury in the next life."

"Not really. But that's a story for another day." And he wasn't likely to share it. Mia would kill him. "Back to your plan. How do you propose to access their devices?"

"I'll have to get close enough to tap their wireless network. Then I can see what my options are."

"Why didn't you do that while you were there? It's too risky to go back."

"I didn't know I needed to get it while I was there. And the friendly household maid was watching me."

"Field trip!" Nikki yelled from the couch.

The woman was a little scary. She didn't look like she was paying any attention to them, but then she chimed in as if part of the conversation the whole time.

"No more field trips."

"I can't hack from here. I need to be closer," Data said.

"How close?"

"Neighbor's house? On the street? Not totally sure till I get there." She pushed away from the desk. "I also think I should go with Nikki the night of the heist. If there are any problems, being closer would be better."

"And?"

She lifted a shoulder. "I'm thinking since you need a car anyway, you could make it a van. Like the FBI uses in movies. We can outfit it with my equipment and I can make sure Nikki gets in and out safely. Then it becomes our getaway vehicle."

A bright glint sparkled in her eyes as she spoke. He loved watching her enjoy herself.

"You're having fun with this, aren't you?"

"I don't get out much. Not like this. My work is usually done from my room. I don't have to go anywhere or see anyone."

"This isn't a movie. This is very much reality," he reminded her.

"Doesn't mean I can't have fun."

That statement alone was a swift reminder of how

Nikki and Data spending too much time together could be a bad thing.

"Yeah, you like to have fun, don't you, Jay?" Nikki asked, her voice filled with innuendo.

"My idea of fun has never revolved around hiding in a van or avoiding the authorities."

"Then you haven't really lived, man."

"Don't feel too bad. I haven't either," Data said.

"Having both of you on site for the heist increases the risk for the entire operation to be blown. I don't know that I'm comfortable with that."

"Good thing your comfort isn't the top priority. Getting the painting and keeping Nikki safe is." Data grabbed her bag. "Field trip tomorrow?"

"You got it," Nikki answered.

"You're leaving?" he asked.

Data looked at him. "I've given you my entire day and then some. There's nothing else for me to do tonight. I'll be back in the morning with the equipment I need."

He'd thought they'd spend more time together. He didn't want her to go. "Can I give you a ride?"

She bit her lip, then said, "Probably not a good idea. Boundaries, you know?"

Jared wanted to follow her out, see where she lived, know more about her, but he let her go. She was right. They had boundaries for a reason.

Or so he reminded himself.

THE FOLLOWING MORNING, Audrey was still questioning what was wrong with her. She'd almost accepted Jay's offer to drive her home. She could argue that it would've saved her bus fare, but she'd just be lying to herself. She wanted to spend more time with him. But letting him see her real life would end whatever thing they had buzzing between them. He'd take one look at her roach-infested apartment building and be reminded how out of her league he was.

Better for him not to have that shoved in his face. She was enjoying their flirtation and wasn't ready to let it go.

She'd tried waking her roommate before she left, but the girl wouldn't move. She needed to make sure Misty wouldn't flip when Audrey was a little late with rent. She'd never been late before, and at this point, she was barely there, so it felt more like she was using her room as storage for her clothes. She left a note and hoped it would be okay. If Misty booted her out, she had nowhere to go.

The morning rush-hour crowd filled the bus, pushing and shoving, knocking into her backpack. When a seat finally opened, she slid into it and held her bag on her lap. She didn't own much, but her equipment was high end. She was always torn over the risk: leave it in her room where it might not be safe because of Misty's guests or carry it with her where it might not be safe on the street, but it was easier than sending Jay on another shopping trip. And if she had it with her, she wouldn't have to worry about Misty selling it to cover her rent.

As much as she wanted to spend more time with Jay, enjoying the buzz, she hoped he wouldn't be at the apartment when she got there. She needed to keep her head clear and he made that hard. By the time she arrived, the sun beat down and no breeze blew to cool her off on her trek from the bus stop. Nikki buzzed her in and she wondered why they didn't give her a key.

Nikki was decked out in her running gear.

"I thought we were heading out right away."

"We are. I figured I could go for a run around the Scotts' neighborhood. Less suspicious than standing outside the house."

"I kind of need to be standing outside the house. That's how I'll gain access."

"I'll go for a run and then conveniently bump into you on the street. You know, Suburban Susie and her friend Barbie don't get together nearly enough." Nikki's voice rose to a godawful pitch. "No one would think anything of two neighbors chatting on the street. The only thing that would make it better would be if you were walking your dog."

"I don't have a dog."

"I bet Barbie would. One of those little yappie ones."

Audrey laughed. "While you have a point about standing on the street, I don't think I can do anything to look like I belong in that neighborhood. I mean, I did just fine dressed as the cable company employee, but as a resident? I doubt anyone would buy it. With my luck, the cops would roll up on me inside five minutes."

"Walk like you belong there and no one will question it. Own it, Barbie."

"Why do I have to be Barbie? You're the one with the model's body and gorgeous face."

Nikki shook her head. "You're cute."

"I wasn't trying to be cute."

"No. You're cute, cute. Like girl next door. Maybe

you're visiting your grandma." As soon as she spoke the words, Nikki clamped her mouth.

How much did I say when I was drunk the other night?

"That I can do." She glanced down at her usual jeans and T-shirt. "Do I look okay?"

"Hmm. Give me a minute." Nikki ducked into her bedroom and came back with a skimpy tank top.

"I am not wearing that."

"Use your body as a distraction. It always works. Put it on."

She sighed and peeled off her shirt. Just as she had the tank halfway on, the front door swung open and Jay walked in, catching a full view of her. At least she was wearing her good bra today.

He cleared his throat and turned his back. "Sorry. I didn't realize the communal space was considered a dressing room."

Nikki let out an exaggerated gasp. "Oh, my stars. You saw her in her unmentionables. That's it. You must ask for her hand in marriage now."

"What?" He turned quickly.

Audrey had the tight tank in place.

Nikki continued her charade. "How am I to marry the girl off now that you've scandalized her?"

Audrey laughed at Nikki's antics. When this job was over, she was going to miss her. She'd forgotten how much fun it was to have a girlfriend. "Don't worry, Jay. I'm okay with living my life as sullied spinster."

A slight shade of pink rose high on his cheeks. "You two are acting stranger than usual."

Nikki waved a hand. "What's usual? You've known us a week."

"And in that week, I've spent more time with you than I have with most people in my life." His gaze bounced between them. "Strange."

He had a point. Nikki was on a roll this morning.

"I'll be ready to go in a minute." She ran back to her room, leaving them alone again.

Audrey wondered if it was intentional.

"Interesting look." His gaze roamed over her.

Instead of the skin-crawling feeling she got when other guys made the same assessment, her skin warmed pleasantly. She tugged the neckline higher. "Nikki has a plan for being in the Scotts' neighborhood without being suspicious."

"How is that—" he gestured toward her top "—not suspicious?"

She grabbed her T-shirt and pulled it over the tank. "I'm Barbie, who's visiting her grandma. If someone questions me, I'm supposed to distract them with this top."

"That would work." He chuckled, low and a little dirty.

"Why are you here?" she asked to try to change the subject.

"To make sure you two don't get in trouble."

"I don't get in trouble."

Nikki reappeared. "No one is getting in trouble. Data is going to get the info she needs and I'm going for a run. We chat in front of Scott's house and no one thinks anything of it."

Audrey gathered her stuff and wondered how Nikki

managed to never slip up and use her real name in front of Jay. She was grateful for it, but if roles were reversed, Audrey wasn't sure she wouldn't screw up. "Do we have a car?"

"I can get one again," Nikki answered.

"How do you plan to get one?" he asked.

"Better if you don't know," Nikki said with a wink.

"Christ. I'll get you a car." His voice was full of exasperation.

Audrey stifled a laugh.

"As much as I'm sure we'd love being chauffeured around by your personal driver, it might be better not letting more people know about our plans."

Jay turned to Nikki. "I'll rent a car. No one will know what you're up to and nothing will look suspicious. Plus, I'll be able to keep an eye on both of you."

NINE

If NOTHING ELSE, Jay thought, working with these women was never boring. He rented a car and returned to pick up Data and Nikki. They were both slightly perturbed by the delay, but he needed to keep as much of this job under his control as possible. He'd known going in that Nikki was a wild card, but Data had struck him as more reserved and thoughtful.

The more time they spent together, the more he saw her other sides. She was drawn to adventure, even if she didn't fully participate. Made sense given her work. People hired her to cause trouble, but she didn't get personally involved.

They drove to Scott's neighborhood and Nikki jumped out a few blocks away with the intention of literally running into Data.

Once she left, Jared glanced at Data in the passenger seat. "You okay?"

"Yeah, why wouldn't I be?"

"You're quiet."

Her mouth lifted in a barely-there smile. "I'm always quiet."

A block from Scott's house, he turned the corner to drop her off. "I'll pick you up around the corner on the next block when you get the information you need." He took out his phone and dialed her number. "Keep the line open so I can hear what's going on."

"Jeez, the thieves on TV get special comms that they stick in their ears and all I get is a phone call. Disappointing." She'd debated bringing comms with her, but since she'd thought only she and Nikki were going on this excursion, comms wouldn't have been needed.

"Yeah, well, we weren't planning on building a team for this job." He made a mental note to look into a better comms system if they were going to keep working together. As she reached for the door handle, he asked, "Aren't you going to take the T-shirt off?"

She huffed and put her phone and earbuds on the dashboard. She peeled off the shirt and tossed it on the console between them. Then she proceeded to tuck her scanner into her waistband. With one earbud in she said, "Testing…can you hear me?"

The rise and fall of her chest mesmerized him and he didn't realize she was waiting for a response.

"Hello?" She tapped his forehead.

His gaze shot up to hers. "Sorry. Yes, I hear you. But it might be more effective to run that test once you're out of the car."

"Whatever." She climbed out and started walking toward Scott's house.

He waited until she turned the corner and then he circled around to find Nikki. She was jogging at a quick clip but as long as Data walked slowly, they'd reach each other at the right place. Nikki definitely had a feel for this. "Nikki is about a block down, keep a lookout to adjust your pace," he said into his phone.

"Roger." Then she giggled. "This kind of spying feels weird, doesn't it?"

"Only when you talk like that."

"How should I talk?"

"I think being yourself is always the way to go."

She responded with another laugh.

"What's funny about that?"

"You're never yourself. At least not around us. I know nothing about you."

"I could say the same."

"True. It's probably best that way."

"Maybe. What would you want to know? If you could ask me anything, what would you ask?" He wouldn't answer most questions. Self-preservation was too important, but he wanted to know.

"Are you single?"

He had no problem answering that question. He didn't want her thinking he'd been involved with someone while flirting with her. "Yes. You?"

"Of course."

"What do you mean, 'of course'?"

"People like me don't date. Could you imagine me bringing some guy into my life and when we talk about work, he'd be like, 'You're a hacker? Cool.' Somehow, I doubt that's the way it would go."

"Probably not if you were dating a lawyer or police officer. But surely you know other hackers."

"Been there. Done that. Different goals. If I let a man in my life, he won't be in my line of work."

Jared wondered what the story was there but didn't ask. Data didn't bother to ask why he was single, which was good because he didn't have an answer. He figured he'd know when he met the right woman.

While she was open to questions, he couldn't help himself. "What's the one thing a man could do that one hundred percent would turn you on?"

She coughed on the line. "Getting kind of personal there."

"You had your shot. You could've gone there. Are you going to answer? Or are you afraid?"

"Psh. Afraid? Of what? You'll use the information against me?"

I absolutely will.

"A man who paid my bills. Being debt-free is quite the turn-on."

"That's a cop-out."

"Uh…"

She was flustered, but he waited, sure she'd answer. In his ear, he heard an ungodly squeal.

"Barbie? Is that you? Oh my God. It's been forever."

Nikki had horrible timing, and she was in rare form.

"Susie. It's so good to see you." Data's tone was dry and bland, in total contrast to Nikki's bubbly character.

"Are you in the right spot?" he asked.

"Of course. We know what we're doing," she answered quietly while Nikki continued to babble about crazy weekend plans he hoped weren't real.

He drove through the neighborhood, blocks away to avoid drawing suspicion. The day was hot, so no one was milling around. No nannies pushing strollers, no housewives walking dogs. "Anyone near you?"

"We're fine, Jay. Just two chicks standing on the

street catching up. If you stop interrupting, I'll have what I need in two minutes."

The entire time she mumbled at him, Nikki's narrative continued in the background. "Have you seen that video? Oh, I laughed for at least ten minutes. Every time I'm feeling down and the Xanax isn't quite enough, I watch it again. I'll send you the link."

"Speaking of videos, you'll love this one." Data's voice became singsongy.

He imagined her holding up her scanner as if it were a phone. He chuckled.

"You naughty girl," Nikki said.

Jared's ears perked up.

"Is that...oooh." Nikki's husky comments made him question how much of their conversation was a ruse.

With Nikki, he never knew. And then Data chimed in.

"Oh, yes, it is. It's from my private collection. Guaranteed for a good time."

He cleared his throat as the women burst out laughing.

"It's not nice to mess with the man who supplies your paycheck."

"It wouldn't be so easy if you weren't creepily listening in on us," Data said.

"I'm here to make sure everything runs smoothly."

"We didn't need you. I'm done."

"It was great seeing you again, Barbie. We absolutely must get together soon," Nikki crooned.

"I'll pick you up on the next block," he said to Data. Nikki would run back to where he dropped her off.

Jared idled at the curb waiting for Data. She glanced around and then climbed into the car.

"Did you get what you needed?"

"I told you I did." She pulled her scanner out. "Did you want to see the video from my private collection?"

Was she seriously pushing his buttons right now? Two could play that game. He leaned across the console, where her T-shirt still lay, and whispered, "I prefer the real thing to a video. I'd be more than happy to act it out with you."

Her face flushed. She parted her lips but said nothing.

THIS WAS A TEST. He was teasing her, but she didn't care. Backing down wasn't an option. So she closed the short distance between them. She'd wanted to kiss him for days. Every time he stepped into her space or leaned close, she'd considered what it would be like.

Now her lips met his, soft and coaxing. She angled her head and slipped her tongue inside his mouth. He reached up and held her head, taking control of the kiss. His tongue stroking hers was like a drug pulling her under. She shifted to get closer. If the console hadn't been between them, she would've climbed onto his lap.

Her head buzzed with anticipation.

No, that was actual buzzing. Jay must've noticed at the same time because he pulled away.

"Your phone," he whispered gruffly.

She eased back into her seat and picked up her phone. "Hello."

"Everything okay? You're supposed to be here."

Audrey swiped at her lips. "Uh, yeah. You must've run too fast. We're on our way."

Jay already had the car in gear and sped down the

street. No tires squealed, but fast enough to make up for their make-out time. He stared straight ahead without acknowledging the kiss or her.

Audrey flipped down the visor and looked at herself in the mirror. Her skin was still flushed and maybe her lips were a little kiss-swollen, but no other evidence of what they'd done. At the next corner, Nikki stood playing on her phone.

When they pulled up, she climbed into the back seat. "What happened?"

"Nothing," Audrey and Jay answered together.

"Uh-oh. Are Mom and Dad fighting?"

Audrey twisted in her seat to look at Nikki. "Don't call us that." It was too close to how they'd both referred to Jay and Ms. Green. *Ms. Green.* Why didn't they know her name? And where was she? They hadn't seen her for days. Not that Audrey was complaining. She didn't much like the woman.

Nikki rolled her eyes. "We have everything we need now?"

"I believe so. When we get back to the apartment, I'll poke around and see what I can find."

After a few minutes of driving in silence, Nikki climbed halfway into the front and turned on the radio. Audrey tuned out the music and considered what had happened. *I kissed Jay.* That didn't seem like a smart move. As he'd pointed out, he was her paycheck. Getting involved with him could make things messy.

She glanced at him. Still no sign of what he thought about their kiss. Except for the muscle twitching in his jaw. That was usually an indication of irritation. Or frustration.

Neither one a good sign for her.

Damn. Hadn't she already decided she was going to make herself indispensable to him? She hadn't been thinking about time in the bedroom either. Well, she *had* been thinking about it, but not in relation to being indispensable. And now, this kiss made her think even more about getting naked with him.

With the exception of the blaring music and the occasional grunt or cheer while Nikki played a game on her phone, the ride back to the apartment was silent. When Jay parked, Audrey hurried out to follow Nikki. Part of her hoped Jay left to go brood somewhere else. He'd cool off and they'd be fine.

"I don't know about you guys, but I'm starving," Nikki said, taking off her shirt as she walked through the living room.

The woman had no boundaries.

Audrey turned to close the door, but Jay was coming in.

"Someone better make or order food. I'm going to shower." Nikki disappeared into the bathroom.

Audrey moved toward the computer. Jay stood near the desk, staring at her. She had work to do, but attempting to accomplish anything while he glowered a foot away was futile.

The water turned on in the bathroom and Nikki began singing, off tune.

Audrey knew she should say something. Maybe apologize. She licked her lips and was immediately reminded of his taste.

"About the car—"

That was as far as she got because he was suddenly

there, backing her against the wall, pressing his body to hers. "Yeah?"

Her chest rose and brushed his. What had she planned to say? That it was a mistake? "Maybe we shouldn't have done that."

"Why not?"

"It might complicate things. Between us. With this job." She was a little breathless.

His mouth was *right there*. Close enough to taste again.

"I don't agree." He brushed his lips on hers. "I think we both enjoyed the kiss more than we thought. Pleasure doesn't have to be complicated."

He gripped her hips and kissed her fully. She wrapped her arms around his neck and toyed with the short, dark hair on the back of his head. He skated his hands up her sides.

His growl deep in his throat made her pulse spike.

Nikki's singing stopped, pulling Audrey's attention. She slapped a hand on Jay's chest. "Nikki's going to come out in a minute."

He kissed along her jaw and nibbled on her neck. She wanted nothing more than to see how far he'd go, up against the wall in this apartment where anyone could walk in. But she had work to do and Nikki would never let this go.

"We have to stop."

He dragged himself away from her. From under hooded eyes filled with lust, he asked, "Why?"

"Nikki is on the other side of that door. And while you probably don't care what she thinks, consider that she'll tell Ms. Green about it. I doubt that would bode well for either of us."

Acknowledgment crossed his face. "Fine. But we're far from done here."

He pushed away from her and cool air pricked against her skin. Smoothing down her shirt, she shook off images of his words.

A moment later, the bathroom door opened and Nikki bopped out, oblivious to what was going on in the living room.

"I'm going to pick up some lunch. Dinner. Whatever," Jay said, still staring at her with heated eyes.

"I'll let Nikki know." Audrey avoided looking at him. She booted up the computer to figure out how to get malware into Scott's house.

"Let Nikki know what?" Nikki asked as she came in the room.

Jay was already gone. Audrey waved in the direction of the door. "Jay went to get food."

"Better be something good. I'm starving."

"You're always starving." Audrey opened a window on the computer and began poking around.

"What's that?" Nikki asked, plopping in the chair Jay normally sat in.

"A list of what the Scotts have on their DVR. Looks to me like Mrs. Scott lied when she said she barely watches TV. I doubt Randall is the one watching *The Bachelor*, *Dancing with the Stars*, and *General Hospital*." The last made her think of Gram. She should go visit.

"What do you care what the woman watches?"

"I don't. The DVR is connected to their Wi-Fi. Now I can hack into everything."

TEN

JARED DROVE FOR blocks without a plan. Kissing Data—
twice—had firmly scrambled his brain. He'd been
attracted to her personality long before they met in person. Something about her snark was fun. Then, having
the chance to actually work with her, see her in action,
did something to him. How could he not be attracted
to such a competent woman? He'd wanted to take her
to bed, but part of him was glad she'd stopped him. If
Mia found out he'd even kissed Data, she'd throw a
hissy fit. No way could she have planned for him to be
attracted to their hacker.

But what he'd said to Data was true, too. They
weren't finished. He couldn't even guarantee they'd
wait until the job was done. They just needed to step
back and make sure they were on the same page. A little
stress relief would do them both some good.

He stopped at a sandwich shop and ordered a bunch
of subs because he had no idea what either woman
would eat. Back at the apartment, he let himself in and
put the food on the table. Nikki was in her usual spot on
the couch, this time playing a video game. She pounced
as soon as the bag made contact.

"I hope you bought a lot. I'm famished."

He glanced over to where Data sat at the computer,
typing madly with her headphones on.

"Don't bother. When she gets like that, she's oblivious to everything around her. If she's hungry, she'll figure it out."

He leaned against the back of the couch. "How long does she stay that way?"

"Hours? Days? Who knows?"

"Does she move at all?"

"Depends. If she has snacks and drinks at the desk, only to run to the bathroom." She paused as she unwrapped a sandwich. "It's kind of like watching a new breed of animal at the zoo. You never know what's going to happen."

It didn't look like Data had any sustenance surrounding her, so he set a sandwich and can of pop near her. She didn't even look up.

He didn't know quite what he'd expected. That his proximity would break her concentration? He'd been known to have that effect on some women. They had chemistry as evidenced by their kiss, but she didn't acknowledge him at all.

Moving back to the table, he asked, "What's she working on?"

"Not totally sure. She was dicking around with their DVR because that's how she's getting access to everything else in the house."

Watching her in her zone was mesmerizing. He could sit there all day and stare. Just then, she froze and her gaze shot up to meet his. Her look screamed, "Stop staring." He winked and offered her a smile, so she switched to a glare.

The need to kiss that attitude away strengthened, so

he grabbed the keys for the rental car. "I'm going to return the car. I'll be back later."

"Wait," Nikki said with a mouthful of pastrami and lettuce. "I want to do a trial run to time getting in and out."

"What do you need?"

"A dummy painting—or at least the frame—hanging on a wall. The entrance and exit like I'll be going through. It all looks good on paper but we have to plan for everything because I'm not getting my butt tossed in jail because you and your...whatever she is can't plan a heist."

"Okay. I'll set it up. We'll find a way for you to run through as many times as you need to be comfortable doing this." He looked back at Data who had returned her attention to the screen in front of her. They had time to address things later.

After returning the rental and being dropped off back at the apartment, he went for a walk. The sun hung low and the air was still warm. He needed to think and talk with Mia. He dialed her number and when she answered, he asked, "Is everything going well with the artist?"

"Yes. The painting is fabulous. How are the other things coming?"

"Good. We think we have the system figured out, but Nikki wants a run-through. I told her we'd get something set up. She needs the painting or something of the same size and space to mimic the actual job."

"Where are you?"

"Taking a walk."

"You're out in public talking about this?"

He rolled his eyes. Mia worried about the most ridiculous things. "No one is around. Even if someone was walking beside me, he wouldn't have a clue what I was talking about."

"Can she do her imitation at the apartment?"

Jared briefly calculated the distance she would have to cover at Scott's house with the layout of the apartment. "Not really. We can try, but it won't give her the real effect. Any other ideas? I don't suppose we have an empty warehouse available, do we?"

Mia was so quiet that he thought he'd lost her.

"Mia?"

"I'm here. I think I might know of a place. London, our painter, works out of a loft that would offer plenty of space. Let me check."

Jared stopped. "You're going to let her know the entire plan? And introduce her to Nikki and Data?"

"Ugh. Can't you call her something else? What is the woman's real name?"

"Data? I haven't asked."

"At this point, it makes sense to, don't you think?"

"I don't know. Are we sharing our names with them?" He shoved his free hand in his pocket and rocked back on his heels. As tempted as he was to ask Data her name, he knew Mia wouldn't want to share.

"They don't need that information."

"And you don't need her real name." But he did. *Need* was a strong word, but he'd never pursued a woman without even knowing her name.

"You're awful protective of our *employee*."

He didn't like the emphasis she placed on her last

word. As if he needed to be reminded of their professional relationship.

Hell, maybe he did need to be reminded since he was having anything but professional thoughts about her.

"I like her, Mia. And not as an employee. I respect the hell out of her abilities. But beyond work, we click."

"You absolutely cannot click with her."

He chuckled at the euphemism.

"I'm not kidding, Jared. We're too close to making this happen."

"I won't do anything to jeopardize our plan." He turned to head back to the apartment.

"Be sure you don't. I told you I didn't expect you to be part of this."

"I am part of it. My father is every bit as guilty as yours. They both deserve to pay." Just thinking about their fathers had his stomach in knots. Sure, when they'd been kids, they had no reason to think about what their fathers did for a living. But the entire time they were being raised to be upstanding, successful members of society, Cesar Towers and Dwayne Benson were stealing from anyone not smart enough to see it coming. Hell, he'd been finishing law school when shit hit the fan. He should've suspected. He and Mia both despised that even as adults they had never questioned what their fathers did or how they'd been so successful.

They'd been sucked into their lies as easily as their victims.

"Then don't let anything get in the way."

He laughed again. "I can take care of myself."

"I'll let you know if I have a place for a trial run."

They disconnected and he stood in front of the apartment. Mia had a point—she always did. As he debated going up, the door opened and Data stepped out.

She pulled up short when she saw him standing on the sidewalk.

"Done for the day?"

"Yeah. I think I have everything about ready to go."

"Okay. We're trying to secure a location for Nikki to do a trial run for timing."

She nodded. "See you tomorrow."

"You need a ride?"

"No. I'll catch a bus on the next block."

"That's crazy. My car is right here."

She hesitated, biting down on her lower lip.

"It's been a long day. A ride from me will certainly save time."

"Fine. It doesn't matter if you know where I live because I'm probably going to have to find a new place anyway."

He pointed his fob at his car and unlocked it. "Why?"

"Just because."

So they weren't at the sharing portion of this relationship. He got behind the wheel. "Where to?"

Instead of answering, she punched in an address on his navigation system. The robotic voice directed him. He decided to use the time alone to get to know her better.

"Why hacking?"

"Why fixing?"

"I'm a negotiator."

"Whatever you need to tell yourself to sleep at night."

"How often does your mouth get you in trouble?"

"Almost never. Hard to do when you don't interact with people."

IT TOOK EVERYTHING Audrey had not to stare at Jay while he drove. His profile was strong and beautiful and begged to be stroked. Instead, she forced her gaze out the side window, which didn't help because then she thought about their kiss earlier. *Kisses*.

"You don't interact with people at all?"

"In person? Other than at the coffee shop, not if I can help it. I don't like them much."

His quiet chuckle drew her attention.

"What's funny about that?"

"You've been spending a lot of time with Nikki."

"Because you set up the equipment at the apartment and told me to work there. And as far as I can tell, you make Nikki live there."

"We want to keep her out of trouble until the job is done."

"And I interact with her because she's there. I'm not totally rude. Doesn't mean I like people." She said the words, but she didn't feel them. They weren't a total lie. In general, she didn't like people, but she liked Nikki.

"I guess hacking makes sense then. Distance from the human race. Why the coffee shop? Nothing but people there."

"That's my legitimate money. I work regular hours, get a paycheck, pay taxes. Hacking pays the bills."

"Where'd you get your start?"

She sighed, debating on how much truth to dole out.

"I needed money fast. Not too many legit jobs can do that. Once I started, I didn't see the point in stopping. Like I told you, black hat jobs pay well."

"I'm aware of what side of the law pays best."

"How did you get your start in negotiating?"

"Law school."

Damn. He's a lawyer? Pulling a heist like this? "Don't you worry about getting caught on the wrong side of the law?"

"Are you?"

"I play in the shadows. Nobody really cares about the person sending the malware; they want the person who hires me. I'd think that as a lawyer, you'd be out in the open dealing with people."

"I'm not a practicing lawyer. The law degree is pertinent only insofar as having the ability to know where the lines are so I can decide whether or not they should be crossed." He got off the highway and sped down Western Avenue, his sleek car eating up the distance. "Although I'm not always one hundred percent lawabiding, this job is the first time I've gone that far over the line. I prefer to walk the line."

"Then why?"

"Some things are worth breaking the law for."

She knew that, too. But she couldn't imagine it was money. He definitely had plenty. Her curiosity got the better of her and she twisted in her seat to fully face him as he parked in front of her crappy apartment building. "What is?"

"Huh?"

"What's worth it for you?"

"Family."

She hadn't expected that. She didn't know what she had expected, but it wasn't that his answer would be the same as hers.

He stared at her, his dark brown eyes asking her to reveal her secrets even though he didn't speak the words.

The silent request had her spilling. "The first time I hacked, it was to steal money to give to my mom's dealer. He threatened to kill her and she was desperate. I was thirteen. Helping her meant selling my body or stealing."

"Did she clean up?"

"I doubt it. Not long after, I went to live with my grandmother." Still leaning on the console, she figured it was only fair for him to give up some secrets, too. "Based on the cringe you offered when I suggested Ms. Green was your girlfriend, I assume she's the family worth doing this for?"

He nodded. "We're cousins."

"Really? I'd never guess. I don't see much of a resemblance."

"Our mothers are sisters. Mia looks like her mother. I take after my father." He paused. "In appearance only."

Audrey felt like he was handing out pieces of a puzzle of his life, but she had no idea how they fit together. "So, you're breaking the law for her?"

"In a manner of speaking. It's been her plan for a long time."

Although he didn't offer more explanation, Audrey understood there was more to it. "You mean, you guys aren't like just freaky art collectors?" She put some teenage girl vibe into her speech, earning her a smile.

"I'll tell you a little secret." His curled finger beckoned her closer, so she inched forward. "I couldn't care less about art."

"That's not much of a secret," she whispered. The intimacy of the space urged her on. "Tell me a real secret."

"All right." His voice dropped. "My cousin would kill me if she knew I was doing this."

Without waiting for her to ask what *this* was, he closed the miniscule distance between their mouths. Only their lips and tongues touched, but pleasure skittered across every inch of her. Heat built from her mouth straight down to her toes.

When they paused to take a breath, he leaned back against the headrest and closed his eyes.

She stifled a laugh. "Not quite how I envisioned my night ending."

"Doesn't have to end," he said, eyes opening to slits.

"Yeah, it does. We both know you don't belong in there." She hitched a thumb over her shoulder. "It's one thing to flirt and kiss in your fancy apartment or in your luxury car, but we aren't part of each other's worlds. Let's not pretend we are."

She reached for the door handle. He grabbed her free wrist.

"This isn't over."

She answered with a smile.

He let go of her and said, "We do a dry run with Nikki tomorrow. I'll text you the address when we have it set. Bring whatever you need to simulate the night of the heist."

"No problem." She left the car and went inside her apartment. She didn't look over her shoulder or run to the living room window to see if he'd waited for her to get inside. She held no illusions about what they were to each other.

Even if she did have the silly thought that made her seem like a teenager coming home from a first date.

Then a note on her bedroom door caught her attention.

I need the rent~M

Damn. She'd hoped Misty wouldn't notice how late she was. She dumped her bag on her bed and went to get at least fifty bucks to keep Misty off her back. When she stepped out on the street, Jay's car was still sitting in the same spot. What was the likelihood she could get by without him noticing?

Zero, based on the passenger window sliding down. She dragged her feet back to the car and lowered herself to lean on the door.

"Forget something?"

"No. I'm running to the corner to get some cash. I owe my roommate rent."

"Should you be running anywhere in this neighborhood alone?"

"I live here. I'll be fine. Have a good night." She tapped the door and stood.

"How much do you need?"

She bent again and looked in the car. He held out a stack of crisp hundred-dollar bills.

"I don't need your money," she lied.

"And I don't need my asset getting hurt running around out here. Take it."

She snagged the bills, counted out three, and returned the rest.

"I have every intention of recouping my losses. And I don't mean the money. Sleep well."

She stepped back on the curb. He rolled the window up but didn't pull away. Lowering the window partway again, he said, "Go inside, Data."

She rolled her eyes even though he couldn't see it, turned, and went in. It had been so long since anyone cared about her, it caught her off guard.

He's just protecting his investment.

She was okay with that.

ELEVEN

THE FOLLOWING DAY was a welcome break from all things Randall Scott and the break-in. Mia secured a location but thought it would be better to do the trial at night. The simulation would be more realistic and fewer people would be around to witness unusual activity.

So Jared spent the day dealing with clients and wrapping up a few jobs he'd been neglecting while babysitting Nikki. A local contractor was getting screwed over by politicians, the usual Chicago dealings. But they held no interest for him. Other things were occupying his mind these days and it didn't bode well for his business. He texted Data with the address and asked if she needed a ride, but she declined.

He hoped things wouldn't get weird between them. He didn't want to hear Mia's nagging. They were all adults and could act as such. If Data didn't want any more than what they'd done, he could back off. He didn't want to, but he would.

After the sun had set and night had fallen, he drove to the warehouse building Mia directed them to.

He stood in front of the door and checked his watch. For a second, he had a flash of his dad telling him to always wear a watch. Every idiot had a phone, but a man of means wore a watch.

"Fancy meeting you here," a voice called from behind him.

Forgetting about his watch and his father, he turned to see Data coming up the walk.

"Did you have a good night?" Data asked.

"If you must know, I didn't sleep well."

"Too bad. I slept like a baby. Soooo relaxed." She stretched her arms over her head.

She was toying with him. And he liked it.

Lowering himself to her ear, he said, "You'll pay for that."

"Will I? Sounds like a threat."

"More like a promise. Because you'd only push and tease like that if you wanted me to push back."

THE DOOR IN front of them opened, and a woman in paint-splattered jeans asked, "Are you Ms. Green's friends?"

"Yes."

"I'm London. Down the hall. 1C. They're waiting for you."

London led them down the hall, which was mostly silent. She opened a huge metal door to a loft littered with art supplies. "Everyone's here. Do you need anything else?"

"No, thank you," Mia said.

"Do you mind if I stay to watch?"

Mia glanced at Jared. He shrugged. What did he care if she stayed?

Nikki came from around a corner dressed all in black, her long dark hair tucked inside a knit cap, and no shoes. Instead, she wore black toe socks that looked like they were rubber.

She bent and stretched, as if doing a rapid-fire yoga class.

Data stood beside him, watching Nikki. She nudged him with her elbow. "Don't get your hopes up. I'm not that flexible."

He swallowed a chuckle.

"Are we ready?" Mia asked. Without waiting for a response, she continued, "The frame with a blank canvas is hanging on the wall in the hallway upstairs."

Data stepped forward. "If you come in through the window in the den on the first floor, you can take the stairs up, like we originally thought. The motion sensors will be disabled during the reboot. Take the painting and leave the way you came while I trip the alarms for the front and back doors simultaneously."

"You said two minutes from your go until the system reboots?"

"At least two. I'll do what I can to stretch it. You might have up to five."

"Two it is." She picked up a rope and looped it tightly around her waist.

"I have questions," he said. "One, aren't you going to put on shoes?"

Nikki kicked up a leg. "Shoes make noise. With these, I'm silent."

"Two, what's with the rope?"

"If I have to leave from a different exit, say a second-floor window, I like to be prepared."

"How are you going to climb down a rope from a second-story window without leaving evidence?"

She flashed a grappling hook at him. "It's quick release. I drop down, and then press this button. They'll just think they left a window open."

It looked like they had all their bases covered. Nikki took another blank canvas, rolled it up, and tucked it in with the rope at her back.

"Ready? Go." Data pressed the stopwatch on her phone.

He blinked and Nikki was through the room and up the stairs in silence. The whole group of them followed her at a distance.

London gasped. "You can't do that."

"What?" Nikki froze with a knife in her hand.

London rushed forward. "First, if you cut the painting, you'll lose important identifying marks. Mathis is one of the artists who always marked the edges of the canvas. Second, how are you getting the new painting in?"

Nikki's jaw dropped.

They *hadn't* figured out everything. Damn it.

Mia pushed through the crowd, pointing a finger at Nikki and then at Data. "You said you had a plan. You knew what you were doing."

"I'm getting her in," Data said. "That's my job. What she does once in there has nothing to do with me."

"And I told you I usually go in and take what I want. I don't leave gifts."

Exasperated, Mia threw her hands in the air. To him, she asked, "Well?"

"Calm down."

Mia's eyes flashed. He knew it was a mistake to say

those words to any woman, but his cousin, in particular, deplored them.

He took a deep breath and hoped Mia would follow suit. "London, this is your area of expertise. How should she do it?"

London looked at Mia. "I made this one to your specifications. Without seeing how the original is framed, I'm guessing."

"My specifications are exact. I've seen it."

"Well, your owner is a freak. Artwork typically isn't framed like this anymore. We use metal clips to hold the canvas in place. This is more complicated." She moved across the room and held the frame. "Nikki needs to take the frame from the wall, take out the spline, which is basically a rope that provides tension to give the canvas a tight fit, and then remove the corner pieces, pop out the canvas and replace it with the new one." She pointed to the rolled canvas at Nikki's back. "Unless you know how to stretch a canvas, that needs to be on a frame already—which the forgery is."

"Oh hell." Nikki threw the canvas on the floor.

"We're screwed," Mia concurred.

"No, we're not. We have time to figure this out," Jared said. "We have some of the best minds I've ever come across standing right here. Data didn't think she could bypass the security system and she figured it out. We have someone who created a perfect duplicate. And we have a master thief. We can do this."

Mia didn't look convinced. Nikki took the frame off the wall and flipped the painting over. She banged the edge.

"What are you doing?" London asked.

"I thought maybe I could pop it out and then pop in the new one."

With a small sigh, London said, "This isn't a movie."

"I got it!" Data yelled.

Everyone turned to look at her.

IT WAS A little unnerving to have four people stare at her, but Audrey pushed forward. "I know the movie Nikki's thinking of. *The Thomas Crown Affair.*"

They returned blank looks, except, of course, Nikki. Didn't these people watch movies?

"The thief runs through the museum, grabs the painting, pops it out of the frame and puts it in a briefcase. But in the bonus content, the director talked about how they cut the scene that showed how the frame was partially broken, allowing the painting to be folded."

Nikki nodded. "Explains a lot. I always had a problem with that scene."

London took the frame from Nikki and within minutes had the canvas out. She ran her fingers over the edges of the wood.

"Can it be done?" Audrey asked.

"Maybe. It's soft wood." She turned to Nikki. "Give me your knife."

Jay and Ms. Green stood in silence while London worked. Suddenly Nikki jumped in.

"I get it. Like a hinge. It'll make it half the size. Still a little big for me to carry, but I can make it work." She stared at the empty spot on the wall. "What about the original?"

London continued to saw at the wood and then folded the canvas over itself. It did look hinged.

Jay chuckled. Audrey liked the sound far too much. He tapped Ms. Green's shoulder. "I told you. Give them a few more minutes and I bet they'll have it figured out."

He looked at Audrey over the top of the other woman's head and winked.

"Why don't we leave them to it?" he said.

Audrey mouthed thank you to him. Ms. Green rubbed her the wrong way every time she was around. She made it hard for Audrey to think. How she and Jay could be related, Audrey couldn't quite wrap her head around. They both came from money, but Jay fit in with the rest of them better. Not perfectly, and mostly Audrey believed he excelled at faking it.

Ms. Green didn't even try to fake it. She let everyone know she thought she was better than them.

Once the Greens left, Audrey asked, "So how do we do this?"

"Let's pre-cut a frame and then you can re-stretch it, right?" Nikki asked London.

The woman nodded. London's wide, pale crystal blue eyes and her long, shiny light brown hair was the opposite of everything about Audrey.

"So all we have to do is figure out what to do with the original."

"How long do you think it would take to cut the wood to do this?" Audrey asked.

Nikki shrugged. "Even if it was easy, I still have to take time to pry it out of the frame."

They stood in silence for a minute.

"This needs alcohol," London said. "Come on. I have wine. The cheap stuff."

"I think I like you," Nikki said.

They all went to the living room—or what passed as one since it was mostly just a big, open space. London went behind the staircase to a refrigerator. She was tall with a willowy frame, looking like a demure, innocent woman, but it was deceiving because she had hefted the painting and flipped it around like it weighed nothing.

"Why are you helping us?" Audrey asked.

Nikki smacked her. "You really don't know how to keep your mouth shut and just accept a good thing, do you?"

"Ms. Green paid me well." London grabbed three mismatched coffee mugs and poured wine. "If I help you, she'll hire me again. With the money she's offering, I can have enough within the year to have my own gallery."

Audrey nodded. She remembered what it was like to have goals. Vaguely. Now her one and only goal was to keep her head above water and get Gram the best care possible.

London pointed to a couch. "Let's brainstorm."

Nikki yanked off her hat and weird shoe things. She sat in one corner of the couch and pulled her feet up. "Before we get to that, let's gossip."

"We don't have time," Audrey said as she sat in the other corner.

London sat between them.

Nikki rolled her eyes and turned to London. "Data here wants to avoid talking about the Greens because she thinks it's some secret that she's screwing around with Jay."

"Nikki!"

"I didn't need her to point that out. It was obvious when I walked in with the two of you."

"Great." Audrey didn't think anything was obvious.

"So are you like, the mistress?"

Nikki snorted and choked on her wine.

"The Greens are not a couple. They're family."

"Hmm," London said, narrowing her eyes. "Not siblings."

"No."

"As busy as you've been with other things, I'm surprised you had time to find that out," Nikki poked. "Is he good?"

Audrey's entire body flushed.

"He's hot," London said. "All that tan skin with the dark hair and eyes. I bet he turns rich brown in the sun. Mmm-mmm. What a palette. I wouldn't mind painting him."

"Whatever floats your boat." Audrey hoped she conveyed the nonchalance she aimed for.

"Then you don't care if London does a series of nudes?"

Audrey lifted a shoulder. "It's a free world."

She hoped that would be the end of it, but both women were still staring at her. "Look, Jay and I are attracted to each other. We've kissed a little. And yes, it was good."

Nikki thrust her fist forward for a bump. Audrey complied.

"But it's not going anywhere. You know as well as I do, the Greens are not part of our world. They're taking this trip on the wild side, but they're not staying. And I won't ever belong in theirs."

"So you're taking a good time while you can. Good for you," Nikki said.

"Wait, what do you mean, they're not part of your world?" London looked at each of them.

Audrey opened her mouth but was at a loss to explain, so she pointed at Nikki.

"Let's start with this, how much do you know about what we're doing?"

"Very little. Ms. Green commissioned me to make a replica Mathis painting. Based on what I've seen tonight, you're going to steal the original and replace it with my forgery."

"Bingo. I'm a thief. Data is a hacker. We live in the world of grays."

Audrey coughed.

"Okay, maybe we lean toward black, but we're not exactly evil. When you compare us to murderers and pedophiles, we're definitely gray."

"And you don't think they're criminals," London said with a hint of question in her voice.

Audrey listened to Nikki's explanation and wondered. Jay definitely felt darker gray than she did. He was a fixer after all. Everything she'd ever done for him leaned more gunmetal gray than ash gray, but she doubted he got his hands dirty. "I wouldn't say they're exactly white."

"No, definitely not," London agreed. "But Ms. Green does strike me as the kind of woman who's more likely to shop for a piece of art than to steal it."

"I don't like her," Audrey admitted.

"She does have a stick up her butt," Nikki said.

"I can deal with that. Uptight people don't bother me.

It's that she acts like she's better than us. As if she's above criminal activity, but she's the one orchestrating all of this," Audrey explained.

"I agree with Nikki. Uptight, yes, but she didn't make me feel like she's better than me."

"Maybe it's just me then." She drained her mug of wine and refilled it. "Enough talk about the Greens. Let's figure this out."

For the next three hours, they tossed ideas at each other, drew pictures, destroyed canvases and frames. Some of the destruction was probably due to the two bottles of wine they consumed, but they finally came up with a workable plan that would hopefully make the Greens happy and garner them all piles of cash.

TWELVE

Two NIGHTS LATER Jared stood in London's loft again, watching Nikki do her thing. Carving a hinge on the forgery worked so Nikki could carry it on her back. This time it was a success.

Nikki bounced back down the stairs.

"Pretty brilliant, right?" London asked.

"Still taking too long," Nikki muttered.

With a wave of her hand, Data said, "That's practice. You'll get the time down. Look how far we've come in two days."

Nikki shook her head and paced. "I don't have a good feeling about this."

"I'll head back to the apartment and work on slowing down the reboot. That'll buy you time."

Jared watched the women's interaction. Whatever Mia thought about creating a team, this was good. They worked together seamlessly. They bolstered each other when necessary. Mia would be able to have the role she'd wanted all along—hands off.

"Do you need anything else?" he asked.

"More time to prep," Nikki said.

Data shoved her gently. "Go have a drink. I'll text you when I have something figured out."

She grabbed her stuff and headed toward the door.

"Wait up. I'll drive you." He followed her to the hall-way. Nikki's unmistakable snicker sounded behind him.

"I don't need a ride."

"It'll save time. You've been staying at the apartment, haven't you?"

"I crashed the last couple of nights because we were working late. It's not like I moved in or anything."

"It wasn't an accusation." He led the way to his car. "I don't care that you've been there. It was part of the reason we rented the place."

"All right, but I really can get there myself."

He held the car door open for her. "We have some unfinished business." He drove to the apartment, his brain racing.

"In all seriousness, I have work to do. I have to find a way to get Nikki more time."

"I'm all for the job coming first. Nikki has London helping her. I can help you."

"Help? Is that what we're calling it?"

"Two heads are better than one." He laughed.

"You're juvenile."

"And yet you like me. What does that say about you?"

"I'm desperate?"

"I doubt that." He enjoyed the easy banter they shared. No pretense about who they were or what they wanted.

At the apartment, she slipped into hacker mode faster than he could lock the door. She sat in front of the computer running algorithms and rewriting code for more than an hour. He made a pot of coffee, opened a new package of Oreos, and sat with her. Although he thought he might be of some help, he began to doubt it. She ignored his presence.

When she finally got up and stretched, she looked a little defeated.

"Not working?"

"Not enough. I can't figure out how to steal more time."

"Take a break. Switching gears might be the way to go."

"Maybe you're right. Wanna play a video game?" She went to the TV and game system and booted everything up.

Not quite the break he'd been hoping for, but he'd take it. Rolling up his sleeves, he asked, "What are we playing for?"

"Why can't we just play for bragging rights?"

"Where's the fun in that?"

"A hundred bucks," she countered.

"I don't need the money."

"What do you want?"

"You. Naked."

"Strip gaming." She rolled her gaze to the ceiling in thought. "We'd need some rules."

"How about if I kill your character, you get naked?"

"Where's the fun in that?" she echoed. Stepping closer, game controller in hand, she pressed it to his chest. "How about for every enemy I kill, you pay me twenty-five bucks, and for every one you kill, I remove one article of clothing?"

"Ten bucks."

"Twenty."

"Bring on the weaponry." He sat on the edge of the couch determined to have her naked within the hour.

MAN, DID SHE love it when a guy assumed she would suck at playing video games. Jay made it almost too easy. He was going to pay her to destroy him.

At least that was the plan. The little voice in her head tempted her to let him win a few battles, but the greedy part of her brain won. If she came out on top, she'd be able to call them even on the money he'd given her for rent and possibly even have a little left over.

"Set up your character," she said. "Mine is already saved."

"How many hours have you played with Nikki?"

"Not that many. When I'm here, I'm usually work-ing."

"Or drinking."

She slid him a look. "Once."

"What was that about anyway?" he asked as he scrolled through the menu of character selection.

"Had a bad day." She went to the kitchen, started another pot of coffee, and grabbed a couple bottles of water. It was going to be a long night.

When she returned to the couch, she set a bottle of water in front of him and used the controller to log in.

"Not willing to say what the bad day involved that caused you to get drunk?"

"Are you spilling details about your life?"

"Depends on what you want to know."

So many questions flitted through her mind, but she couldn't ask. Doing so would invite him to ask her, and she wasn't the sharing type. Nikki had caught her in a weak moment. "Let's play."

Their characters on screen moved through a battle-field, or what was left of one after previous teams had rolled through. Within seconds she had rapid-fired and killed two enemy combatants. "Forty bucks in under a minute. Maybe I should forget hacking and just play video games against you for a living."

He didn't respond because he was busy making two of his own kills. "Start stripping."

"I'm not stopping to take things off in the middle of the round." But then she had second thoughts and kicked off her shoes. "Two items down."

"Better watch it. Seeing your socks might have an overwhelming effect on me."

His sarcasm was dry and she found herself wonder-ing what would've happened if she'd taken off her shirt instead. Keeping her eyes on the screen, they battled it out for more than a half hour, yelling and cheering and slapping the occasional high five because they were teammates after all. When the round ended and they to-taled their scores, Jay had six kills and Audrey had ten.

"Two hundred bucks. I think I like this."

He didn't even bat an eye. He opened his wallet and set two crisp one hundred dollar bills on the table in front of them. Did this man only have hundred dollar bills? Who did that? Staring intently at her, he said, "Your turn. Six items."

"Uh, only four more. I already took off my shoes." She peeled off her socks. "That makes four." Then she thought about her options. Which two articles made the most sense?

With a smile, she stood and took off her jeans. Jay barely moved, just a slight shift forward, watching. When she straightened, her shirt hung low enough that she was still covered. Then she reached under her shirt and removed her bra.

She tossed it at him and said, "That makes six." Pointing at the money, she added, "Put that toward what you gave me the other night."

Why she thought it was a good idea to walk past him to get to the kitchen, she didn't know. Maybe it was her subconscious wanting to toy with him.

"I don't think so," he said, standing up. "We have more unfinished business." He led her to the bedroom.

At the door, he paused and looked into her eyes. "What's your name?"

"Why?"

He gripped her chin in a firm, but gentle way. "Because I like to know who I'm sleeping with."

"You know who."

"I do know you, but I want a real name."

She debated telling him. It was one thing for Nikki to know, but this was different. Staring up at him, though, she trusted what she saw, so she whispered, "Audrey."

He lowered his mouth, murmuring her name on her lips as he opened the bedroom door and pulled her through.

THIRTEEN

AUDREY POPPED UP like a piece of bread flying from the toaster. Where the hell had that energy come from?

"I got it." She scrambled off the bed.

"Where're you going?"

"I have an idea to get Nikki more time."

He forced himself up on his elbows. "We have phenomenal sex and you're thinking about Nikki?"

She stepped into her panties and tugged her shirt over her head. Then she came back to the bed and crawled over him. "Like you said before, switching gears was just what I needed."

Her grin lit her entire face. She began to slide away, but he caught her.

"Okay, Audrey." It was like he couldn't get enough of saying her name now that she'd entrusted him with it.

"You can't call me that."

"Why not?"

"Because then they'll all know we had sex. This is supposed to be a business arrangement, remember?"

The reminder was a cold shot to his system. He hadn't forgotten, but he'd definitely put it out of his mind. It had been glorious to not think about Mia and this job and their fathers for at least a little while.

"There's nothing that says business partners can't be friends."

She snorted. "I don't think anyone would think this is being friendly. It was way beyond friendly. Unless, of course, you treat all your friends that way."

"Not a chance. When can we be more than friendly again?"

"Get dressed." She tossed his clothes at him without answering his question.

Before he could even sit up all the way, she was out the door. Whatever idea she'd had lit a spark in her. He hoped it would work. They were running out of time. Mia had chosen the date based on the calendar of society events. Scott and his wife, as well as Mia and Jared, would all be at the same place at the same time, allowing little room for surprises. If this first mission failed, he didn't know what Mia would do. He feared she'd get reckless, which was the opposite of who she was.

Reluctantly, he dressed and followed Audrey to the living room. She was already back at her computer. She'd scooped her hair messily on top of her head, and the blue light from the screen eerily illuminated her face. He detoured to the kitchen and poured them each a cup of coffee. Setting a cup next to her, he glanced at what she was working on. Scott's routine and schedule.

Mia had had the man followed for a month. She paid some private investigator to shadow his movements under the guise of trying to prove insurance fraud. They had detailed notes about the comings and goings around the house, regular routines, visitors—Mia had thought of it all. He'd thought she'd gone a little overboard, but based on Audrey's sudden interest, it might turn out to be useful.

"What's your brilliant plan?"

"I didn't say it was brilliant. I simply said I had one. In fact, it's kind of crazy."

The front door opened on her last sentence and Nikki strode in. "What's crazy?"

Jay opened his mouth, but he almost used Audrey's real name, so he got stuck.

"What's the biggest problem you have once you're inside?" Audrey asked.

Nikki's posture changed and the frustration she'd worn hours ago returned. "The damn frame. Everyone knows it's the frame. Everyone also knows that anyone who steals a painting either cuts it out or takes the whole thing. Removing it from the frame is dumb."

It wasn't dumb. It would prolong their ability to keep the thefts—and ultimately their plan—undetected. But he didn't say anything.

Audrey continued, undaunted by Nikki's outburst. "What if we take care of the frame ahead of time?"

"What?" Nikki asked.

The sun was beginning to rise and a golden glow created a halo behind Audrey. "We go in ahead of time and remove the spline. With the spline gone, you can pop that sucker right out. I don't know why we didn't think of it earlier."

Nikki didn't comment, but she stepped closer to Audrey. As she neared, Jay saw the signs of exhaustion on her face. Even with dark smudges, though, her eyes were alert.

Was she actually considering this?

"You're suggesting we break in twice?" He spoke it like a question, but he already knew the answer. The lack of sleep had taken its toll on all of them.

"Not break in. Walk in. I just have to figure out how." She pointed to the papers spread on the desk.

"How is that keeping a low profile? In and out. Undetected. No one knows the painting's been swapped for a long time to come."

Audrey rolled her eyes. "These people leave their house all the time. We just need to have a plausible reason for coming in. While someone keeps the maid busy, another person takes the painting down, removes the spline and loosens the edges. Simple."

She'd lost her mind. "No."

Both women turned to him, arms crossed.

"What do you mean, *no*?" Audrey asked.

For a moment his mind blanked, thinking of her as Audrey. The name suited her—soft and quiet but strong. Unfortunately, it was strength staring back at him now.

"It's too risky."

"I live for risk," Nikki said. "No one is asking you to do anything. You hired us to do a job and we're doing it. That's how being an independent contractor works."

He opened his mouth to correct her, but clamped it shut. She was right. They were independent contractors, regardless of how much he felt like they were building a team.

Audrey's words from the bed echoed in him. *They* were a team. He wasn't part of it. "If you go in there, you risk exposing the entire plan."

"That implies we're amateurs who don't know what we're doing." Nikki scoffed.

Audrey bit her lower lip. Eyes fixed on him, she finally said, "Nikki's right. We're good at what we do."

She gathered the papers and took them to the long table. Nikki grabbed a pile, too, and they spread the papers out.

"What are you thinking?" Nikki asked. "Cable guy again?"

"I don't think that'll work. I didn't get much past the front door. We need to get all the way in. Plus, it's not like we can say they called for an install. Too much risk."

Jay stood there not believing his ears. Grabbing Audrey by the elbow, he said, "We need to talk."

She sputtered as he propelled her back to the bedroom for privacy. Once the door closed, he released her arm.

"Look, I know you wanted another round," she started, "but we have more important things to handle."

He barely suppressed a growl. "What you're suggesting is reckless and dumb."

She shook her head, anger flashing in her bright eyes. "It'll buy Nikki the time she needs."

"And if you get caught?"

"We won't."

His frustration mounted.

"We got this. Nikki and I will have it planned."

"Audrey—"

"Don't make me regret telling you my name." She pursed her lips. She ran a hand down his chest. He felt her warmth as if he were still shirtless.

"Trust me. We got this."

Maybe it was the spark in her eye, the same one when she made a difficult shot in a video game or ran a line of brilliant code. He didn't know where exactly it came from, but he said, "Okay."

Reaching around her to open the door, he added, "Let's hear it."

Audrey's confidence soared when Jay acquiesced. She'd thought he'd put up a bigger fight. As she reached the living room, Nikki smiled.

"Did you two kiss and make up?" she taunted.

Audrey's cheeks flamed, but she focused on the papers on the table. With her head down, she didn't address Nikki's question. "We need something to get us in there without notice, with the security down."

Jay came up behind her and set a fresh, steaming cup of coffee next to her. She hadn't even noticed him go to the kitchen.

"What am I, chopped liver?" Nikki said.

"I'm a little afraid to see you hopped up on caffeine. I brought you a bottle of water."

Audrey bit her lip to stop the smile. If she didn't know better, she'd think they were siblings. "Exterminators would work."

"Do they have routine exterminators?" he asked.

"No. I'm suggesting we make them need an exterminator."

Nikki hopped onto the table and sat with her legs crossed. "That seems like a lot of moving parts. Getting them to call a company, intercepting the call, pretending to be exterminators…"

"No. Simpler than that. If the maid, or God forbid, Mrs. Scott, walks into the kitchen and sees a mouse, do you think either of them is going to hang around to supervise the exterminators?"

"We still have to take the call."

"We wait for the exterminators to show up. Knowing Mrs. Scott, she'll pay extra to get them in right away. While the guys are in there laying traps and spreading

poison, you walk in, take down the painting, remove
the spline, and loosen the canvas from the frame. In
and out in five minutes. The guys working have no idea
who lives there."

A grin crept onto Nikki's face. "I act like I belong
there, do what I want, and they won't comment."

"Then next Saturday, you can follow our plan when
no one is home."

"Why not just take it with me while the exterminators are there? I can do it."

"First, one of the exterminators would notice you
carrying a painting out, or worse, replacing the original with the fake," Jay said. "Second, there are other
things at play. The date is set for a reason. That part is
not negotiable."

He stayed on the other side of the room, arms crossed
on his chest, ankles crossed at the floor. The image was
so different than everything she'd experienced with him
earlier. He was pissed.

"Fine." Nikki sounded disappointed.

Audrey wondered what other things were at play.
Were they planning another heist at the same time?
Maybe a string of them all at once? It *would* be brilliant. She briefly imagined rich assholes all over the
city being taken for a ride. But then she considered that
meant that Jay had other teams like this all over the city.
What did that mean for her?

"Why?" she asked.

"Why what?" he responded.

"Why is that date nonnegotiable?"

"You don't need to know the reason. It just is."

She tried not to be irritated, but that answer was

getting old. Her mind raced again, back to the idea of multiple heists.

"How do you expect to get them to call an exterminator?" he asked, breaking her from her useless musings.

Audrey shrugged. "I guess we get a couple mice and set them loose in the kitchen when the maid is around."

"So you want yet another trip to expose us." It wasn't a question. More like an accusation.

She clenched and unclenched her jaw. *Men.* If he would just leave them alone, they'd be halfway done with this already. She inhaled slowly through her nose and released, so she wouldn't snap at him. No matter how much she wanted to. "You're the one who is insisting on that night for the heist. Nikki's right, if we do this, we could get it out now."

"No."

She flicked her hand up. "If you'd stop interrupting me, we'd get to the part where I say we have their schedules. The neighbor's dog routinely gets out and runs into their yard. If we tempt the little bugger over, it will set off the motion sensors. The Scotts will see the dog on the monitor and either call the neighbor to come get him or they'll take him back themselves. They won't pay attention to me. At that point, I slip by and let a couple mice loose through the kitchen window or door."

"Then we sit on the house and wait for the mice killers to show," Nikki added. "I feel bad for the little guys."

Jay pinched the bridge of his nose. "That's still a lot of moving parts."

"Well, unless you have something better…"

"If we can get the spline out from the frame, next

Saturday will be a breeze. Every time I ran it at London's, the spline is what takes forever. I lose at least three minutes on the damn thing." Nikki leaned over and slid some pages around, uncovering the layout of the house. "And as an added bonus, I'll know if there are trip wires on the painting."

"Excellent information to have." Audrey had almost forgotten that they didn't know if the painting was hooked up to the alarm. They'd been banking on Nikki getting the switch done while the system rebooted.

"When do you plan to do this?" Jay asked.

Audrey looked at Nikki who shrugged.

"Later today, I guess. Early enough that they can see the mice and call the exterminator, but not so late that the mice hide and don't get noticed." Audrey shuffled the stack of papers. "They usually eat dinner around seven. So the maid will be prepping around six? Does that line up with when the dog likes to come over?"

Nikki scanned the schedules of activity. "The dog has been in their yard all times of the day, so I guess it's a matter of the dog needing to go out. What do we know about the neighbors?"

"As far as I know, nothing. We didn't have them under surveillance," Jay supplied. "But based on the number of times the dog was reported in the Scotts' yard, it seems that whenever the door is opened at the neighbor's house, the thing escapes."

Nikki's grin returned. "So we just have to get them to open the door to let him escape." Turning to Audrey, she asked, "Are you good with dogs?"

"Why?"

"Ring the bell at the neighbor's house, when someone

answers, comment on their dog, pet it, and then let it run past you. Look all contrite and chase the dog into the Scotts' yard. While you're running around after the dog, making a huge disturbance, I can let the mice loose."

Audrey shook her head. "There's a chance Connie will recognize me."

"Connie?" Jay asked.

"The maid." She pointed at Nikki. "You do it."

Nikki shook her head. "I don't do dogs."

She was dead serious. Audrey had never seen her so grave.

"You don't have to actually do anyth—"

"No."

"What about you?" Audrey asked Jay.

He shook his head. "We're hands off. We can't be seen there."

Audrey filed that bit of information away to think about later. The Greens were up to something, but she couldn't fit the pieces together. Not yet anyway.

"I bet London would do it. And she's about as non-threatening as a person can get," Nikki said.

Jay released a heavy sigh. Audrey didn't know if he was resigned to the fact that they were going through with this or if he was still irritated by the idea. He unfolded his stance and took her near-empty coffee cup.

"If you're planning on this for today, I suggest you both get some sleep. You've been going at this all night. If you're exhausted, you'll make mistakes. We can't afford mistakes."

"I'll nap when I get back." She checked the time. Today she normally went to visit Gram and she wanted to make sure the move to the new room was working. "I'll grab mice on my way back."

Nikki hopped off the table. "I'll call London."

"I wasn't kidding. You both need to sleep."

Audrey and Nikki both rolled their eyes.

"I've participated in hackfests that ran for over forty hours straight. No sleep," Audrey said.

"And I once spent thirty hours in a broken elevator shaft waiting to gain access to an office," Nikki tossed out.

Jay threw his hands up. "Fine. You win. You're both superwomen who can function without sleep unlike mere mortals." Then he pinned them with a stern look. "But if you get busted, you're on your own. No job. No payout."

His warning swirled the coffee in Audrey's stomach. He had a point. She wasn't normally this exposed on a job.

"We'll be fine," Nikki said.

"See you in a few hours." Audrey picked up her bag.

Jay followed her out the door. "Can I give you a ride?"

"No, I'm good."

"It's not like I don't already know where you live."

"I'm not going home."

On the sidewalk, he pressed the button to unlock his car. She really wanted to take him up on his offer.

"Where are you going that can't wait? Your time would be better spent sleeping and preparing for tonight."

"I don't need you telling me what I should and shouldn't do. My errand can't wait." She slid her bag across her body.

"Last time you ran *errands*, something happened and you spent the night drunk."

She hated that he'd witnessed her weakness. Well, at least the aftereffects of it. "I'm fine. I'll get the mice and Nikki, London, and I will handle our business. You don't need to worry about us."

He stepped closer and tucked some errant hair behind her ear. "I do worry. More than I should, I think."

She didn't want sincerity from him. Why was he making this difficult? "Well, I don't need your concern. I can take care of myself."

"Of that, I have little doubt. But there's no shame in asking for a hand." He flicked his thumb toward his car. "Or a ride."

"I'm fine with public transportation. Thank you for the offer."

"I'll meet you back here later."

"Why? You're hands off, remember?"

"I still have a vested interest in what happens."

She didn't want to read too much into what he said. She reminded herself that he was out of her league. They were good for a quick roll, but she wouldn't fit into his world. At some point, he'd figure that out.

"See you later then." She turned and headed to the bus stop. She refused to turn around because she felt his gaze on her all the way down the block.

FOURTEEN

JARED HAD PLENTY to do. He texted Mia and asked her to meet him at his office. His consulting business always had new calls, many of which he'd been putting off since he and Mia had forged ahead on this endeavor. He should've been tired after pulling an all-nighter, but he was actually full of energy. Maybe it was the idea that they finally appeared to have the kinks worked out of the plan to get into Scott's house. More likely, it had been the amazing time with Audrey.

Having her leap out of bed instead of enjoying the afterglow stung his ego, but it had been his idea for her to switch gears to find a solution. It had worked. Now, however, he couldn't stop thinking about when he could get her back in bed for an extended period of time.

He drove to his office to attempt to get some work done. Of course, Mia, being Mia, arrived within minutes of him. To her on time was late, so as usual, she was early. Why had he thought he'd have some time to do anything else?

"What's wrong?" she asked as soon as she whisked into his office.

"Nothing."

"You don't ask me to meet you here unless something is going on." She closed and locked the door behind her.

"Data has a plan to get more time for Nikki, but you're

not going to like it." Although he wanted to pat himself on the back for remembering not to use Audrey's real name, he braced for Mia's scathing comments.

Her eyes were cool, no sign of irritation, which was different these days. "Go on."

"They plan to go there today—"

"Absolutely not. They've already been in Scott's neighborhood twice. People will get suspicious. Especially if even the slightest thing goes wrong next Saturday."

Jared took a deep breath and waited patiently until she quieted. "I know they aren't doing things the way you would, or even the way you prefer, but it's not a bad plan. It will buy Nikki the time she needs next week. She's run drills over and over. The frame is a problem. And we're running out of time."

Mia massaged the space between her eyebrows, but said nothing.

"The thing is, with the plan they've devised, they could theoretically get the painting out today."

"What? No," Mia said, dropping her hand from her face.

With a raised hand, he tried to reassure her. "I told them there were other things at play, nothing specific. But I can't help but think it might make sense."

"It's too risky. We have to have airtight alibis."

"We could."

She paused for a moment and he thought she might go for it. He also knew, though, that Mia hated people messing with her plans.

"You know it's more than that. I want to be with him, knowing that we're ripping him off."

"Don't you think all of that is riskier than letting Data and Nikki grab it today?"

"I know it's petty, but I want this. They need to pay." When she looked up, the cold confidence she usually exuded was missing. She looked like the devastated young woman who'd just learned her father was a thief and a majority of her life was a lie.

"They will pay. Don't do anything rash. Let's get through this first job and see how it goes."

Mia narrowed her eyes and tilted her head to the right. "No one plans and avoids pitfalls as much as I do. We're only in this mess with the painting right now because you insisted we hire people and let them run the show. Hands off, you said." She took a step closer and stared him down. "Are you still hands off?"

A grin cracked across his face. He didn't even try to hide it. "Mostly."

She threw her hands up. "I told you no screwing the help."

"Really? You're seriously calling Data and Nikki 'the help'? No wonder they don't like you."

"What do you mean, they don't like me? They don't know me. I've only interacted with them a handful of times."

"They haven't said anything. Just the impression I've gotten. Maybe you should spend some time getting to know them."

"That defeats the purpose of keeping us separate and away from the thefts." Her face tightened with disapproval.

"You can't have it both ways—hands-off and in charge."

"You shouldn't underestimate me. This is not going to end well."

"Nothing's ending yet. Data and I are enjoying each other, taking a much-needed break from scheming. Everyone needs some stress relief on occasion." He winked. "You should try it."

Another slight shake of her head and a minor eye roll. "Tell me what they want to do."

Jared laid out the plan, from the mice to the exterminators to Nikki loosening the painting. While he spoke, Mia sat in one of the armchairs across from his desk. She slid back and crossed one leg over the other, hands folded primly in her lap.

When he finished, he said, "What do you think?"

"I think there is too much that can go terribly wrong."

"I've seen them in action. They know what they're doing. This is why we chose them."

The reminder seemed to do the trick, gaining her acceptance.

"All right, then. Keep an eye on them, especially Nikki. The girl has stickier fingers than a three-year-old eating cotton candy. I don't want our timeline blown." She stood. "And you should make sure you are nowhere near the Scotts' house. Make dinner reservations with a client or friend. Very public."

He nodded. He knew she wanted him to be clear if the women were caught. They said their good-byes and Jared stretched his feet out onto the corner of his desk. He had emails to handle and clients to collect from, but he wanted a few minutes to revel in his night with Audrey, short as it was.

Tonight would be a different story.

AUDREY DIDN'T NEED to visit Gram today but she needed
distance. When she was in the middle of a job, she
would sometimes skip a visit, but today the break was
necessary. Jay was invading her space a bit too much.
Sure, she'd wanted to have sex with him. That was no
secret. But playing video games and sharing coffee
and…sleeping together? Even though he hadn't said it,
she knew that was what he'd been expecting. As if she
should automatically want to snuggle up to him.

What the hell is he thinking?

And like a typical man, once he played with her
body, he acted as if he owned it. Telling her when to
sleep and what she should and shouldn't risk. She had
a mind of her own. She'd been doing fine by herself for
years. Who needed his input? Definitely not her.

Gram reached over and laid her wrinkled hand over
Audrey's. "Where is your mind today?"

Audrey suppressed a laugh. Gram's mind was gone
more than half the time they visited, but today of all
days, she was lucid enough to notice Audrey being distracted.

"I have a lot going on, that's all."

Gram closed one eye and tapped her head. "I know
that look. It's man trouble. I thought you said you found
a good one."

Audrey blinked a few times before remembering the
tale she told Gram about Jay. Of course, the old woman
would remember that. "You know how it is. I'm busy
and he wants more of my time."

Her go-to reason for keeping anyone at arm's distance.

"Sometimes it's worth giving up a little of your time

and space. Make room for other people. You wouldn't be so alone."

She opened her mouth to argue and realized it wouldn't have any effect. Why would she want to fight during the few precious minutes she had Gram back?

Gram fell silent as she focused on the TV again. Audrey liked to come here to be with Gram whenever she had to sort things out. If her grandmother was lucid, she might offer advice. More often than not, though, Audrey could think without the pressure of outside forces.

Like Jay.

The chemistry between them sizzled. He was the perfect reason why she never mixed business with pleasure. Everything muddied and she couldn't afford to lose focus. She needed his job to pay for Gram's care.

At some point, she dozed off in the chair beside Gram and woke suddenly when applause for a game show blared on the TV. She jolted up and rubbed a hand over her face. Gram was snoring away. Audrey checked her phone. She had to hurry to go find some mice and get back to the apartment.

She'd missed a text from Nikki. London's in!

Audrey kissed her grandmother's papery cheek and left without waking her. She grabbed some more equipment from her apartment. Then she went to two different pet shops to find the mice. She chose the fattest, ugliest ones she could. If Connie thought they were cute, she might try to catch and release them herself.

By the time she made it back, it was late afternoon, and she needed more coffee. The positive effects of her miniscule nap on the chair were fading fast. After being buzzed in—really, when would they think to give her a key?—she entered a scene of chaos. London was bouncing around rambling and Nikki was laughing hysterically.

And no sign of Jay. Maybe he decided to leave them to handle it.

She greeted the other women, who from what Audrey could discern were attempting to come up with some kind of SWAT-level silent hand movements to communicate. As she made her way toward the coffeemaker, she called over her shoulder, "I have some comms we can use. Small earpieces with wireless connectivity."

"Ooo," London cooed. "This is so cool. I've never been part of a team before. Not since I was a cheerleader in high school anyway."

Audrey leaned against the kitchen counter and looked at London. She could totally see the artist as a cheerleader. "We never would've been friends in high school."

"Why not? I like you."

Nikki fell over in a peal of laughter.

"We like you, too," Audrey reassured her. She turned to make her cup of coffee when the front door opened again. She knew it had to be Jay. Ms. Green only showed up when she wanted to check up on them, and since everyone knew she wouldn't like this plan, no one informed her. Except Jay probably had.

The thought had Audrey spinning back around to make sure Ms. Green wasn't there. Audrey was having a hard enough time without having to listen to her snippy attitude. Luckily, Jay came through the door alone bearing bags that smelled wonderful.

"Food!" Nikki called and jumped over the back of the couch.

Jay set the bags on the table and backed away. He looked up and when his eyes met hers, the chemistry she'd been thinking about earlier zipped right through her. He left Nikki and London to rifle through the bags and he joined her in the kitchen.

"Did you get some rest?" he asked, trailing his thumb across her cheek in a gesture that made her want to lean in.

"I napped."

"You got the mice?"

He stood so close that she was having a hard time focusing, so she took a sidestep along the counter.

"Of course." She sipped her coffee. "London is going to lure the dog, Nikki is going to be lookout, and I'll get the mice in the house. Then we'll stand by to eavesdrop on the call so we know who to expect and when." She winked at him. "I told you, we got this covered."

He inched closer and lowered his head. "I hope you'll meet me back here afterwards. I've been thinking about the many ways I want to have you."

Her blood warmed and she tightened her grip on her mug. She focused on being casual, borderline flippant. "You had me last night."

"And you ran from the bed."

"Is your ego bruised?"

"Of course not. My performance was so good that you were inspired." He brushed his lips over the shell of her ear. "I plan on inspiring you a whole lot more tonight."

Her pulse jumped and all her girly bits throbbed.

Yeah, his performance had been pretty damn good, and she wouldn't mind a repeat.

"Hey, get a room," Nikki called from the table.

Jay eased back and Audrey took a deep breath, releasing the tension her body held.

Nikki snickered. "I guess technically you have a room." Pointing toward the bedroom, she added, "But you better make it a quickie. We have to leave soon."

Audrey's whole body flushed. She felt stuck in a spotlight. And she didn't like it.

"Just working off some stress," Audrey said as she carried her coffee away from Jay and toward the women. At the table, she scooped up some French fries from Nikki's pile and dragged them through ketchup.

From over the top of her burger, Nikki watched her with questioning eyes. She didn't need to explain herself. Or what she was doing with Jay. She wasn't even sure what was happening with Jay.

He kept his distance, remaining at the kitchen counter while she took her spot beside Nikki.

"I feel bad for these guys. They're going to die and they haven't done anything wrong." London dropped a few fries into the cage of mice.

"They might get out before the exterminators show. They're pretty smart," Audrey offered.

"When the maid starts yelling and screaming about the mice, she might just scare them right back out the door. She'll still assume there's a whole pack living somewhere in the house," Nikki added.

Audrey didn't have the heart to tell her that Connie didn't strike her as the kind of woman to scream over seeing a mouse.

"Wait a minute," London said. "We don't need to be mice killers. You said yourself you just need a distraction to get in. Instead of going tonight, what if we wait until the Scotts are gone tomorrow. Then I start running through the yard, causing the commotion you need, chasing my dog that got away after being startled by the neighbor's dog? The maid comes out to yell at me and I keep her engaged. Nikki goes in and does her thing."

Audrey dropped her burger. It was simple. But beautiful in its simplicity. London was likely to be exposed no matter what, so this might work.

"It saves us an extra trip." Looking at Nikki, she said, "Can you get in without notice while London has Connie occupied?"

Nikki scoffed. "I've walked out of a house with a bag full of jewelry while a whole family sat at the dinner table. Sneaking past one maid? Easy."

London clapped. "I'll borrow my neighbor's dog."

"I thought you were just going to pretend to have a runaway dog." Audrey picked up her burger and resumed eating.

"I have to make it plausible. Won't she get suspicious if she doesn't see a dog?"

"What if it runs away for real?"

She waved a hand. "She's well trained. Offer a snack and she'll come running."

"Then how will you get her to run away from you?" Jay asked from his post in the kitchen.

London's brow furrowed and she rested her chin on her fist.

"What if I call her from the neighbor's property? She'd come even if a stranger called her?" Audrey asked.

"Sure."

"Then I'll stay out of sight and call her, offering a treat. Then you come yelling through the yard."

"But then the dog goes straight to you. No chase," Jay said.

The dude was a total party pooper, but he had a point.

Nikki waved. "Then I call her from the edge of the house. Then Data calls her again—before she actually gets to me. By then, I'm sure Connie will be out."

Audrey held out her hand for a high five. Over her shoulder, she said to Jay, "I told you, we got this."

"That's at least as much exposure as your other plan. Maybe more."

"But these poor mice won't have to die for the cause," London said. "Should we go tonight? It's still early. I can go get the dog now."

"Too risky," Nikki said. "The Scotts are almost always home for dinner. Connie won't let dinner burn to help you. Tomorrow late morning when Mrs. Scott goes to whatever crap she does, we go in."

Audrey polished off her food. She hadn't realized how hungry she was. "We have a plan."

FIFTEEN

JAY WATCHED, SPEECHLESS, as the women worked out the kinks in their plan. Not that there were many. He'd been right—they'd created a team. Audrey, Nikki, and London bounced ideas and joked around while he remained on the perimeter. He didn't like it, but he couldn't interfere.

His job was to make sure they didn't take too many risks or get caught.

"Hey," Nikki called. "Aren't you eating?"

"No," he responded. "I have dinner reservations in a bit."

Audrey twisted slowly in her chair. "We were supposed to go release the mice soon. Does that mean you hadn't planned on joining us?"

"No. As you've said repeatedly, you've got this."

She raised an eyebrow. "Were you leaving us alone because you trusted us or because you thought it was likely that we'd get busted?"

He didn't know how to answer honestly. Of course he trusted them not to get caught, but the dinner reservations were his protection in case they did. "I have other business to conduct besides taking care of the three of you."

Nikki snorted. "You're only interested in Data."

Audrey blushed and closed her eyes. She really hated being the center of attention.

"All three of you are an important part of the team," he said.

"Okay." London stood. "I'm going home. I'll be here in the morning with Daisy."

"Daisy?" Audrey asked.

"The dog. That's her name. Daisy."

Audrey gathered her trash.

"Wait," Nikki said, reaching for Audrey. "You're not leaving, too, are you?"

"Uh, yeah. We're not doing anything tonight and I'm tired."

"Stay. I'll be bored."

"You'll be asleep as soon as we're all gone."

"Come on. We can have a girls' night."

He cleared his throat, reminding them of his presence.

Nikki leaned around Audrey. "I'm sorry. Were you planning on coming back?"

"Yes, I am." He neared Audrey and placed a hand on her hip. "We have plans."

The pink on her cheeks deepened. He flexed his fingers, pressing into the soft flesh. Her swallow was audible. "I don't have a change of clothes for tomorrow. I have to go home."

Nikki still held Audrey's wrist. "But you're coming back. We can play video games and watch movies."

The request seemed out of character for Nikki. As far as Jared knew, she was as much of a loner as Audrey and London. It made him wonder if she had some other plan in play.

"I'll drop you off to save time," he offered. "And if you spend the night here, you can sleep in."

Nikki laughed. "You're always using euphemisms. We know you don't plan to sleep."

Audrey pulled away from both of them. "That's where you're wrong. I'm going to sleep a lot. I'm exhausted."

Audrey threw away the wrappers from her food, and London said her good-byes with a promise to be back early.

JARED SAT THROUGH dinner with Carolyn, counting the minutes until he could get back to the apartment and Audrey. While he'd planned to meet with a client, Carolyn had called and asked to catch up. There had been a time when their parents tried to match them, but he and Carolyn were nothing more than friends. So he spent his evening offering an occasional chuckle and swallowing tasteless food.

Carolyn leaned over and touched his arm. "Is everything all right?"

"Yes. Why?"

"You seem to be in another place. Is it work?"

He gave her a smile. His family and their friends believed he ran a consulting firm, but no one ever asked for specifics. Consulting was a vague enough term to not inspire questions.

"I'm working on a difficult project right now. The client keeps wanting to take risks I think are unwise."

"What do you do in a situation like that? I mean, you can't stop him from doing what he wants, right?"

"She thinks things through, but I wish she'd heed my advice more than she does."

"*She?* Jared Towers, are you fooling around with a client?" Her tone was nothing short of scandalous.

"Of course not. I would never mess with a client. Mixing business and pleasure is rarely a wise move." He'd learned a long time ago that serving up half-truths worked wonders with making people believe what he said. At the moment, all he could think about was mixing up some pleasure with Audrey. "Tell me what's going on with your life."

"Nothing much with me. Daddy's planning on selling some of his property. That's why I wanted to get together with you."

While the dinner with Carolyn had been impromptu, it was proving to be useful. Her father, Steven Draper, had been a confidant of his father's. Steven hadn't stood behind Jared's father when everything had come out. He did, however, profit from their fathers' scheme, so Mia had kept an eye on him. They weren't even sure how much he'd known while it was going on.

"Why's he selling? The market's been on a downswing."

She wiped delicately at the corners of her mouth and smoothed her napkin on her lap. He knew those moves. She regretted bringing it up.

"What is it, Carolyn? Is he in trouble?"

She leaned closer and lowered her voice. "I'm not sure. Something isn't right. I overheard him talking at his weekly poker game. The bunch of them."

He didn't need an explanation of who the *them* were. Cesar's cronies. Half of whom *were* on Mia's list. Steven's poker night was legendary and Jared had tried to score an invite for years, but Steven always claimed a young man like him didn't belong at the table with the old codgers. He'd always believed there was more to it.

"I'm sorry. I shouldn't have said anything." She shook her head, her chin-length blond hair swaying.

He patted her hand. "It's all right. Tell me."

"I'm worried about my dad. I don't know why he continues to be friends with those men. After everything you've told me, I don't understand. My dad isn't like them."

Jared wasn't so sure, but since he wasn't positive, he wanted to give Carolyn and Steven the benefit of the doubt. "What did you overhear?"

"Max Ingram and Harry Ross were talking about how they're planning to liquidate some of their assets as soon as possible without raising any red flags. I'm not sure if my dad joined in the discussion because that's what guys do at the poker table or if something else is up. After everything with your father… I'm worried."

"Do you think your dad is doing something illegal?"

"I don't think so. At least not directly. But you didn't know what your father was doing, right?"

Jared shook his head. Carolyn had been one of the few people who immediately believed him when he said he'd had no idea.

"He might be helping them, though," she continued. "Max said something about sending a few paintings and sculptures to auction and how he could do that and hide his profits. Harry said the price of gold was up so the jewelry he kept from his last ex-wife in the divorce would bring him a pretty penny."

The wheels in Jared's head were spinning triple time. This was why Mia was insistent on rushing through the jobs. She knew they were liquidating. Was it possible their fathers knew something about their plan?

"I don't trust them," Carolyn whispered.

"As you shouldn't. They all knew what my father was doing. They encouraged it and profited from it. And they got away with it. If they're making moves, there's a reason. You need to distance yourself. I would hate to see you get caught up in the middle."

"What about my dad?"

"Will he listen to you?"

She lifted a shoulder. "Would you talk to him? He might listen to you."

"I don't know. We haven't spoken in a long time. I doubt he would take advice from me."

"Please, just try. I know you've been through a lot because of your father, but my dad has always liked you."

"I'll try." It was the best he could offer. But the information she'd given him was food for thought. If Mia already knew about this, why hadn't she said something?

They finished their dinner without mentioning fathers again. Jared's mind wandered to Audrey. After paying the bill, he said good-bye to Carolyn and called Mia as soon as he got into his car.

"Please do not tell me there was a problem," she said without a greeting.

It took a minute for his brain to process what she was referring to. "They abandoned the mission tonight. They came up with an alternate plan for tomorrow. I'm calling because I had dinner with Carolyn Draper."

"And?"

"She told me that at her father's last poker night, she heard the guys talking about liquidating their assets. Know anything about that?"

She sighed heavily in his ear.

"I knew it. What's going on?"

"I think they're being pressured to sell to help our fathers. We don't know how much they had stashed overseas. I'm beginning to think it's not as much as we originally imagined."

Jared absorbed the information. Their fathers were in trouble. It was hard to lie low when you didn't have money to hide with. "Is this why you're rushing to get these jobs done?"

"Yes. I heard Jerome Bauer was getting appraisals on a few pieces from his collection. It piqued my interest, especially since one of the pieces going up for sale is one I earmarked for us. Once I started to dig, the network of lies unraveled."

"What are you saying?"

"In addition to the money our fathers hid in offshore accounts, their backup plan was in physical items left with their friends. Expensive items, like art and jewelry that could be sold when needed."

"Brilliant," Jared muttered with awe and disgust. "Do you know what each man is holding?"

"I'm not one hundred percent sure, but I have it narrowed. I want to get this done now more than ever. This isn't about just making amends. We have the chance to strike them from thousands of miles away. If Carolyn heard them talking, they might be moving faster than I anticipated."

"Which means our fathers might have a move planned." Right now, they knew where their fathers were—Montenegro, chosen because of the lack of extradition. He'd always thought it an odd choice for his father. Maybe they had simply used it as a first stop. "What do you want to do?"

"Let's get through this first job Saturday. If it all goes well, we'll reassess and see how fast we can get to the rest. I want them to feel it, Jared."

"I know. Me, too." They disconnected as he arrived back at the apartment. He let himself in. The living room was dark except for the glow of the TV. Nikki was sprawled on the couch, mouth hanging open, sound asleep. As he walked toward the spare bedroom, he loosened his tie, hoping Audrey was waiting for him.

He eased the door open and saw the moonlight cascade over her curled up form on the edge of the bed. She hadn't even gotten under the blanket. It was as if she didn't want to leave a mark. He took off his clothes, hung them on the chair at the desk, and climbed onto the mattress behind her.

Kissing her neck and her ear, he caressed her hip, and smoothed a hand along her thigh, quietly waking her.

"Audrey, wake up."

"Hmm. Did you enjoy your dinner?"

He paused, trying to determine if he heard a hint of jealousy in her voice, and decided it was his imagination. "It was fruitful."

She snickered. "Who talks like that? Dinner is not fruitful—unless you're chowing on a fruit salad."

"Is productive a better word?"

"I guess productive makes sense since you indicated it was a business dinner."

"But I was thinking about you the entire time."

She turned over to face him. "That's what I wanted to hear."

SIXTEEN

LATER THAT NIGHT, Jay pulled Audrey close and nuzzled her neck. She immediately stiffened.

"I'm not asking for lifetime commitment here. Relax."

"You want to cuddle?"

"I'm not fond of that word. How about I want to hold you and talk for a while."

His touches were mesmerizing and she relaxed against him. She was exhausted and lying there for a moment would allow her to recharge.

"What was the best hack you've ever done?"

Her foggy brain struggled to focus. "I don't tend to do things that make a big splash. I like small, quiet jobs."

"But you're good enough to cause real damage."

"I like to fly under the radar. Keeps it simple."

"If you can do more, why not? Bigger jobs have to be more profitable. And if you're all about the money…"

"Who said I'm all about the money?"

He kissed her temple. "Babe, every business conversation we've ever had told me how important money is to you."

"The only people who say money isn't important are those that have enough."

"Touché."

"You're one to talk about bigger jobs. You went to law school, but you're not a lawyer."

"Lawyers are snakes."

"No argument there. But why bother?"

"I wanted to know the ins and outs of the law. It's the best way to serve my clientele."

The conversation had become a little too real for her liking. This went beyond having a good time and relaxing. Sitting up, she tried to lighten things by saying, "This heart to heart has been great, but I need a shower."

THE MORNING LIGHT streamed through the window, waking Audrey. The sun cast across the expanse of tan skin of Jay's naked chest.

They'd spent the night together. She didn't do that. It was personal, sharing a bed with someone, waking with him. She reminded herself it wasn't her bed, so it didn't count. But even with the laughing and talking, being with Jay was easy. He didn't pressure her for anything. When she refused to answer something or dodged a question, he let it go. Probably because he had at least as many secrets as she did.

They clicked in a way that nagged at her and made her uncomfortable. She was having a hard time separating the physical connection from everything else between them. She'd never had that problem before, at least not since high school. Sex and emotion didn't have to go hand in hand. But with Jay there *was* more. He saw into her, the parts she liked to keep hidden.

His arm tightened around her and pulled her closer, as if even in his sleep he couldn't get enough of her.

He cared for her. Not about her, but for her. He made

sure she ate and slept and relaxed. In the couple of weeks they'd known each other, he'd shown her more care than anyone in her life had since Gram had gotten sick. And he'd done it without expectation of anything.

Ah, damn. I'm falling for this guy.

She couldn't fall for him. It would be a mistake of epic proportions. He came from a world she existed on the fringes of because she was useful to people like him. They could have this time here in this rented apartment, but she would never be on his arm in public. She would never know his family, his friends.

Her heart thumped. *Get out!* it screamed at her.

She slid from his grasp and went to shower. She halfway convinced herself she wasn't falling for Jay. How could she? She wasn't even sure if she knew him. He was the kind of guy who always knew what to say to get what he wanted. With the heat of the water, she washed away the ridiculous thoughts she had in bed. She had work to do. They had a painting to steal. When she got to the kitchen, Nikki was already awake and drinking coffee.

"Morning," Audrey said.

Nikki smirked over the rim of her mug. "Better for you than me."

"Don't be jealous," she said with a bravado she didn't feel. Vulnerability crept around her edges.

"Not in the slightest. I'm happy you enjoyed yourself. I just wish you were a little quieter about it."

"Sorry," Audrey answered with a grin of her own.

"That was real sincere." She dropped a few pieces of bread in the mouse cage. The bell rang and she went to answer it.

Audrey focused on getting as much caffeine into her system as quickly as possible so she wouldn't fall asleep while talking to a damn dog. She downed an energy drink and then poured a cup of coffee. Moments later, London walked through the front door at the same time Jay came up behind her.

He took her cup from her and drank.

"Hey, that was mine."

"Too much caffeine is bad for you." He pointed at the empty energy drink can on the counter.

"I wouldn't need so much caffeine if someone hadn't kept me up most of the night."

"But the sleep you got was of the highest quality."

"Still full of yourself." But she couldn't stop her smile.

The small dog in London's arms squeaked out a bark. Setting the animal down, she said, "Maybe you guys should try calling her so she gets used to you."

"I don't want her to get used to me," Nikki said from her perch on the back of the couch.

Audrey bent and slapped her thighs. "Hey, Daisy. Come here, girl."

As the dog clicked by, Nikki pulled her legs up on the edge of the couch so her entire body was balanced on the back. The dog came to Audrey immediately and she rubbed the dog's head. "I really don't think you have anything to worry about here, Nikki. She's not vicious."

"That's what every dog lover says."

Audrey straightened. "At least call her once so we can gauge how quickly she can change focus. Once she gets to me, we need her to turn so London can give chase."

"Daisy," Nikki said sharply.

Her ears perked up, but she didn't move.

London crossed the room and picked up the dog. "She's not going to come to you if you sound like you might kill her."

"I don't want her to come to me."

With a sigh, London went to the other side of the apartment. Cradling Daisy in one hand, she pointed at Audrey. "Go by the hallway so Nikki can stay up on her pedestal. Then call her."

She set the dog down again. Audrey called her. When she got halfway across the room, Nikki called. She turned, walked a few steps and Audrey beckoned again. The poor animal looked ridiculous, but it was exactly what they needed her to do.

"You sure this is going to give me enough time?" Nikki asked, stretching her legs out on the couch as if it were a balance beam and she was a gymnast.

"Once they catch Daisy, London can engage Connie in a conversation for a couple minutes. If Daisy does her part, we have at least eight minutes."

"If she doesn't?"

"We have about five. Maybe."

"Psh," London said with a wave of her hand as she gathered Daisy in her arms again. "I can have a ten-minute conversation with anyone. You have time."

Hopping off the couch, Nikki said, "Then let's do this."

As London and Nikki headed for the door, Nikki pointed at Daisy. "Don't you have a cage or a bag or something for that?"

"No. Daisy is great in the car. She rode on my lap on the way here." London stroked the dog's head.

"Keep her away from me or I'll toss her out the window."

As they left, Audrey laughed, but she wasn't sure Nikki was exaggerating. She shoved the bag of dog treats that London had brought in her pocket. Jay reached out and yanked her back to his body.

He kissed her deeply and when he pulled away, he whispered against her lips, "If things go sideways, get out of there."

"We will."

"No. I mean if you can only save yourself, do it."

She didn't say anything since she didn't know how to respond. It was kind of nice that he was worried about her. And it had to be concern, right? She'd already completed everything he needed for the alarm. He could have anyone run it Saturday night. But the fact that he was okay with her bailing on Nikki and London bugged her.

"I want to be looped in on the comms. I'd like to hear how things are going."

She set an extra earpiece on the table. "You need to be in range for it to work."

"No problem." He held up keys. "I'm driving."

Her heart thundered. She'd needed more of a reprieve. She needed space to deal with her feelings and thoughts. Now she was going to be trapped in a car with him.

"TAKE THE RATS, just in case Daisy doesn't cooperate," he said.

She sighed but picked up the cage. "They're mice,

not rats. I think it'll break London's heart if we have to sacrifice them."

"Better them than us."

With cage in hand, she gave him a skeptical look and walked out.

Mia would kill him if she knew he was riding along again. But he couldn't stay behind. If they ran into problems, he could run interference, but mostly he wanted to make sure Audrey was safe. While she talked like some badass criminal, she admittedly rarely interacted with people. She'd chosen a line of work that required minimal contact. He didn't know if she would have any clue how to get herself out of a jam.

Nikki could handle herself. Not much fazed her— except apparently a small dog. He drove the borrowed car back into the north shore suburb, letting the women out in separate places. They each planned to enter the property from a different direction, with Nikki and Audrey climbing through neighbors' yards. If they were stopped, they would explain they were looking for their friend's dog. London's calling the dog would set minds at ease.

It was a good plan. Better than the crazy letting loose of rodents and waiting for exterminators. It didn't stop him from worrying, though. Audrey had burrowed under his skin in a way he hadn't seen coming. He wanted to see where they could take things, and he wanted to protect her. He knew she'd balk if he said that, but it was true. Whether or not she needed his help.

He put the earpiece in and within moments heard Audrey. "I'm in place. You, London?"

"About fifty feet away from the front of the house."

"Give me two to avoid cameras and get in the yard," Nikki responded.

The silence was killing him. He wanted to see, make sure everyone played her part. Driving in circles near the house—but not too close—was maddening.

Then all hell broke loose in his ear, just the way it was supposed to. London's squeals were almost enough for him to yank the earpiece out, but then Audrey's quiet whisper of "Daisy, here, girl" came across and his nerves settled. London made so much noise he was surprised the entire neighborhood wasn't outside.

London began talking to someone and soon there was another voice joining the fray.

"I'm in," Nikki said.

"You should get out now, Audrey." As soon as he spoke it, he knew she was going to be pissed.

Nikki snickered. "Yeah, *Audrey.* Beat it."

"Not funny," she muttered.

"Damn," Nikki whispered.

"What?" he and Audrey asked simultaneously.

"It's not here."

"What do you mean?" Audrey asked.

"The painting isn't where you said it would be."

His brain scrambled. Mia wouldn't have been wrong about this. She was meticulous in her observations.

"Get out and we'll regroup." Audrey sounded nervous.

"Give me a minute."

His heart began to race. If Nikki was caught in the house, the entire plan would be ruined.

London finally caught the dog and just as she'd said,

she engaged the maid in a conversation about dogs and their owners.

"Found it. Should've known this stupid plan wouldn't be as easy as we thought. I walked right past it in a hurry to get to the stairs. They conveniently moved it to the den."

He released the air trapped in his lungs.

"It's in my hands right now," Nikki said. "I can have the whole thing out of here in less than two minutes."

"No," he said sharply. "It has to be Saturday and you have to replace it."

She huffed a sigh. "I'll have you know this goes against every cell in my being. To have the mark, the prize, in my hands and walk away. It's dumb."

"Hurry up," Audrey said. "Connie's patience is wearing thin with London. She's starting to back away. Time for you to get out."

"What are you still doing there? You're supposed to be on your way back to me." He drummed his fingers on the steering wheel.

He heard rustling and then her harsh whisper came back. "Well, it's not like Nikki has eyes on the situation, and London can't very well warn her. I'm heading out now."

"I'm out. London, say good-bye," Nikki said.

Jared sat at the corner where Audrey was supposed to come out. He scanned the neighborhood and saw no one milling around. Then she peeked around the corner and dashed to the car, carrying the mice with her.

She scooted into the passenger side and set the cage at her feet.

He pointed at the mice. "You probably could've left them behind."

"London wants to keep them." She pulled her comm from her ear and pinned him with a look. "I told you not to use my real name."

He also removed his earpiece. This wasn't something he needed to broadcast to everyone. "Are you going to tell me that during all of your girl bonding, you didn't tell them your name?"

"That's not the point."

"They know we're sleeping together. I don't see what the problem is."

"It was a simple request." She crossed her arms and looked out the window.

He pulled away from the curb, his jaw clenched. Everything had gone more or less as planned, but he was still irritated. Yes, her request was simple, but it wasn't as if her name was a state secret.

On the next block, Nikki was jogging like she belonged there. When he pulled up, she ran to the car and stuck her head near the passenger window.

"Care for a ride?" Audrey asked.

"Love one." She climbed in the back seat.

Another block down, they picked up London. As soon as all three were in the car, they debriefed.

"No additional alarms on the frame. Them moving the painting was the best thing for us. I actually save travel time. Saturday night will be a breeze as long as you can get me in," Nikki said.

"Shouldn't be a problem," Audrey responded.

"Still don't see why I couldn't take it now."

"That's what we're all wondering, but it's obviously above our pay grade." Audrey was filled with snark.

He drove to the apartment and dropped them off before leaving to return the car. Audrey needed space to cool off, and he needed to get his emotions in check. They had eleven more jobs to pull after this one, and nothing would work if he kept worrying about her.

After switching back to his own vehicle, he texted Mia and let her know the women were amazing. Everything had gone as planned and Saturday was looking better than expected.

SEVENTEEN

"You're in a *mood*," Nikki said as she did her usual flounce on the couch. For a renowned burglar, she sure did flop and flounce a lot. Before Audrey could say anything, Nikki jumped back to her feet.

"Jay pissed me off. How did he not piss you off?" Audrey asked.

Nikki shrugged. "I can admit that I usually prefer to run the show myself and call the shots, but I'm fine letting someone else be the boss for the right price. It's his gig."

"There's something else going on."

"Is this because he used your real name? I thought you stayed Data with him."

"I told him in the heat of the moment. He's not supposed to use it willy-nilly like that."

"What's the big deal? You told me and London your name."

Audrey huffed. "He knows where I live—the building at least. Now he has my real name. It removes a layer of anonymity. My life is based on being anonymous."

"So even the score." Nikki stretched her arms over her head. "I think I need a run."

Audrey nodded but wasn't listening. *Even the score.* Why the hell hadn't she considered that before? Obviously because she respected boundaries more than Jay did. But it wasn't just his use of her name. Something about their insistence that the job go on Saturday and his sharp reaction when Nikki mentioned nabbing the painting today.

She didn't like not having all the pieces and this puzzle definitely had some holes.

As Nikki changed into her running gear, Audrey went back to the computer. She'd figure out what the Greens were hiding.

She was vaguely aware of Nikki leaving. With her headphones on, blasting music to keep her tired brain focused, Audrey attempted to remember every bit of information she'd gleaned about the Greens. Normally, when she had to track someone down, she at least had a name or a trail to follow. What did she have here? The rented apartment she was working in. She shook her head. They were smart. They'd bury their names.

The one constant they had was Scott and Saturday night. "Let's figure out where Scott is going to be Saturday."

She started to dig through Randall Scott's social media and found nothing of note. Someone else ran the social media for his business. His personal accounts were bare. But his pretty wife would want to show off.

Audrey found the wife's accounts and as expected, they were chock full of information and photos. Event after event she attended on her husband's arm to show the world how fabulous they were.

No mention of her plans for Saturday, but Audrey had plenty to scroll through. In one picture, she hit pay dirt. Ms. Green. Two photos later, Jay. "I knew it." They traveled in the same circles as Randall Scott. Now it was time to get names.

Audrey wanted to kick herself. Digging into a person's life was routine for her. Why she hadn't done it with Scott before embarking on this job was crazy. Then again, the Greens had made her digging unnecessary. They'd handed her all of the pertinent information. At least the information they wanted her to have, carefully omitting anything that would lead to them.

A reverse image search was easy enough to perform and she had Ms. Green's name within minutes. Mia Benson. Benson. The name sounded familiar, but nothing immediately came to mind. Then Jay's real name popped up. Jared Towers.

Fuck. Towers and Benson. Those names were synonymous with high-end con artists. No different than Madoff. Her heart thumped. Whatever she thought she'd learn, this wasn't it. *Maybe I'm wrong.* She wanted to be wrong.

She searched for Jared Towers and Mia Benson. Window after window popped up. Some were benign articles about their work, but most of the information linked them to their fathers. While Audrey recognized the names, she'd never paid much attention to the full story. Millionaires stealing from people didn't have an effect on her. She'd never had anything to steal.

Desperate to give Jay the benefit of the doubt, she read every article on their fathers. Forty minutes later, she had no benefit left to give. Towers and Benson stole from hardworking people and left them broke. When the police entered the picture, they fled the country. Most speculated they'd gone to a country without extradition.

Audrey's blood ran hot. She clicked on story after story of families ruined because of those two men. People who lost their homes when they believed they were saving for retirement. Others whose kids had to skip college to work. Her heart broke a little with each instance. And she was helping Jared carry on the family tradition.

No, she wasn't. She'd find another way to pay for Gram's care. She went through the apartment and gathered all of her things. She wouldn't be returning.

When the door opened, Nikki jogged through. "Guess what I picked up on the street?"

Jay—Jared—walked in behind her and held up a bag of food. He took one look at Audrey and rushed across the room. "What's wrong? Did something happen?"

Ignoring his questions, she looked at Nikki. "Did you know?"

"Know what?"

"Who they are." She pointed at the huge screen on the wall. "Jared Towers and Mia Benson, heirs to two of Chicago's biggest thieves."

"Damn," Nikki said.

Jared set the bag of food on the table. He reached up as if to touch her, but she backed away.

"I'm out of here. Don't call me. Don't contact me."

"Why?" he asked.

The confusion on his face told her he really didn't have a clue.

"You lied about who you are."

"I never lied. I just never gave you all the information. Neither have you. Or Nikki."

"It's not the same and you know it."

"How is it different? You're entitled to privacy but I'm not?" The confusion flipped to irritation.

"This isn't about privacy. This is about lying about who you are. Regardless of whether I use Audrey or go by Data, I'm a hacker. I serve whoever will offer the biggest paycheck. Nikki goes by one name. She's a thief." She pointed at him. "You were pretending to be one of us." She huffed.

"What's the problem? We're all the same. That's what you're getting at, right? You thought I wasn't a criminal, but I am."

"The problem is the type of criminal you are. You steal from people who can't afford it. You rob people of their lives."

His face grew red and his eyes flashed. He got up so close they were nearly nose to nose. "Do not confuse me with my father. He stole people's livelihoods. I don't."

She snorted. "Sure."

"I am no more my father than you are your mother."

She snapped back from his words. How dare he bring her mother into this? "Fuck you, Jay. Jared. I don't work for liars."

"Oh, that's rich. You just admitted you'll sell yourself to the highest bidder."

As soon as the words left his mouth, he regretted them. Devastation stole across her face for a brief moment before she schooled her features.

He normally had much better control over his emotions. Worse, he didn't even mean them. He'd wanted to strike out for being compared to his father.

She swallowed hard. "Glad to finally see the real

you. Our business is done." She pushed past him to the door.

"The job isn't done. If you walk out that door, you won't get your money." He thought for sure the lure of the payout would make her stay.

Over her shoulder, she said, "Then I guess it's a good thing there are plenty of rich jerks out there who will pay me."

She stomped out of the apartment.

Nikki took a seat at the table and started taking out food. "You sure screwed that up good."

"Me? What the hell did I do?"

Nikki shook her head. "If you don't know, I can't help you. Your cousin's gonna be pissed, though. You just lost your hacker."

"You're not going to follow her bizarre moral code and leave?"

"I don't care who I work for as long as the cash is good. You do have the money to pay me, right?"

He nodded. "I don't spend money I don't have."

"Good." She took a bite of pasta. "However, I won't be going into this job without someone who can get me in and out of the house."

"I'll handle it." He left Nikki sitting there and went to see Mia.

Nikki was right. He had screwed this up, but he didn't know what he could've done differently. He hadn't even considered the when or how of revealing his full name. He hadn't wanted her to know for this exact reason.

Although Mia had planned to be at the museum most of the day, especially while Nikki and Audrey were at

Scott's house, it was late enough that she should be home; she rarely worked this late, even though she loved her job at the Art Institute. He knocked, and while waiting for her to answer, he tried to figure out a plan.

The door opened and Mia simply said, "What went wrong?"

"Shit went sideways." His words were clear, all business, but his mind was hazy, his heart squeezed tight.

She stepped back from the entrance. Inside, he smelled dinner cooking. No table was set, though, so she was making dinner for herself, giving him the freedom to talk.

"The trip to Scott's went off more or less without a hitch, but when I got back to the apartment, Audrey was pissed. She figured out who we are and shared the information with Nikki."

"Audrey?"

"Data. Her real name is Audrey. She left. She said she's out. She won't work with liars."

"You slept with her."

It wasn't a question. Not quite a statement either. More like an accusation.

"That has nothing to do with this. She thinks we're continuing our fathers' legacy," he said defensively.

"How stupid are you? Sleeping with her has everything to do with this. When did you learn her real name?"

He opened his mouth and realized the trap she had laid. Rather than answer, he continued, "Nikki is still there, but we need a new hacker."

"I told you this would be a problem. You never want to listen to me. Accused me of being a control freak. I stepped back, let you run this, and now look where we are. I warned you not to sleep with her. I said don't let them meet. We're not building a team."

"They work so well together. You saw it. If we didn't have them in the same room, they wouldn't have come up with the solutions they did. Certainly not that quickly." It had been a smart move. They were a team.

"But now we have less than three days. Can Nikki do this alone?"

"Someone has to force the reboot of the system and then trip the alarm."

"How hard can it be to find someone to do that as long as you can show him how?"

"It would mean bringing in another person."

"Do we have a choice?"

"Not really," he admitted, but he didn't want to replace Audrey. He wanted her to see it through.

"Then find someone. Preferably someone you won't want to screw. To make matters worse, we need to move the timetable up on all the jobs. They're making a move and I want to take away all of their options."

He nodded. Thinking about the additional hassles this had caused, he said, "I'm sorry."

"You truly care for her, don't you?" She ran a hand down his arm.

"We have something special." *Had.* She'd walked out and told him not to contact her again. That was pretty decisive. His heart said it wasn't over yet, though.

"Not to be a dick, but how special could it have been if she didn't even know you?"

Hearing Mia use crude language startled him. It

wasn't like her. "She didn't know my name or my family, but she knows me."

"Then I'm the one who's sorry."

"But you're not revoking the 'I told you so' though, are you?"

"Of course not. I do thoroughly enjoy being right. Stay for dinner." She led him into the gourmet kitchen.

He followed even though he didn't have an appetite, but the thought of being alone with his regrets didn't appeal to him either.

Mia pointed to a stool at the counter and poured him a glass of wine. She was the only person he knew who routinely cooked her own meals. And she did so in her designer clothes without spilling or splashing food on them. It was like she was surrounded by her own little force field.

While she served, he sipped the wine, knowing the drink wouldn't take the edge off his hurt or anger at losing Audrey.

"Is there anything you can do to fix this?" she asked.

"With Audrey? I have no idea."

"Obviously getting her to come back would be best. She created the plan and knows how it's supposed to go."

"Maybe once she cools off I can talk to her." For a moment, he'd thought Mia was actually concerned about his relationship, but it was all about the job.

"If you can't convince her, how difficult will it be to find another hacker we can use going forward?"

He didn't like the idea of someone else taking Audrey's place. In the few short weeks they'd been working together, they'd built a team, and starting over didn't sound like a good idea. But Mia was right. If they had to move fast, they didn't have time to wait for Audrey. "I'll put some feelers out for other people I've worked with. Since most of the legwork is done, they can probably work remotely, but I don't know if that can continue for the other jobs."

"Why not?"

"Look at the issues we've had on this job."

She waved a wooden spoon in his direction. "Let Nikki plan the next one. Give her the mark and let her figure it out. Once she knows what's needed, you can inform the hacker."

"In theory that makes sense, but remember Nikki insisted on meeting Audrey. She wanted to know who was at her back. I doubt she'll trust someone who only works remotely."

Mia placed two dishes on the counter and they both stared at the neatly arranged chicken and rice.

"Do whatever you have to for this to happen. We've come so far, Jared."

"I'll figure it out." He reached across and placed his hand over hers.

"I wish our lives were different. Then you could have Audrey and the two of you could get your nerd on at the computer where the most complicated thing you'd have to navigate would be code."

He saw complete understanding in her eyes. And maybe a bit of longing?

"That's never been my life. But with her, I felt like I could have some semblance of normalcy."

She gave him a disbelieving look with one eyebrow nearly reaching her hairline. "Seriously? The hacker and the negotiator—two people full of secrets and hidden lives who work mostly on the dark web. That's your idea of normal?"

He laughed. "I know it sounds ridiculous, but because of the lives we lead, we make sense together. Even though it's only been a couple of weeks."

"If there's anything I can do to help, I will. But my priority is getting the art and helping the people who have suffered because of our fathers. When the jobs are done, we can think about finding happiness and building new lives for ourselves. Until then…"

"I know. I let a distraction get in the way. But I'm not sorry about it. I was falling for her." He knew everything coming out of his mouth sounded crazy. On paper, his relationship with Audrey made no sense. They didn't belong together, but he didn't care. But who they were, where they came from, that part made sense. They got each other on a deep level because of the messed-up families that had shaped them.

Most women couldn't connect with him in that respect. They couldn't understand what drove him. Audrey understood because she was driven in a similar way.

He wasn't just falling for her. He loved her.

Unfortunately, his need to help Mia with her plans might've cost him the best relationship he'd ever had.

EIGHTEEN

JARED DECIDED TO avoid the apartment and Nikki for the next day. She would want to know what the plan was and he didn't have one yet. He gave Audrey the night. He hoped that even if she was still pissed, she would consider coming back. He drove to her apartment and went to the door. The bells weren't marked. He didn't know which was hers.

He could ring bells at random and hope to be allowed in. He could call her and hope she would answer. Hope. It seemed as though that was all he had right now. As he considered his options, the door swung open. A thin woman in workout gear and with a heavily made-up face came out.

"Excuse me," he said, taking a step back. "I'm looking for my friend, Audrey. Can you tell me which apartment is hers?"

"I could, but since I don't know you, that would be dumb."

He realized she was right. If he were a terrible ex-boyfriend, this would be how he'd go about finding her. "I owe her money for a job she did for me. She left yesterday and was upset."

"Oh," the woman said with a smile, "you're the asshole."

"Yeah, I guess I am."

The woman tilted her head to the side, her bright red hair cascading over her shoulder. "Based on the ranting I heard last night, you owe her more than some money."

"Is she home?"

"No."

"Do you know where she is?"

"Yes."

He waited patiently.

She narrowed her eyes. "If she were really your friend, you would know the only place Audrey goes is to spend time with her grandmother."

"We didn't share a lot of personal details, if you know what I mean. Can you tell me where her grandmother lives?" When she just continued to stare at him, he gave her his most charming smile and added, "Please. I'm not here to cause trouble for her."

"She owes me a couple hundred dollars." She held her hand out expectantly.

He pulled out his wallet and pressed the bills into her palm.

"A place called Horizons, but you didn't get that information from me."

"Thank you."

She waved as she headed down the sidewalk, shoulder bag thumping against her body. She hadn't given him her name, so he didn't know if she was Audrey's friend or just a neighbor, making it easy for him to not explain where he'd gotten the information.

On his way to his car, he googled Horizons to see where he was headed and what kind of place it was. The internet informed him it was an assisted living facility for the elderly. He gathered information on the residence and quickly realized the reason Audrey accepted any well-paying job.

He pulled up to the facility and parked in a visitor spot. Since he had no idea what Audrey's last name was, much less her grandmother's, he didn't have much choice but to sit and wait for her to come out and hope she used the main entrance. As far as he knew, she didn't drive, so coming out this way made the most sense since the bus stop was on the corner. While he waited, he learned more about the assisted living facility and the kind of patients they cared for.

At the hour mark, he became restless and stepped from the car to walk around. The sun beat down on him. Even the breeze was thick and warm, adding to his restlessness. He removed his suit jacket and rolled the sleeves of his shirt to his elbows. He stretched his legs and thought about what he wanted to say to Audrey. For the first time in his life, he was at a loss for words. In his work, he figured out what people wanted or what they were afraid of and used it against them.

He didn't understand why Audrey was pissed off. They'd spoken on numerous occasions about the secrets they kept. He didn't know what she wanted, other than money, and now he understood the importance of that. Although she'd never actually said it, he'd figured out she feared turning into her mother, which was what made it an easy comparison to make during their argument. Understanding how to get at people was what made him successful at his job.

It was a low blow to bring her mother into the fight, but she'd come at him with gloves off. He'd fought back the only way he knew how, and for that he had regrets.

But in order to fix this mess, he needed to understand why finding out his real name made her so upset.

She finally came through the front door and a tug pulled the middle of his chest. He'd missed seeing her and talking to her, even though it had only been a day. She walked quickly, head bowed, but he knew she paid attention to her surroundings. Stopping abruptly a few feet away, she stared at him with a stony face.

"Stalking me now?"

"It's not like that. I asked your friend from your building where I could find you."

She gave a disgusted snort. "I don't have any friends in my building."

"Someone knew enough to give me the name of this place."

"Why are you here?" She wrapped her arms across her middle, making sure to put up every barrier he'd already fought past.

"I wanted to see you, talk to you."

"I have nothing left to say."

"I do. We have a pretty good thing going here. I know you feel it, too."

"What exactly is good? The part where you pretend to be some art thief in order to get me to help you be like your conniving father? Or the part where you sleep with me, say you want to know who you're having sex with, but don't offer me the same courtesy?"

He sighed. "I didn't lie to you. For the purposes of this job, I am an art thief, but it's nothing like what my father did."

"You're an insanely rich dude who has nothing better

to do but to take from other people simply because you can. How is it not the same? Please, explain."

"I can't. It's not just my story to share. And as far as sleeping together, I've never been more myself than in those moments with you." He couldn't tell her everything without Mia's consent, but the truth in his confession was freeing.

She shook her head slightly, squinting as she looked into his face. "How long did you practice those pretty words?"

Her question stung. "Not at all. This is the real me, asking you to trust me. Come back."

"You don't get it, do you? I can't trust you. I gave you my real name and asked you to keep it between us. You blurted it out first chance you had."

"I was worried about you. I used your name because that's how I think of you now."

She flicked up a hand to head him off. "I wasn't finished. You ask that I trust you, allow you to keep your secrets, but you've been trying to expose mine from the beginning. Showing up here is a perfect example."

"Let me ask you this—would you have taken the job if I did tell you who I am, where I come from?"

She rolled her lips in and licked them. "To be honest, I doubt it. But I guess we'll never know for sure. Even if you didn't lead with that, you could've told me later. Like you, I prefer to know who I'm sleeping with. You didn't give me the opportunity."

"I'm sorry." He stepped closer, wanting to touch her, but holding back. "I wasn't just protecting myself, though."

Her arms flinched as they tightened around herself.

"Your cousin doesn't seem like she needs much protection."

She had no idea, but he couldn't explain that either. He was losing this battle and he didn't like it. "Is there anything I can do to change your mind?"

"I don't know. Right now, I don't even want to look at you."

"Even if you're angry with me, this job needs to go forward. If you don't come back tomorrow, we'll have to replace you." This time he indulged and ran a hand down her arm. "It would kill me to bring in someone to take your place."

Then he stepped away with the hope that she'd come back. Even if she remained pissed off, he could take time to convince her to give him another chance. But if she walked away for good, he'd have to learn to deal with it. No matter how much it might destroy him.

AUDREY SHOOK ON her way to the bus stop. She didn't have the energy for another face-off with Jared. Diane was kind enough to give her a shift at the Grind. If nothing else, she had to make rent. She also had to figure out an affordable place to move Gram. She didn't have any headspace for Jared and his hurt feelings.

As she scrolled online looking for another hacking job, she received a notification for a wire transfer. Confused, she logged in to her account. She'd already been paid for all of her jobs. When she saw the deposit, she knew immediately it had been Jared. Damn man. Did he really think he could pay her and leverage her to come back?

She'd earned this money, though. Had she been

thinking straight, she would've demanded a partial payout when she left. But she'd been too focused on her hurt feelings. She'd fallen for a guy without having a clue as to who he was. People sucked and she knew better. Except sometimes selfish people felt guilty. With a smile, she closed the app. The deposit was for a third of their agreed amount. She had her cushion to figure out her next steps.

The coffee shop was slow since Diane didn't need her for the peak morning hours, so to keep her mind off everything, she cleaned up the counter and restocked condiments.

When she turned, Nikki stood in front of her. "What are you doing here?"

"Looking for you, of course."

"How did you find me?"

"The first time we met, you were wearing this shirt. If it had been a Starbucks, I might not have tracked you down so easily."

"I guess covert operations are out of my area of expertise." Audrey smiled. "Can I get you some coffee?"

"Only if it'll buy me five minutes of your time."

She knew Nikki wasn't here for a social call. And while she was still upset at Jared, Nikki hadn't done anything to her. She waved at her coworker. "I'm taking my break."

Nikki glanced around and headed to a small table in the corner near the bathrooms.

"Did he send you?"

"Of course not. I wouldn't do his bidding."

"Then why are you here?"

"To ask you to come back and finish the job."

"No."

Nikki raised a hand. "Hear me out."

Audrey crossed her arms and nodded.

"I get that you're pissed. I'm not a hundred percent sure on the why of it, but I can back you on calling him a liar. Personally, I don't care who I work for as long as their money is good."

"Their money isn't good. Their fathers stole it from hardworking people who couldn't replace it." Every time she thought about it, her stomach twisted. She'd done a lot of questionable things, but never against anyone who didn't deserve it or couldn't afford it. "Doesn't that bother you?"

Nikki shrugged. "My moral compass is a little off. I was raised by a con man who taught me everything I know. I was picking pockets before I learned to multiply. If people are stupidly naïve, maybe they have it coming."

Audrey had been stupidly naïve. All those thoughts about Jared and how he made her feel. Stupid, stupid, stupid.

"But this time, they're—we're—stealing from a total jerk," Nikki added.

That knowledge had made the job appealing.

"Think of your grandmother."

Audrey narrowed her eyes. This was why she didn't let people in. They used information against her.

Nikki continued, "She's obviously important to you and you're worried. I don't have anyone like that in my life."

Something about the way she paused made Audrey

think that maybe at some point there had been someone like that.

"I like to work alone. But we started this together, and in all honesty, I'm not sure I trust someone else to come in and have my back. I'm the only one with my ass swinging in the breeze if everything falls apart. At least if you're there, I know you'll get me out."

Nikki made a compelling argument. Audrey liked her, but she didn't know if she could continue to work with Jared.

"I'll think about it. I don't want to leave you hanging, but there's so much that's not right with them. It's all smoke and mirrors."

"But the cash is real."

She knew that, too, and she wanted the money. She wanted it enough to reconsider. "I'll tell you what. If you can get Jared to back off—no showing up at the apartment, no contacting me, nothing—I'll come back. As soon as the job is done, they arrive with cash in hand." She stood to go back to work. "You make that happen and I'll come back."

One of Nikki's eyebrows winged up. "Like I'm gonna argue with that? I lose a babysitter and get my hacker back? Win-win. Consider it done. He might not like it, but his cousin is all business. She'll make it happen."

Audrey released a long breath before going back to work. She hoped she wasn't making the mistake of a lifetime. The rest of the payment from this job would give her time to find another source of income. And Jared's absence would allow her to keep her head straight.

Hopefully.

NINETEEN

Mia

MIA PACED HER OFFICE. Being surrounded by beautiful pieces of artwork was the most calming thing in the world for her. But Nikki had called. That woman didn't communicate with anyone, so Mia had immediately known something was up. They could have Data back. More importantly, Nikki demanded they get her back.

"It was my one requirement," Nikki had reminded her. *"If I don't work alone, I need to know who's got my back going in. I'm not dealing with a stranger now. Audrey will get me in and out."*

Mia couldn't argue with any of it. *Audrey.* That was the name of the woman who had made a mess of things, including Jared. If the two of them had kept their pants on, they wouldn't be in this position. She didn't like having to capitulate to the demands of Nikki. She might be a brilliant thief, but the woman was a disaster.

Mia had texted Jared and asked him to meet her for a late lunch. She'd break the news to him then. He was levelheaded. He'd understand. Hopefully, the logical part of his brain would take control and they wouldn't have any further problems. As she gathered her things for her lunch meeting, her brain cataloged the thefts she wanted to make happen.

Her timeline had to move up exponentially. Where she'd thought they had six to twelve months to accomplish this, she now worried they only had a few months at most. Maybe she should have Jared create additional teams. She hadn't considered it before, but that was when she'd thought they had all the time in the world. Their fathers were on the move and she had the chance to bring them back.

Exposing themselves to more people as the moneymen behind a bunch of heists might be worth it if it brought their fathers to justice.

In the back seat of the car, she called London. Another team didn't mean they would need another artist.

"Hello."

"Are you capable of creating other types of art? Other than paintings?"

"Depends on the medium."

"Can you create sculptures, vases, pottery, or jewelry?"

"Jewelry's not my thing, but I'm open to discussion. I assume you're looking for something specific?"

Mia liked that London exhibited caution with her words. Didn't ask about copies or forgeries. Safe. "Yes, I am looking for some very specific pieces."

"Then let's talk after the thing Saturday night."

"What would you know about Saturday?" So much for being cautious. It seemed as if everyone was busy filling in every detail all around.

"I told the girls I'd be at the apartment to keep them company."

"Hmm. I'll stop by later to give you specifics of what I'm looking for. Time is of the essence. The sooner you start, the better." She disconnected and wondered how much London knew about what had happened with Jared and Audrey. Ultimately, it didn't matter. Regardless of who executed the thefts, they would need the forgeries. She would give London the full list to get started. Then she'd worry about who would make the switch.

The car pulled up at the restaurant and Jared was standing outside waiting for her. He wore his usual suit, but he looked rumpled. And not in a good way.

As she neared, she took him in. "You look like hell."

"Thanks. I love you, too."

"This has nothing to do with love. What is going on with you? So you slept with a woman who no longer wants you. It's not like you to get this bent out of shape." She pointed at him up and down, at a loss for words to describe the sight before her.

He held the door open for her to enter the restaurant. "What is this urgent meeting about?"

"It's about how to make our plans come together, but you're not going to like it." She walked past him and the maître d' immediately led them to a table. No small talk or names needed to be exchanged. They were regulars at the upscale establishment. Many high-profile people used the restaurant for business meetings. Celebrities had been known to indulge in private meals away from the prying eyes of public scrutiny. Politicians met to handle backdoor deals. Discretion was the name of the game here.

Jared held the chair for her to sit. Even in his obviously sleep-deprived state, he remained a consummate gentleman. She sighed. Her cousin was a good man. He deserved to be happy.

Sometimes she got so caught up in her own plans she forgot to look around her and see the people she cared about.

After the waiter poured water and Jared stared at her for a few minutes, she began, knowing she was about to break his heart. "Audrey is back at the apartment with Nikki."

"She is?" His entire face brightened.

Her heart broke a little for him in that moment. "Down, boy. There were conditions for her return."

Jared crossed his arms and leaned on the table.

"You can't be there, and as soon as the job is over, we pay her in cash."

"How am I supposed to make sure Nikki stays out of trouble if I can't be at the apartment?"

He was grasping for something—anything—to cling to. She'd never seen him so invested in anything, much less a woman he'd known for a few weeks.

"The information came through Nikki, who tracked her down. Nikki wants to work with her, so I'm fairly certain she'll keep herself in check." She reached across the table and rested a hand on his arm. "I'm sorry you're upset. I wish there was some other way. I don't know how in a couple of weeks this one woman has swept in and managed to tie you up in knots."

He nodded. "I don't know if I can explain it. We have something real and different. Maybe it was the fantasy of what we were doing. Like a vacation fling on an exotic island. Perfect for the moment, but not meant to be."

She hated hearing him sound so defeated.

"So we're set then?" she asked. "Things can go forward as planned?"

"Of course. For the record, I went to see her. Nikki isn't the only one who can find people. I asked her to come back, even if it wasn't to me. For the job."

"But you hoped it would be back to you." It wasn't a question. She saw the truth written clearly on his face: he'd fallen for the hacker.

TWENTY

AFTER HIS LUNCH with Mia, Jared went back to his office. He needed to keep busy, keep thoughts of Audrey at bay. The best way to make that happen was to immerse himself in work. The thrill of engagement with his adversaries never disappointed.

Sitting behind his desk, he sent a text to one client while dictating an email to set up a meeting with Alderman Rooney. Although Jared had never had any direct interaction with Rooney, the man had a reputation for being willing to deal on any number of matters. O'Brien Brothers Construction had been getting the runaround for months on a city contract they'd been promised. Thomas O'Brien had reached out to Jared a couple of weeks ago. At the time, Jared had put him off with a city-politics-are-slow excuse.

Today, he banked on his reputation getting him an appointment with Rooney. He fired off a few more emails before he got the response he expected: Alderman Rooney had an opening in his schedule in an hour. *Nice try, Rooney. Giving me no notice and a small window for an appointment are child's play.* Jared immediately had his driver pick him up.

He took the time on the drive to revisit his notes on what Thomas wanted. It seemed rather straightforward— the alderman expected some kind of kickback but wasn't brazen enough to come right out and ask for it. Jared looked forward to negotiating a solution.

Surprisingly, the alderman didn't keep him waiting. Once he arrived, the secretary ushered Jared right in.

"Mr. Towers. It's good to finally meet you. Please take a seat," he said, gesturing to the chairs in front of the desk.

Good to meet him? Anyone who recognized his name rarely responded positively. "Alderman Rooney," he said with a nod.

"What can I help you with today?"

"A man who gets right down to business. I can respect that. I'm here on behalf of O'Brien Brothers Construction."

Rooney raised a hand. "Let me stop you right there. As I've explained to Mr. O'Brien, the contract is outside of my control."

Jared chuckled. "We both know you have the power and friends to push a contract through. It just depends on how invested you are in the project."

"Mr. O'Brien knows I am *very* invested in this project."

If they already struck a deal, why the hell am I here? Jared's restlessness and impatience grew. "Then what's the problem?"

"The union. They're breathing down my neck, threatening to picket and call in favors with inspectors. I can't afford to have too many extra eyes on this, if you know what I mean."

He did and he had a solution. "I think I can arrange to satisfy all parties. However, the O'Brien contract will have to be increased by fifteen percent."

Rooney leaned back in his leather chair and studied

Jared for a full minute. Jared kept total eye contact until the man finally said, "Done."

"I'll have Thomas send over the revised bid." Jared rose and extended a hand. "It was good doing business with you."

"You're not nearly as bad as some of my colleagues painted you to be."

Jared offered a slick smile. "I'm only as ruthless as necessary."

As soon as he exited the office, he made a call to his union connection.

"Hello."

"Hi, Bill. Jared Towers. How are you?" Standing on the street, waiting for his car, he put his sunglasses on. Mia may have thought he looked like crap, but his appearance didn't hinder his ability to make things happen. Heartbreak didn't inhibit his negotiating skills.

"Busy. Summer is construction season."

"Excellent. That's exactly the purpose for my call. I need to get some union cards."

"Ah, man. I wish I could help. But you know we don't do that anymore. Buying your way into the union is a thing of the past."

They both knew that wasn't the entire truth, and for some reason, it irrationally irritated Jared. He took a deep breath and walked down to the corner where he saw his driver pull up.

"They'll pay their dues like any other member. It's not just for show."

"I don't know if I can swing it."

"You know you can. Your usual finder's fee plus five

percent for the headache." He was done dancing around. He'd known Bill for too many years to play games.

"Make it ten and every man on the crew needs a card."

"You'll have the information by next week." He disconnected and climbed into the car. He sent Thomas a text letting him know what the next steps were.

By all accounts, he'd brokered a successful deal, but he found no joy in it. Working with Nikki and Audrey had ruined him.

Hell, who was he kidding? It was all about Audrey. He liked seeing her face while they worked. He enjoyed everything about her company. He had to find a way to get her back.

AUDREY HAD SPENT so much time in her own head for the last day or so, it felt weird walking back into the apartment, but as soon as Nikki buzzed her in, she realized little had changed. Nikki opened the door with a doughnut hanging from her mouth, TV blaring in the background.

"Doughnut?" Nikki asked around a mouthful.

"I'm good. Thanks." She glanced at her workstation, half expecting Jared to be sitting at the desk.

"He agreed to your terms." Nikki waved the doughnut. "He had them delivered to keep me in place."

Relief warred with regret. And she hated it. She didn't *want* to want to see him again. But she did.

"It feels like forever since I've been here." *A day. It's only been a day.* She rolled her shoulders. "Let me see where we left off."

"We left off being brilliant." Nikki flicked the spline

from the painting across the room. "You'll have me in and out in no time on Saturday."

"I still have to perfect forcing a reboot. Right now, it only works in theory."

"You got this." Nikki winked and jumped over the back of the couch.

Audrey sat at the computer and put on her headphones. She had the malware set up and ready to go. She accessed the Scotts' internet and uploaded the virus. While that ran, she wrote the email from the security company about the upgrades. Then wrote and revised and rewrote. She asked Nikki to read it, but Nikki was zero help. She needed a pair of eyes to check the language and make sure it contained the right mix of business and "don't worry."

Sighing, she tossed her headphones on the desk and wheeled back. As much as she hated to admit it, she needed someone else to look this over. Jared or Mia? Regardless of her feelings about Jared and what happened between them, she still liked him more than Mia.

She sent him a link to the message through their private chat and asked what he thought of it. Texting felt too personal since that was how they'd been communicating. Before they met, everything had been conducted online. This would put them back in a position to be nothing more than a business transaction.

She bounced back and forth between watching the virus upload and checking the chat for a response from him. The compulsion sickened her. The rapidity of his response didn't matter. To refocus her attention, she ran the plan for the reboot again.

A few minutes later, he sent the email back with

some minor revisions. No other comment, no flirting, nothing.

She tried to not let it bother her, but she'd expected him to put up more of a fight. Yeah, they'd only known each other for a couple weeks, but their chemistry was different. Maybe to him it wasn't. She was just another woman. It wouldn't be the first time she'd misread a situation. Even as she had the thought, though, she didn't believe it. They might not be a perfect match meant to be together forever, but he'd never treated her like a one-night stand.

Which was exactly why she was so upset about his deception.

Nikki left her alone for the day as she worked. Audrey was grateful for the time to process while accomplishing tasks she needed to have done for Nikki to be successful on Saturday. With everything running as planned, she gathered her things and said good night to Nikki.

"You can stay if you want," Nikki said.

"No. It's better if I don't." Glancing at the spare bedroom reminded her of being with Jared. No, she couldn't stay here.

"See you tomorrow?"

"Yep." She let herself out of the apartment. As she walked toward the curb, Jared was there. Standing in front of her, a look of frozen shock on his face. Her heart stuttered and her breath caught in her lungs.

Her body went offline, which proved why she couldn't see him again. She wanted to lean in and feel his hands on her.

"Sorry," he said, taking a step back. "I figured you'd be gone."

"I am." She turned away to go to the bus stop.

"Would you like a ride?"

"No," she answered without turning around.

"Audrey," he called. His voice was filled with the same pain she held in her chest.

She turned her head and looked over her shoulder.

"Thank you for coming back."

"I'm not doing it for you." She wasn't completely sure why she was doing it. Money for Gram, of course. But there was also Nikki's plea. She wasn't used to anyone other than Gram relying on her for anything.

"Thank you anyway."

Then he let her go without another word. Getting what she'd demanded didn't make her feel any better. In fact, she felt worse and she didn't know what to do about it.

TWENTY-ONE

FRIDAY FLEW BY as days often did when Audrey worked on an intense project. Traveling back and forth between her room and Nikki's apartment was more time consuming and exhausting than she remembered. Then again, even from her first days with Nikki and Jared, she spent most of her time at the apartment. And Jared always offered her a ride.

Saturday morning slapped her awake. Her entire system buzzed with anticipation. She'd never worked on a job so hands-on before, not through to the conclusion to see the reward. She both loved and hated it. The adrenaline rush was amazing, but the fear of failure stabbed at every turn.

The bus wasn't as crowded as it normally was during rush hour, so she relaxed and spread out a bit. She and Nikki had a few last-minute details to hammer out, like how they were getting to and from Scott's house. She'd put in her request for a van a long time ago, but no one had mentioned it since, so it looked like she and Nikki were on their own. Even though going to the house made Jared, and probably Mia, uncomfortable, it was the right thing to do. Proximity made troubleshooting easier.

In addition to figuring out transportation, she also still had to trip the alarm at the house to get the password. She wanted to do that when she was relatively sure she'd get Mrs. Scott to pick up. The wife didn't seem too suspicious of anything, so having the alarm go off during the day when there was nothing wrong would simply be an annoyance for her. Mr. Scott might demand the company come out and look at the system.

When she arrived at the apartment, she rang the bell. No one answered. Damn it. She had things to do. She fished her phone from her pocket and called Nikki. The phone rang in her ear, but it was a voice from down the block that caught her attention.

"I'm coming," Nikki called. She was running, her long, dark hair swiping like a horse's tail with the beat of her steps.

As she neared, Audrey asked, "Shouldn't you be conserving your energy for tonight?"

"Hell, no. I'm too pumped, edgy. I needed to burn off some steam." She jogged in place a minute and then began a series of stretches. Nikki bent and pulled a key from a pouch at her ankle. They laughed and joked on their way in. Their voices died when they got in the apartment and saw Mia standing in the living room. Why the hell hadn't she answered the bell? Too good to answer her own door?

"Hey," Nikki said.

Audrey went to her computer and got to work.

"I'm here to make sure everything is ready for tonight," Mia said.

"As ready as we can be," Nikki answered.

"Transportation," Audrey said. "Calling a ride share from the house you just robbed isn't a great plan."

"There's a van parked downstairs for your use." She placed a key on the table. "Anything else?"

"More time would be better. Why does this have to go down tonight?" Nikki asked.

Mia took a deep inhale through her nose. Audrey watched the muscles in her jaw jump. After taking a moment to press her lips together, as if debating what to tell them or how much of the truth to give, she said, "The Scotts will be at a charity event this evening in the city. They will be there for at least a few hours. Jared and I will also be in attendance, where we can notify you if they leave early."

Audrey was stunned. That actually sounded like the truth. "You know the Scotts personally?"

It was a test. Audrey knew they did. These people all traveled in the same circles. She'd seen the freaking pictures.

"We're acquaintances. Do we know each other enough to talk when we see each other? Yes. Do we plan family vacations or holidays together? No." She stared at Audrey. "Anything else?"

"I guess not."

Mia turned back to Nikki, who was chugging a bottle of water. "When do you plan to go in?"

"After dark. Probably around ten. I'm still fine-tuning the canvas situation."

Mia shook her head. "I thought this was all figured out."

"It is," Audrey said. She didn't like the way Mia constantly doubted them. "Nikki is just covering every angle, seeing if she can come up with a better option. We can run with what we have. But as she's said, more time would give a chance to develop a better design."

"Walk me through it one more time," Mia said, pointing at the floor plans.

As Nikki started explaining, Audrey tripped the alarm on the Scott house. She let it blare for a minute and then placed the call from a new burner phone.

"Hello, this is Frontier Security. We're showing that your alarm just went off."

"It's nothing," Mrs. Scott said. "My husband said something about system upgrades causing possible problems today. Was this you?"

"Can you give me your password, please?"

"Gertrude."

"Please spell that."

While the woman spelled it out, Audrey tapped away on her keyboard hard enough to make it sound like she was investigating the issue.

"Yes, Mrs. Scott. I'm sorry for the inconvenience. We are showing there are upgrades to the server in your area. The upgrade should be done by tomorrow. Again, I'm sorry for any inconvenience."

"Ugh. I have a call on my other line and it's showing from your company as well. Don't you people communicate?"

"I'm sorry, Mrs. Scott. I've updated the system. You should be fine now."

Audrey disconnected, hoping she left enough time for Mrs. Scott to click over and yell at the operator there. Protocol would be for them to call Mr. Scott before notifying the police, so that part was a gamble, but Audrey believed the plan would work. Besides, she now had their password.

After disconnecting, she went to the table where Nikki and Mia were still discussing the plan.

"You're confident this will work?" Mia asked.

"Yes," Nikki said. "If you didn't think we were competent, you wouldn't have hired us."

Audrey stifled a laugh, glad Nikki said what she'd been thinking during every interaction with Mia.

"I know. I just need this to go off without a hitch." Turning to Audrey, she said, "Jared mentioned that you had some comms?"

"Uh, yeah."

"Will they work for us if we wear them at the function while you're back here in communication with Nikki?"

"Not the ones I have, no. I can get some, but they'll cost."

"Get them." She pointed at Nikki. "She has a card."

Nikki leaned over to the counter, picked up a credit card, and handed it to Audrey. It was a prepaid card in Nikki's name. Nikki Smith. As if. No one knew Nikki's last name. These people were slick.

"Okay. I'll run out and get them now."

"We'll stop back here on our way to the function."

Audrey stiffened and it must've been obvious because Mia said, "I'll leave Jared in the car. You won't have to see him."

It was very accommodating of her, but it didn't make Audrey like her. She checked the virus and then turned to leave to get the comms.

"I'll walk you out," Mia said.

Audrey barely stopped the eye roll.

In the hall, Audrey braced herself and asked, "Was there something else?"

"Yes." Mia stopped and faced her. "I wanted to say that a large part of Jared's deception had to do with me. I didn't want our identities known to you for obvious reasons."

"Okay."

Then the woman did something completely uncharacteristic. She reached over and laid a hand on Audrey's arm. Mia's entire being softened. Her eyes, her hand, her voice. "For what it's worth, he really does have feelings for you."

Audrey didn't have words for that, so she just nodded.

Then Mia pulled back, putting the ice queen back in place. "Use the card to take a cab where you need to go. Don't waste unnecessary time on buses."

Audrey left the building with even more confusing thoughts swirling in her head. Why the hell would Mia tell her about Jared? Why should it matter if he kept a secret because of her?

Because that's what you do for family.

But their family was a bunch of jerks. She didn't know if she could get past what their fathers had done. If Daddies Benson and Towers had ripped off their own friends, she wouldn't have cared. What got to her was the fact that they intentionally targeted people who couldn't fight back.

Out on the street, she waved for a cab and put Jared out of her head. After tonight, their business would be concluded and they could go their separate ways.

JARED SHOULD BE breathing easy right now. Audrey was back on board to get Nikki in and out of Scott's house. However, he couldn't focus on work, and he had to keep his hands off the job because Audrey was still pissed. Although it had only been a couple of days, he'd been sure that she'd cool off and understand why he didn't tell her everything.

Even now, she thought she knew everything, but she didn't. Maybe if he came clean, and laid out the whole plan like he'd wanted to from the beginning, she'd get it. They could go back to where they were.

He wasn't sure how to convince Mia that was a good idea, though.

Losing Audrey hurt more than it should have. After everything came out about what his father had done, he'd gotten used to a constant sense of loss in his life—family, friends—but having Audrey push him away stabbed at him.

He sat in the back seat of the car as they neared Mia's place. Schooling his face, he tried to get in the right mindset for seeing Scott. If—no, when—the painting was discovered to be a forgery, the house would be checked. A breach in security could be linked to tonight. He and Mia had to be above reproach. Even if it made them sick to do so.

The driver pulled over and opened the door. Mia swept into the car wearing a sparkling red ankle-length dress. Her heels would take her petite height to be almost at his eye level.

"Are you ready for tonight?" she asked.

"I'm not the one you need to worry about. Are they ready?"

"You tell me. You're the one who knows them better." She gripped her small purse in her lap. "Speaking of which, we need to stop by the apartment. Audrey has comms for us to be able to communicate with them while this is happening."

"She said the comms had to be in close proximity."

"I authorized the purchase of better equipment."

"Have you mentioned the next jobs to them?" he asked. If they could keep everyone on for more work, he might have a chance to reconcile with Audrey.

"Not yet. I want to see how tonight goes. When we rendezvous back at the apartment tonight, we'll broach the subject."

The car parked in front of the apartment. He reached for the door handle.

Mia touched his arm. "I promised her you'd wait in the car."

He released the handle and swallowed his resentment. "Fine."

"Let's get through tonight and then we can try to fix things. Okay?"

He nodded, but in his heart, he wasn't sure this could be fixed. He stared over at the black van he'd purchased for these jobs and remembered when Audrey had mentioned getting an FBI-level van. He'd delivered the bare minimum of a vehicle. It wasn't outfitted with anything. He didn't want her at the heist in case things went sideways. And now she couldn't stand being in the same room with him.

No way would she believe he'd fallen in love with her.

The thought had him straightening in his seat. He had fallen in love with her. That explained why this was so difficult. Why he worried whenever she was out of his sight. Why he needed to see her. Without thinking, he jumped from the car and sprinted to the door of the apartment.

He let himself in. To say what, he had no idea. He walked in as Nikki was running the plan down. "I'm going to creep up on the house and Audrey will be in the van on the street to give me the all clear."

"You're not supposed to be on site," he blurted.

Audrey shot him a dirty look. "You're not supposed to be here."

"I left him in the car," Mia responded. "Unfortunately, he listens about as well as the rest of you."

"London and I are both going to be in the van. We're Nikki's backup. I don't like leaving her on her own for this. If something goes wrong, she has no way out."

London hopped off the breakfast counter where she'd been perched.

"How are you going to help?" he asked.

London shrugged.

"I have no idea. But Nikki won't be alone," Audrey answered.

"Okay, kids," Nikki interrupted. "Let's move this along."

Audrey handed comms to Mia. "You'll be able to hear everything we do, but we won't hear you unless you press the button on the comm. It's tiny, so not the most convenient, but I think the noise from the party will be distracting."

Mia stared at the piece in her hand. "I just tuck it in my ear?"

"Like this." Audrey stepped close, took the earpiece and positioned it in Mia's ear. Taking the other one, she came near him.

Her face showed no emotion. If he declared his love right now, would she even hear him? She held out the earpiece and placed it in his upturned palm, her fingers barely grazing his skin.

Before she could drop her hand, he grabbed her wrist and tugged her toward the spare bedroom. "Can we please talk?"

She yanked free once they were in the hallway. "We don't have time for anything personal. As you've said about a million times, this job has to go tonight. I need to be focused."

"So you at least admit that I'm a distraction." He wanted to lighten the mood, make a joke, but she wasn't having it.

"I didn't say you were a good distraction. I can't afford the interference and brain space."

"Then tonight. After the job."

She shook her head. "I don't know what else there is to say."

He had so much more to say, but she was right. Now was not the time. He lowered his voice. "Thank you for not throwing me out."

"Kind of hard to do. You pay for the place after all. I'm just a visitor."

"Back when you were Data and I was Mr. Green, you always said you wanted to see inside my lair."

She huffed. "But this isn't yours either. It's a way station. A brief stop before heading back to your real life."

Her words struck him hard. She was right. They had a nice fantasy thing going here, but it wasn't real. This wasn't his life.

He pulled a pen from his pocket. Taking her hand again, he wrote his address on her palm. "That's my lair. My home address. Come whenever you want."

She held up her hand and wiggled her fingers. "Not a smart move. What if I get arrested tonight?"

"I'll take my chances." Strolling past her, he said to Mia, "Ready to go?"

"Okay, kids, have fun," Nikki called.

Audrey stood, staring at the black ink on her palm.

He led Mia from the apartment and forced himself not to look back.

Mia slipped her arm through his. "Feel better?"

"Not really."

"What happened?"

"I gave her my address."

Mia froze on the sidewalk. The driver stood at the car, holding the door open for them. "What?"

"I told you how I feel. It's real with her. I can't continue to pretend that this is my whole life. Not if I want her to give us a chance."

Mia's eyes iced over. "What if she gets caught? What if she gets pissed off and goes to the police?"

"She already has my name, so having my address doesn't much matter. But she wouldn't do any of that. Don't you see how loyal she is? Even if she wanted to, she wouldn't risk us dragging Nikki and London down, too."

"I hope you're right." She turned and went to the car.

He didn't know how to explain it, but he knew Audrey. Felt it in his every cell that she loved him, too. She just couldn't admit it yet because she felt betrayed. But he'd fix it. She didn't think there was anything left to say, but he hoped that a declaration of his love would change that.

TWENTY-TWO

AUDREY STARED AT that stupid address for a full minute after the door closed behind Jared and Mia. Then she spun to face Nikki. Flashing her palm up, she said, "What the hell is this? He gave me his address."

"Oooh," London said. "That's some serious stuff."

"Girl, you're in trouble," Nikki added.

"Me? I didn't do a damn thing."

Nikki shook her head, ponytail swinging. "If this was about sex, he would've planted a hot and heavy kiss on you and been on his way." She pointed to Audrey's hand. "He just invited you into his life. His *real* life."

Oh shit. Her heart raced and her lungs locked. What the hell was going on? She sank onto the edge of the couch.

"Is she okay?" London asked.

Suddenly, something thunked against the back of her head. Nikki's rubbery shoe flopped to the floor. Audrey turned. "Did you throw your shoe at me?"

"Snap out of it. We have work to do. Money to make. Be lovesick later."

Lovesick? She'd never been lovesick. She didn't pine away for some guy. Her life was complicated enough without adding the messiness of feelings.

But nothing with Jared had felt complicated or messy. At least not until she knew his true identity.

She shoved the thoughts way down deep. Nikki was right. They had work to do. Pushing off the couch, she asked, "What's up first?"

"Food. I'm hungry," Nikki said.

"You're always hungry."

Nikki shrugged. "What can I say? A good heist always makes me famished."

"Aren't you afraid you'll throw up?" London asked.

"Nope." She tossed keys at Audrey. "Let's find me some food and get in place."

Audrey jiggled the keys. Although she had a driver's license, she hadn't driven in years. "I think you should drive."

"What?" Nikki said. "This was your idea. You wanted to be my getaway. Are you telling me you don't know how to drive?"

"I do. Kind of. I've never owned a car. I take the bus everywhere."

"I'll drive," London said.

They both turned to stare at her. Nikki had only included her in the plan because she seemed as if she wanted to be a part of it. She had no reason to be there tonight. Unless she was a plant from Jared or Mia to watch them.

"Why exactly are you here?" Audrey asked.

London's eyes popped wide, looking innocent. "What do you mean?"

"I mean, your part of this job was done once you finished the painting. And yeah, we used your place for a run-through, but that was Mia's doing."

"I don't understand what you're asking."

"Why are you still here? Why risk being arrested?"

"I want to see this through. It seemed like it would be good for you to have an extra pair of eyes tonight." She neared Audrey and took the keys. "Lucky for you, I'm an excellent driver. Besides, I thought we'd become friends."

Audrey was looking to lash out at something, anything, but a little hint of guilt wiggled its way in.

An exasperated gasp came from Nikki. "God. She wants to make sure you're not a spy for Jared or Mia."

"Of course not," London said.

Walking in between them to head to the door, Nikki said, "I invited London, remember? None of this was orchestrated by Mia."

"Okay." Audrey picked up the remaining comms and handed one to each of them. "I don't trust Mia. She's still holding stuff back."

"We just need to get through tonight, and you'll walk away with your bag of cash and never have to see her again. That's what you want, right?"

It was, wasn't it? She closed her fist and tried not to think of the address written there, or remember the warm strength in Jared's hand as he wrote it.

"Come on," London said. "I'll drive and you can give us all the details of your wild affair with our boss." She snickered. "It's like one of Charlie's Angels sleeping with Charlie."

"Wasn't Charlie the fat guy?" Nikki asked.

"No, Charlie was the mysterious guy who took care of the girls."

Audrey couldn't believe they were discussing her life as if it were a TV show from the '70s.

They got to the street and London pressed the fob to

open the van. It looked almost like a soccer mom van, but the back windows were blacked out.

"Charlie was always portrayed as a total ladies' man. How could he not be? Rich, eligible bachelor," London continued.

Audrey climbed into the back of the van. "We are not Charlie's Angels. We're not private investigators. We're thieves."

She glanced around, a little disappointed that it was just a regular van. No equipment. Nothing. She'd wanted a decked-out van and got this. She didn't know why she'd expected more. Jared only offered superficial gestures. She looked at her palm again. Until now.

"Whatever. Same kind of excitement. And Jared is kind of like Charlie. He foots the bill for everything. He worries about keeping us safe. Well, at least keeping *you* safe. And his identity was a secret until you blew it." London started the engine as Nikki got in the passenger side.

"This is a ridiculous conversation." Audrey tucked her comm in her ear and began booting up the laptop.

A low chuckle sounded in her head as soon as it was in place. She knew that chuckle.

"It might be a silly conversation, but I don't mind being compared to Charlie. Which angel are you, Audrey?"

Hearing his voice softly inside her head did something to her. She shot Nikki a dirty look. "You put your comm in early?"

She smirked. "How was I supposed to know where that conversation was going?"

"Audrey, I asked a question."

"First, you're not supposed to be on the comms. Second, I never really watched the show. It was a little before my time."

"I came on to let you know our friends are here at the party."

"Mia could've told us."

"I know, but I like being inside your head."

"Stop talking. You'll draw attention at the party for being the weirdo who talks to himself."

"Please give me more credit. I'm talking into my phone."

She sighed.

"We'll be in touch if Scott or his wife leaves early. Good luck tonight."

"We don't need luck," Nikki said. "We've got skill."

Nikki turned the radio on and began to dance in her seat.

"Stay safe," he responded and then he was gone.

Of course, not really gone. He could still hear whatever they said, but she could no longer hear him. His last words felt like they were meant for her, even though they all heard him. She needed to focus. Having his voice in her head while she worked wasn't smart. What she'd said earlier was true—he was a distraction.

London swung into a drive-thru and Nikki ordered an obscene amount of greasy food. They drove into the suburbs with nothing but the radio making noise. It was game time, and they all had to get in the right headspace.

JARED WALKED THE room with a glass of champagne in hand. What he really wanted was a whiskey, but he needed to keep a clear head, so he held the flute as a prop. He tracked Randall Scott as he joked with other guests. Mia worked the room as she always did.

The conversation in his ear died and he wondered if the women had fallen silent or simply removed their comms. He wished he could be with them in the van making sure all moved smoothly. He was well aware of the fact that they didn't need him. But he also knew Nikki would protect herself above all else. Audrey wasn't wired that way.

The image of the lone hacker was one she portrayed well, but once she made a connection, she was loyal to the core. He wanted to be on the receiving end of that loyalty. He didn't know what else to do to convince her they had a chance. They could share something real.

Mia stepped in front of him. "Stop scowling," she said between the gritted teeth of a fake smile.

He blinked and looked at his cousin.

"They're fine. They know what they're doing." She patted his arm. "In the meantime, you need to play your part. Go ask someone to dance. Drink. Don't stand here looking miserable."

He normally had a better hold on his emotions. He never let anyone see any more than required. Forcing a smile, he said, "Would you like to dance?"

Mia scoffed. "Please. I have more important people to talk with."

"Who are you charming now?"

She turned to the side so they faced the same direction. She raised her glass toward the right. "Bruce Moore was kind enough to show up this evening." Then she tilted her chin up, indicating across from them. "Elijah Davis and I had an interesting conversation about a Caffrey sculpture he plans to sell."

"Would that be the same Caffrey we're interested in?"

"The very same." She shook her head in disgust. "They're liquidating. They must've burned through the cash they took with them. Something's going on."

"Do you think something happened to trigger this? They were safe where they were."

He briefly wondered when their fathers had simply become *they* instead of Dad.

"I don't know what's happened. But I wish I could tell them now. I'm petty enough to want them to know it's coming. That *we* are the cause of their downfall. But, no, to answer your unasked question, I haven't done anything to warn them."

He understood Mia's need to rub their fathers' noses in everything, but he didn't like seeing her lose her grip. They were only one heist in—and even that hadn't been pulled off yet. What would she be like by the time they reached the twelfth?

"I saw Carolyn. You could ask her to dance."

"You mean I could pump her for more information."

"She's always liked you."

"Her mother likes me. Carolyn and I are not interested in each other."

Mia sighed. "I'm aware of who you are interested in. Unfortunately for you, she has chosen to distance herself."

As if he needed the reminder. "I'm working on it."

"By inviting her to your house."

"She needs to know I trust her."

"Do you?"

"Implicitly. I love her, Mia."

Mia's usually cool countenance flickered. "Have you considered how that will play out?"

"What do you mean?"

"With her, you're Mr. Green, shady fixer. Out here—" she swept her arm out "—you're Jared Towers, consultant to the rich and powerful."

"It's the same person. And any of the people here who've hired me as a consultant know, or at least suspect, how shady I can be."

"But is she? Can she play the dual role? Or do you plan to introduce her as your hacker girlfriend?"

He paused because he hadn't given it any thought. He didn't want to bring Audrey into this world. Not because he didn't think she could play the role, but because he didn't want her to *have* to.

"I think Carolyn could use a fresh drink. I'll see you later."

As he stepped away, Audrey's voice came in his ear. "We're going to trip the system now. So if I don't hear from either of you about a problem in the next ten seconds, we're a go."

He glanced over his shoulder to where Scott was still entertaining people with some droll story that required them to force laughter to impress him. He chuckled his way through the retelling, waving one arm for emphasis while gripping his glass of brandy in his other hand. Everything about Scott was pompous. Was that how Audrey saw him?

With a nod to Mia, he crossed the room, picking up

an extra flute of champagne for Carolyn. Mia smiled as she engaged in conversation with Mrs. Scott.

Extending the glass, to Carolyn he said, "You look like you could use this."

"Thank you." She took a sip and then stepped closer. Keeping her voice low, she said, "Please rescue me. Kyle Peters keeps asking me to dance and he has no rhythm. He's on his way back here."

"Never let it be said that I would leave a beautiful woman in distress." Jared set his glass on a nearby table and bent his arm for her to take.

She looped her arm through his and he shot Kyle a look as they passed to get to the dance floor.

In his ear, Audrey said, "System is rebooting. Nikki, get in."

His heart raced, but he took Carolyn in his arms and began to waltz.

"How are things with work?" Carolyn asked.

"Busy. I'm thinking of expanding and hiring some permanent help instead of using freelancers." He had no idea where the thought came from, but it solved all of his problems. Audrey could work for him full time. If she became part of his consulting firm, no one would question their relationship or whether she fit in. *Take that, Mia.*

Of course, he still needed to convince Audrey of the brilliance of his idea. Which would require her to actually have a conversation with him. Later. Make sure she finished the job without trouble. Then they could figure out the rest.

"Tell me what's going on with you," Jared said. "Is your mom still on a matchmaking mission?"

"Like never before."

He knew the topic would get Carolyn to take over the conversation so he could pay attention to the sounds in his ear. He wished Audrey would give updates.

As soon as he had the thought, she said, "The reboot is sixty percent done. You have two more minutes."

She'd done better than she thought. She'd done everything in her power to give Nikki five minutes, and by his count, she was coming damn close.

"Almost done. I have the original out."

There wasn't even a hint of stress or worry in Nikki's voice. He had no idea what would rattle the woman.

"Damn. Move faster, Nikki. The reboot sped up. The alarm will go off early." She tapped furiously on keys.

"I've got time. I'm fine. You said you were going to trip it anyway."

"But we can't risk being in this neighborhood if the cops roll up."

"The canvas isn't going in right. It's too tight."

"If the alarm goes off and they call Mrs. Scott, we're screwed. She'll lay into them about tripping the alarm twice in one day." There was a pause. "I have it. I'm coming in."

What? Jared stopped dead on the dance floor.

"Is something wrong?" Carolyn asked.

He patted his jacket. "Sorry. My phone is ringing."

"Do you need to answer?"

"Would you mind terribly?" He put on his best apologetic face. "It's a business call that I've been waiting for."

"Of course not. Kyle found someone else to dance with and I can run and powder my nose."

"Save another dance for me." He kissed her cheek and pulled out his phone. He discreetly engaged the button on the comm as he pressed the phone to his ear. "Audrey, so help me God if you're going in that house…"

She didn't respond, but he heard rustling.

He stepped outside onto the veranda. "Someone tell me what the hell is going on."

London piped up. "Audrey took off out of the van and ran across the yard toward the house. Something about buying Nikki time."

He swallowed hard and waited. All he heard from Audrey was the sound of heavy breathing.

TWENTY-THREE

"WHAT THE HELL are you doing?" Nikki asked as Audrey climbed through the window.

Before she could answer, the alarm sounded.

"Get out," Jay said in her ear. She was beginning to regret giving him a comm.

"I'm not a freaking runner. Give me a sec." Audrey took a couple deep gulps.

Then the phone rang. She raced to the kitchen.

"Hello?" she answered, grateful that the Scotts still had a landline for the company to call first. She was a little out of breath and she did her best to play it off as irritation.

"This is Frontier Security. With whom am I speaking?"

"This is Mrs. Randall Scott and your stupid alarm is blaring again. Really. I would think with as much money as we paid for this system, we wouldn't be having these problems. I put in my code and it won't stop."

"I'm sorry for the inconvenience. Before I can do anything, do you know your password?"

"Of course I know my password. Gertrude."

A few keystrokes and then silence. "Thank you," Audrey said.

"Is there anything else we can help you with today, Mrs. Scott?"

"No. Thank you."

"Have a good evening."

Audrey hung up and wiped the handset off to be safe.

Nikki laughed, holding up the painting. "We're good. Time to run."

"Oh, God. Don't say run again."

"I told you to join me when I go for a jog."

"I prefer the comfort of my chair."

Nikki slapped her back. "Thanks for the rescue."

Audrey climbed back out the window and accepted the painting from Nikki. A moment later, Nikki joined her on the lawn.

"Why didn't you just give me the password?" Nikki asked.

"I figured you needed the time to finish putting the painting in the frame and hanging it. If you had to answer the phone and pretend to be Mrs. Scott, we'd run the risk of being here longer than necessary."

"Hello," Jared practically screamed in her ear. "Is everything okay?"

"Yeah. We're out and heading to the van now."

Nikki swung the van door open. "I think you liked the adrenaline rush. You wanted to know what it's like to be a burglar."

"You can keep it. I'll stick with the safety behind my screen."

London let out a hoot and drove out of the neighborhood.

Audrey twisted in her seat to face Nikki. "I'm sorry. I don't know what happened back there. The virus tripped the reboot like it was supposed to, but then it was like it figured out it was a trick and sped up. I had no idea the system would do that."

"We're good," Nikki reassured her. "Not the first time I've had a close call. And in the grand scheme of my life, that wasn't very close. I've had to escape a house with the cops at the front door."

Nikki was a fascinating woman. If she ever wrote her memoir, Audrey doubted people would believe the stories were true.

Audrey wanted to promise such a mistake wouldn't happen again, but then she remembered there wouldn't be another job. This was it. The cold reminder brought her back to the present and putting this to bed.

"Jared and Mia, we're on our way back to the apartment with the painting. Will you be bringing our payment tonight?" She sounded cold even to her own ears.

"Yes," Mia answered. "We'll be there within two hours."

Nothing from Jared. Maybe he finally got the message. Part of her expected him to put up more of a fight. She took the comm from her ear. Nikki did the same.

"Are you going to his place?"

"What?"

Nikki pointed to her palm. Audrey stared at the address. "I don't think so. Like I said before, I can't deal with liars."

London glanced out of the corner of her eyes. "You're just done? You won't work with us again?"

Audrey shrugged. "I have nothing against you guys. I'd work with you again. It's *them* I take issue with. They're playing some game we're not privy to. I don't like it. I don't understand how it doesn't bother you."

"It doesn't bother me because I walk into every job not trusting anyone. If you assume everyone is a liar, it makes life easier." Nikki propped her feet on the back of London's seat.

Audrey understood her point, but it wasn't the same. She'd trusted Jared because they were attracted to each other. In truth, her own naiveté irked her more than anything. "This wasn't just business, though. He made it personal."

"Got me there. All that matters to me is that his cash is green," Nikki said.

"You would do any job for the right price?" London asked as she pulled into a parking spot at the apartment.

Audrey couldn't believe this would be her last visit here. Maybe she should go take a shower one last time to enjoy the super-powered jets. And take some quality food from the fridge.

"I didn't say that. I choose what jobs I take and yeah, there have been dudes who've tried to hire me and I've refused." Nikki gathered her things before reaching for the door handle. "I guess these lies or omissions or secrets or whatever you want to call them aren't all that big to me. Not when we're going after a douche like Randall Scott."

Nikki's words wormed their way into her. Was she overreacting?

When Nikki slid the van door open, Audrey stood nearby to see if she needed help with the painting. She wrapped a thin blanket around it.

"How good was my version?" London asked with a tilt of her chin.

"If I hadn't paid attention to which I came with, I might've mixed them up," Nikki answered.

Audrey had no idea if it was true or if Nikki was just being nice. It wasn't exactly in Nikki's nature to randomly compliment someone, so Audrey figured she was being honest. Audrey wanted to go in and see what was so special about it. Of course, she'd seen London's version and it didn't seem all that spectacular, but Audrey was no art connoisseur.

Nikki handed London the painting and let them all in the apartment. London propped it up in front of the TV and they all settled on the couch and stared at it.

The picture that was nothing more than an off-white background with random spots of paint in various shades of green.

"I don't get it," Audrey said.

"It's ugly," Nikki added.

"I could've made that in kindergarten," London said with a sigh.

Nikki jumped up. "Time to celebrate."

"With what?" Audrey asked.

"I prepared." Nikki ran across to the kitchen and pulled out a bottle of champagne and three glasses. "Every successful mission should be celebrated."

She rejoined them on the couch and worked at prying off the cork. "I must like you girls, because I would normally drink this whole bottle by myself."

"Drinking alone isn't healthy," London said.

"No one who wasn't an integral part of a job should be celebrating, and since I normally work alone, I drink alone." She passed a glass to each of them.

London held her flute high. "To a successful heist."

They clinked glasses and sipped. Immediately, Audrey knew this was the good stuff. This was no five-dollar bottle. Nikki relaxed into the cushions and spread her arms wide, allowing her champagne to dangle precariously between her thumb and forefinger.

She always looked so careless, but Audrey knew Nikki had more depth than she let on. She paid attention to everything. Even if she didn't care or have a personal stake in it. It was probably what made her a good thief.

They sat side by side on the couch and stared at the stupid painting they were getting paid a stupid amount of money for stealing. They didn't talk. But Audrey's mind raced with thoughts of Jared and what would happen when he came back.

She needed to stick to her guns, take her cash, and get out.

No matter how hard that would be.

THE CAR HAD dropped them off at Jared's place so he and Mia could pick up the cash and transfer to his car. His entire body was strung tight. Between listening as the job went haywire and not being able to do anything about it and hearing Audrey coldly ask for her money, he was wound up. He'd asked to talk to her. He believed they could clear things up.

But she kept pushing back.

When they got to the apartment, Mia turned to him. "Are you sure you want to come in?"

"I need to. I heard the finality in her voice when she asked for her money. I get it. But I want to look her in the eye to see if it's over." *It can't be. We've barely started.*

They walked through the door of the apartment to find all three women sprawled on the couch staring at the painting. A near-empty bottle of champagne sat on the table in front of them.

"I'm glad you took it upon yourselves to celebrate," Mia said as she neared the painting. "Job well done."

"Hey," Nikki said, "if we're gonna do this again, I want more time to plan. I don't like rush jobs. Tonight could've gone so wrong."

Mia turned and looked at Nikki, then glanced at him. Jared barely met her gaze. His focus was on Audrey, who wouldn't even turn around.

"Actually, we do have a number of jobs, similar to this one, if you're interested. However," Mia continued, "you won't get your wish of more time. In some cases, you'll have less."

"Hell, yeah, I'm still interested," Nikki said. "At least I know things'll be interesting."

London said, "I could do more. Especially if the payday is the same."

Audrey didn't respond, other than to cross her arms. *Still building armor.*

Crossing the room, he handed each woman a bag of cash. First Nikki, who tossed the bag on the floor next to her. Then London, who slid the zipper open and peered inside, but didn't touch.

He stood in front of Audrey with the bag hanging from his fingers. She took it without looking up at him. She yanked the bag open and pulled the cash out far enough to count it.

As if he would cheat her.

"Can we talk now?" he asked, squatting to be at her level.

Her gaze finally met his. For a brief moment, he saw a range of emotions in her eyes: hope, anger, sadness. Then nothing. She turned it all off and that was the saddest thing.

"There's nothing to say, Jared."

It was like she threw his name at him to punctuate the betrayal she felt. He took her hand. "You might not have anything to say, but I do. Give me five minutes."

He stood and hoped she would follow.

She tucked her money in her bag, slung it over her shoulder, and said, "I'm sorry. I can't."

"You can. You're just afraid."

She snorted. "Afraid of what? More lies?"

"The truth." He glanced around, irritated that he had to do this with an audience. "We started something real and you're afraid of it. Why? Because you didn't know my life story?"

"I didn't even know your name." She stepped around him and over Nikki's extended legs. "See you around," she said to Nikki.

At the door, she turned and made full eye contact. For all the armor she held in place, her eyes told the whole story. She was really hurting. He didn't know how to fix that. He'd never meant to hurt her.

So he let her go, even though he wanted to chase after her and make her listen to him. Hold her until she understood how he felt. Kiss her until she thought of nothing but him.

Deafening silence filled the room after Audrey

slipped through the door. She might as well have slammed it for the shock value she created.

Nikki slapped her thighs. "On that note, I'm outta here." She scooped up her bag. "Give me a call when you have the next job lined up. If it's going to be like this, I hope you have someone else in mind to take Audrey's place. I can go in anywhere and take what I want, but not if it's as complicated as you're making it out to be. I don't mind setting off an alarm and walking out the door with my prize. But you lose your secrecy."

She was right, of course, but he had no one else in mind, no matter what he'd told Mia. He'd worked with other hackers, but none of them would fit in here. Audrey was special.

He shored up his own defenses before speaking. "Can you manage to stay out of trouble in between jobs?"

"Of course." She leaned over and waved at London. "Catcha later."

And then she was gone. London quietly gathered her bag and whispered something to Mia before following Nikki.

When he was alone with Mia, he allowed the full force of misery to hit him. "How did I screw that up so bad?"

"It wasn't all on you. I didn't want them to know who we are. In all honesty, I'm still a little uncomfortable with them knowing. But what's done is done." She sat on the couch and patted the cushion beside her.

He grabbed the bottle of champagne and guzzled the rest. "Maybe not if we finally came clean. All the way."

"Why the hell would we do that?" she asked.

He leaned back in the couch. "Because the secrets have ruined the relationship I started with Audrey. If I can pull all the skeletons out, she might learn to live with why we have them stuffed in a closet."

"Giving someone ammunition when they're already pissed off is never a good idea."

"I doubt she could get more pissed off."

"She doesn't need to be. She's angry and hurt. Whether we think she should be has nothing to do with it. If we tell her everything, we expose ourselves and our plan."

"Who the hell would she tell? What more exposure would we face?"

The anger he'd been feeling now had a target—Mia. And for a moment, his questions seemed to stump her.

"I see what this is doing to you. I never meant for you to get hurt." She waved her hand and rolled her eyes. "Although I did tell you repeatedly not to get involved with her."

"Thanks for the reminder." He stood, grabbed his fresh bottle of whiskey from the kitchen, and poured a glass. Returning to the couch, he reined in his anger. Mia wouldn't respond to yelling, but logic might work. And he was desperate enough to try this last attempt to get Audrey back.

"They know who we are, Mia. I don't see the downside of telling them why we're doing this. It's not like we're dealing with law-abiding citizens who would run to the police. They're all complicit in our plan."

He waited in silence while Mia digested what he said. She shifted, twisting to face him fully. "Fine. If you think telling her the entire plan will bring her back, I'm willing to give it a try."

"Really?" He was afraid he'd misheard her.

She offered a curt nod.

"After all this, now you agree."

"We're in a time crunch. It won't take long for our fathers to find out they've been had. If we want to get the rest of the pieces, we need to move fast. Getting someone new up to speed will take time. And if you trust her, that will have to be good enough."

It was a lot to process. He leaned his head on the back of the couch and closed his eyes. He tried to imagine how Audrey might react to hearing the whole story. If he could turn back the calendar a week, she'd be nothing short of giddy. She'd get off on pulling one—or twelve—over on the crooks that were his and Mia's fathers. For all of Audrey's talk about being a black hat, her core was white.

Mia snapped her fingers in front of his face. "What do you think?"

"I'm not sure she'll even talk to me," he finally said. "I wanted five minutes and she wouldn't give me that."

"We should bring them all back—London, Nikki, and Audrey—and lay it all out. Like you said, they work well together."

He opened his eyes and gave her a half grin. "See? I told you to listen to me."

"Don't gloat. Just because you were right this one time doesn't mean you know everything." She rose. "I'll call them and ask them to come back tomorrow." Pointing at the painting, she added, "Do you have a buyer yet?"

"For this one, yes. Not for the others. Since you're moving up the timeline, I'll send a list out and find the buyers we need. The money from this sale will be enough to pay for everything for the next one and still make the first bit of restitution we planned."

"I'd rather take all the money and pay restitution to the people on our list. I'll foot the bill for the jobs."

He knew that was originally the plan, but he didn't want her to blow her entire inheritance to make this happen. He could afford it. He wasn't sure she could. He supposed she made decent money as a curator and appraiser, but he wouldn't let her end up broke because of this.

"We'll do it your way." He stood and stretched, suddenly feeling exhausted. "I'll get the painting shipped out tomorrow as soon as the payment is made."

Mia put the glasses in the sink and the empty bottle in the trash. "On the plus side, the lure of money might be enough to bring her back. Then she would have to interact with you."

He nodded, but he didn't want Audrey to feel obligated to come back because of the big paycheck. Thinking about why she wanted the money, he struck on a thought that would settle things once and for all. He'd remove her need for the cash. Then if she came back, he would know they had a chance.

TWENTY-FOUR

AUDREY WIPED DOWN the tables after the morning rush. The wet rag smudged the address on her palm even more than her shower had last night. She'd scrubbed to get rid of it, but it lingered, much like her thoughts of Jared. Erasing the ink on her hand wouldn't even matter. She had it committed to memory.

A throat cleared behind her. She turned, her customer smile in place. "Is there something I can do—"

She froze when she came face-to-face with Mia. *Don't these people have lives?* "What are you doing here?"

Mia's perfectly made-up face didn't register a reaction to Audrey's rude comment. The woman was an ice queen. Barely a flicker in her hazel eyes. "Can I have a moment of your time?"

"Will it matter if I say no?"

The woman smirked, actually smirked. "I suppose not. I'll talk fast."

Audrey tossed the rag on the table and crossed her arms. "Real fast."

"I'd like you to come back to the apartment this evening. We have another proposition for you."

Audrey shook her head. "I already told you. I'm out."

"I can respect that, but you don't yet have all of the information." At Audrey's eye roll, Mia held up a hand.

"I'm aware that keeping you in the dark was my choice. This evening, I will tell all of you the entire story. Then, if you still want to leave, I'll never bother you again."

She wanted to say no, but Audrey was tempted by I'm-better-than-you Mia standing in front of her asking. The part of her brain that was more curious than cautious wanted to know.

"We'll start at seven. If you don't show, that will be answer enough. I hope to have you there. I think what I have to say might be enough to make you rethink your position."

"Then why not just tell me now?"

"The story requires more depth and privacy than the current conditions allow," she said with a glance around the coffee shop.

"I'll think about it."

Mia gave a brief nod and then spun to leave.

The woman was weird. Always so formal. Audrey wondered if she ever cut loose. What would a relaxed Mia look like?

Even Audrey's active imagination couldn't conjure a picture. With a quiet chuckle, she finished cleaning. Very few clients piqued her interest as much as Mia and Jared had, even before she knew who they were. She owed it to herself to get the answers Mia was offering.

AT 6:50 THAT NIGHT, Audrey paced in front of the apartment. She hadn't thought about whether Jared would be there. Although she'd tried to mentally prepare for seeing him, nothing worked. Jittery nerves assaulted her as if she'd consumed five energy drinks.

She could do this. Mia was giving information and

answering questions. *But she said it might make me re-think my position. My position on what? Working for her or being with Jared?* That was the true source of the nerves—she didn't know what outcome she was hoping for.

"Can't decide if you want to go in?"

The voice startled her, causing a slight jump. She turned to face Nikki. "It's not nice to sneak up on people."

"I'm a prowler. It's kind of my thing. So. Going in?"

"I'm not sure."

"Come on. You know you're dying to know what Mia plans to say."

"I could just wait until she tells you and then you can tell me."

"Not if she swears me to secrecy."

"As if a promise to her carries any weight."

"She might ask me to pinky swear," Nikki dead-panned.

Then they both fell into laughter at the thought of Mia doing anything so childish.

When they sobered, Nikki said, "If nothing else, you'll get closure. Plus, free food."

Nikki had no idea how swaying the free food was. The money from the job would pay for Gram's care for just over six months, but Audrey was pretty tapped out again.

"Okay. Let's do this."

They went in together. As Nikki pulled out her key to unlock the door, Audrey said, "I'm glad I met you. I don't have many friends."

"Let's not get all emotional. Even if Mia does nothing more than fill the time with good food and crappy explanations, our paths will cross again."

It wasn't much of a reassurance, but coming from Nikki, Audrey understood it was the best she could expect.

Inside the living room, London was already sitting on a chair drinking a glass of wine. "You're here!" Her voice was excited as though she thought she'd never see them again.

Mia came from the kitchen carrying a bottle of wine and two more glasses. "There is food on the table and more wine in the refrigerator if you don't like this one."

"I prefer beer," Nikki said and went straight to the kitchen.

Mia looked at Audrey with a soft smile. "I'm glad you came."

Audrey nodded without commenting. She glanced around for evidence that Jared was there.

"He's on his way. Will that be a problem?"

"No. We're all adults." The words felt phony on her lips. She wasn't good at faking nonchalance. Jared caused nothing but mixed emotions in her. In bed, of course she felt like a grown woman, but standing here in the living room, she felt like a teenager hoping the guy she liked would be around and notice her presence. Teen Audrey craved his attention as much as his kisses.

He made her feel like she mattered.

But how much of it was real when it started with him pretending to be someone else?

She didn't even like wine, but she poured herself a glass and drank quickly. Then she went to the table and loaded a plate with food. She didn't know what it was, but the range and variety of colors told her it contained a balance of all the major food groups—nothing like her normal diet—and it smelled fabulous.

When she curled up in the corner of the couch, Nikki joined her with a plate and a bottle of beer. They ate in silence, waiting for Mia to start.

As if she could read Audrey's mind, Mia said, "I'm waiting for Jared. This is as much his story as it is mine."

The door swung open and Jared strode in. The cousins did their weird nod of acknowledgment, and Mia stood in front of the TV. With her hands clasped in front of her, she started.

"I know Audrey made you all aware of our names, and I'm sure along with that, some information about our history. I'm not going to bore you with all of the details, but I need you to understand some things in order to fully see the plan we have.

"As you know, our fathers are con men, thieves, if you will."

"Hey," Nikki yelled, "I take offense. I keep better company."

Mia gave her a look Audrey could only describe as amused. It was…strange.

"We were unaware of our fathers' scheme. Our mothers did not know either. We were all taken by surprise when the FBI came to arrest them. Of course, being the criminals that they are, they had a getaway plan and fled the country."

"Google already told us all of that," Audrey said. Except for the part that the men committed the crimes without their families' knowledge, and she wasn't sure she bought that version.

"We know where they are, and they can't be extradited. We want to flush them out."

Now she had Audrey's full attention.

"After they fled, Jared and I began digging into everything they'd done. If we couldn't make them pay, we at least wanted to make things right. That's where the artwork comes into play."

"How so?" Audrey asked.

"First, we planned to take things from their friends. These are men who benefitted from their scheme but who won't be prosecuted." Mia's eyes narrowed. "I wanted them to know I was going after their friends."

"I love me some good pettiness," Nikki said and pulled her feet up on the couch like she was settling in for story time.

"Your fathers left the country years ago. Why wait until now?"

"We had to wait until we had access to our inheritance from our mothers' family. We needed the funds to pay for everything. The profits from the theft and subsequent sales are going to our fathers' victims. The painting you stole on Saturday will fund scholarships for two teenagers whose families lost their life savings to our fathers."

Audrey's heart sped up. No way. All of this deceit for what? To cover up doing good?

Mia waited for that to sink in for a few seconds. "It was a solid plan. Steal from their friends, maybe make them feel guilty enough to poke their noses out of hiding. Help the people they hurt."

"Why not just give them money?"

"Sometimes it takes a thief to right a wrong," Jared said. "The money is only part of it."

Mia continued, "Then, I recently found that many of my father's friends were planning to sell various pieces of art. After some detailed research, I pieced together that the artwork, most of the pieces I planned to steal, were purchased on our fathers' behalf."

Nikki cackled. "You're stealing from your fathers?"

Jared cleared his throat before jumping in again. "We think the art is their contingency plan. They knew their accounts would be frozen by the FBI and large transfers to overseas accounts might raise red flags. Artwork purchased by a bunch of their rich friends wouldn't even be noticed."

It hurt to look at him. Audrey wanted to smack him. He should've just told her the truth, any version of it. As painful as it was, she kept her gaze on him, still wanting his attention even though she'd pushed him away.

"Are they planning to run again?" Nikki asked. "Since you know where they are?"

"I don't know if they're aware we know their location. However, the logical conclusion is that they're selling art to fund another move," Mia replied.

This was the most emotion Audrey had ever seen from the woman, and she wasn't sure how to read it. It was all so much to process. For the first time since meeting Mia or Jared, Audrey felt like they were being honest. For all the lies they'd fed her, they were pulling some Robin Hood stunt.

Audrey got mad all over again.

JARED STUDIED AUDREY as Mia spoke. She'd been looking for this truth since the beginning. He didn't know exactly what he'd expected, but he knew it wasn't the blank, nearly confused, look on her face. No, that wasn't true. He believed as soon as she heard the plan, she'd jump into his arms. She would see he was nothing like his father. They could be together.

Childish? Yes. But sometimes that was all he thought hope was.

He was so focused on Audrey, Mia had to clear her throat for him to realize he was up.

He stood, feeling a bit like a bumbling fool, and crossed the room to where Mia stood. "There are eleven more pieces of art we want to take."

"Why only eleven?" Audrey asked, finally meeting his gaze. "I'm sure these guys can afford more."

"We chose the twelve men based on the items they purchased—the value of those items—as well as how easy it would be to steal without being obvious. These men are far from serious art collectors."

Another chuckle from Nikki. "In case you didn't notice, there wasn't much that was easy about the Scott job."

It took tremendous effort, but he tore his attention away from Audrey. "There are a number of factors for that. One, it was the first time we worked together. Two, we had no plan. You're all in place now, and this is an operational team. You'll have all of the information up front so you can help us plan. You have each other to rely on and bounce ideas off. We want you all to stay and finish this job with us."

"But it's still a rush job." Nikki was stating and not asking.

"Unfortunately, that's even more true now," Mia interrupted. "If they want to liquidate, the art will go fast. We need to get it before it's sold."

"How do you decide who gets the money?" Audrey asked.

See? More white hat than black.

Jared took a step closer and smiled. "Months ago, I hired you, Data, to dig up information and do backgrounds on some of the victims. We used that to develop a list."

A flash of recognition lit her eyes. When she'd done the research and given him the dossiers, she'd mentioned how different it was than the other work he'd hired her to do.

"Why keep it a secret?" Her voice was filled with venom, especially on the last word.

"The last person they want to see is someone with the last name Benson or Towers. They hate us, and rightfully so. We also can't afford the attention if word got out."

Mia placed a hand on his arm. "We would be in the spotlight. Others would contact us to get their share. With too many eyes on us, we won't be able to finish what we're doing."

"Still seems cowardly."

That stung. But she was hurting so he'd take the hit.

"Cowardly or not, it's safe," Mia said. She held up the remote and clicked the TV on and the slide presentation he'd created earlier flashed on the screen. "These are the men we've targeted."

The women on the couch studied the faces and names.

"Those are some heavy hitters," Nikki said.

Mia clicked again. "These are the pieces we'd like to steal."

"You want these other jobs to happen like this one?

Where we take all of the risk while you mingle at some fancy party," Audrey asked.

"Risk for which you are well compensated," Mia said.

"People expect us at these social functions," Jared added. "It took a long time for people to accept us after what our fathers did. Many still don't, but we won't hide. It would be suspicious if we weren't around. Additionally, we have eyes and ears on the mark."

"But since we're replacing all of the art, it's not like anyone can pinpoint the day or time it was switched," Audrey pointed out.

"And London said she's giving you papers to forge the provenance," Nikki added.

Audrey hadn't known that, so she stared at Nikki.

"What? I know things, like what provenance is."

"I don't doubt you. It seems like a lot of extra hoops to go through for a fake piece of art," Audrey responded. Turning back to them she added, "You'd need the alibi if we were doing a smash and grab. I think you just don't want to get your hands dirty."

"You're right," Mia interrupted. "We all bring a skill set to this deal. We don't break the law. You do." She waved her hand as if suddenly realizing how condescending she sounded. "If I tried to do what you do, I'd most certainly fuck it up."

The curse from Mia's lips stunned everyone into silence. They stared at her for a few heartbeats.

Then Nikki burst into laughter. She smacked Audrey lightly. "See? She's not a robot."

Audrey grimaced.

"Very funny," Mia responded.

Jared sat on the table in front of the women. "We chose you because of your particular talents. Mia knows art. The value, the specifics. I can find the right buyer."

Nikki scoffed. "I know people."

"You know fences who wouldn't get you nearly what any of these pieces are worth. I arrange the purchase with people who have the capital to buy."

"That's a lot of jobs," Audrey said quietly.

"It's a crap ton of cash," Nikki countered.

If he hadn't known better, he'd think they'd been partners for more than one job.

Audrey looked at London. "You can produce art that fast?"

"I already started. I have four pieces in various stages of development."

Audrey nodded. Turning to Mia, she said, "Putting all personal crap aside, I don't know that I want to give up my own business to work for you full time. I've spent years building my reputation and name. If I go dark for that long, I'd have to start over. I don't know that you're worth it."

Although she spoke to Mia, her words hit him. "I can help with that," he found himself saying. "I have an extensive network. People will hire you based on my word. And if they don't, I'll hire you myself."

She turned her cautious gaze on him and flicked one eyebrow up.

"Is this agreeable to all of you?" Mia asked.

"I don't know," Audrey answered, still looking at him.

Her eyes told him she wanted to agree. But she was scared.

She rose from the couch and addressed Mia. "Can I think about it?"

"We need an answer within two days. If you're out, we need to find someone to replace you."

She couldn't be replaced, he wanted to scream but knew it wouldn't help.

Audrey shifted to pass him. He reached up and brushed his hand against hers, afraid to take hold, but needing the contact. She paused but didn't move closer.

"I'll walk you out."

"I can find my way to the street," she said quietly.

He followed her anyway. They walked out in silence while he searched for the right words.

Once they got to the sidewalk, he finally just asked. "Is there anything I can do to fix this?"

"I don't know." She sighed heavily. "Right now, I'm not even sure why I'm still so upset. We agreed to have a good time while we were together. Now I find out all the deception just covered up you doing something good. Like you couldn't trust me with anything."

"You feel betrayed. I understand that better than a lot of people. But know this—with you, I was always one hundred percent myself. I'll respect whatever you decide. But I hope you come back to finish this job, in whatever capacity you want."

"Thank you."

Then she turned and walked away from him. In that moment, he swore to himself if he was ever lucky enough to get her back, he would never witness her leaving again.

TWENTY-FIVE

AUDREY TOSSED AND turned all night with too many thoughts crowding her head. As much as she hated everything that had gone down with Jared and Mia, what they were doing was almost noble. How could she hate them for that?

And she couldn't lie to herself about the thrill of the job. Her usual clients had her hacking into systems and shutting down sites with DDOS attacks. Sometimes they paid her to be nosy and get information hidden in the depths of someone's search history.

But working with Nikki, taking an expensive piece of art from a total douchebag, was fun. The pay was excellent, but the work itself thrilled her.

Could she keep it up for the next couple of months and then walk away? The money would be enough to keep Gram in comfort for a long time. Beyond that, it wouldn't be hard to rebuild her business, especially with Jared's help. She pushed thoughts of him away. She didn't want to rely on him. Even though he had a history of sending the occasional job her way.

Hell, if Gram was taken care of, maybe she could get a normal job. She barely remembered what that was like. Not having to struggle to pay bills and make sure Gram was cared for. It made Jared and Mia's offer that much more tempting.

She gulped an energy drink to power through not having slept and hopped a bus to go see Gram. If Gram was having a good day, she could offer Audrey some advice. But even if she wasn't lucid, Gram always made her feel better. As she walked into the facility, she remembered the bag of cash locked in her room. She was supposed to have gotten a money order. Damn. Now she had to decide if she wanted to try to dodge Mrs. Merriweather.

She signed in and made it to Gram's room unnoticed. The new room was smaller than her old one but outfitted for medical needs if necessary. Audrey couldn't bear to think about that. Instead, she focused on the plush couch and flat screen TV on the wall playing soap operas as always.

"Hey, Gram," she said and waited to see what kind of day Gram was having.

"Audrey? What are you doing here?"

"I wanted to visit. Do I need to have more of a reason?" She moved the rest of the way into the room and kissed Gram on the cheek. "How do you like the new room?"

"It's fine. I miss my old one. Better view," Gram said, gesturing to the windows.

Audrey slid the curtain aside and looked out onto the parking lot. Gram had a point. In her old room she could see the park across the street. With a sigh, she said, "I'll see if I can get you into a room on the other side of the building."

Gram had little to look forward to on an average day. If looking out at the park was important to her, Audrey would try to make it happen. With her luck, a room like that would cost more, sealing her fate for accepting the job with Mia and Jared. "How are you feeling?"

"I'm fine. Tell me what's happening with you. You've been busy."

Audrey was surprised Gram had noticed. Most days, she couldn't tell her what year it was, much less whether Audrey had been by to visit.

"I had a big job. It was time consuming and more complicated than we originally thought it would be."

"Did it go well?"

"Yes, it did. We pulled it off."

"And the man?"

"What man?"

Gram waved her hand. "There's always a man."

Audrey thought of Jared, his plea for her to come back. "He messed up."

"They all do. How bad?"

Audrey sank onto the edge of the bed. "I'm not sure. At first, I thought really bad, but now…there were extenuating circumstances. I thought he lied to me and he kind of did, but he had a good reason."

Gram stared at the TV without saying anything for a moment. Audrey knew she was losing her again. Every visit was becoming more painful.

"No one needs a liar. They'll ruin your life. I've been telling you that ever since you were old enough to walk."

Not quite gone yet. That was her Gram.

"He apologized."

"Do you believe him?"

Audrey thought for a minute, but the answer kept coming back the same. "Yeah, I do."

"Can you forgive him?"

"I'm not sure."

"You can't have much without trust. If you don't have that, get rid of him."

Audrey's heart hurt. She lay down beside Gram just to feel her warmth. Gram's words rolled around in her head. On the job, she did trust Jared. But she couldn't decide if that was because he deserved it or because he had as much at stake as she did. She hadn't decided if she could trust him with her heart. And her heart was at risk every time they were together.

Gram patted her shoulder. "Look here." She pointed to the screen. "This guy's fooled around with every woman on the show. I don't know why they don't all gang up on him and chop his wiener off."

A giggle bubbled up in Audrey. Gram was in rare form today. She would give anything to keep her like this a while longer.

Before the show ended, they both dozed off and when Audrey woke, it was near dark out. Her neck was stiff from the uncomfortable position. She stood and stretched. Although she loved being here with Gram, she had a decision to make.

She kissed Gram's forehead, inhaling the scent of powder she used, and grabbed her bag. In the hall, Mrs. Merriweather spotted her.

"Ms. Abbott," she called, waving her over.

"Hi, Mrs. Merriweather. I have the money for Gram's care. I promise. I just haven't gotten a money order yet."

"Excuse me?"

"Isn't that why you called me over?"

A look of confusion filled the woman's face. "You have no idea, do you?"

"About?" A sinking feeling dropped in her stomach.

"I called you over to thank you and your benefactor. But now I see you were unaware of the donation." Mrs. Merriweather folded her hands primly in front of her. "Your grandmother's care is paid for. A sizable donation has been made to the facility in her name. You have nothing more to worry about."

The words sank in and Audrey felt lightheaded. One deep breath in and out. Then another.

"Are you all right, Ms. Abbott?"

Audrey nodded. Another breath and then she forced out a thank-you. *How dare he do this?* She sped to the bus stop and wondered if the trip to Jared's house was too long for her to plead diminished capacity when she killed him.

By the time she arrived at his house, she no longer cared if it would be considered premeditated murder. He continued to manipulate everything and she was done. His townhouse was one in a long row of townhouses, all looking the same. But she knew they were expensive. It reeked of gentrification. His was a neighborhood she'd never stepped foot in.

When she rang the bell, her anger flared again, this time at herself because she hadn't considered if he wouldn't be home. He might be at his office or at the apartment with Nikki. Even though Mia had given her a couple days to decide, Nikki had said she was on board for more jobs. They might be planning right now.

She wanted to kick herself.

Then his door swung open and she returned to wanting to kick him.

"Audrey?" His voice was filled with shock, as if he questioned whether she was actually in front of him.

Ignoring how good he looked in a pair of low-slung sweatpants and a well-worn T-shirt, she did nothing to keep the threatening tone in her voice at bay. "How dare you? This is your idea of respecting me and whatever I decide?"

He stood gaping at her.

"You have nothing to say?" she continued while waving her arms. She'd come for a fight. He should have his back up to fight her.

"What are you talking about?"

"My grandmother. The part of my life I kept from you. You just plowed in anyway. You had no right!" She was yelling now, but she didn't care.

"Come in."

"Why?"

"Because you're causing a scene on my porch. I prefer my neighbors mind their own business."

"Ha," she huffed. "Interesting coming from you."

"Come in so we can have a conversation. Please."

It was the please that did it. The single word was a little strangled. His gentle voice shouldn't have an effect on her, but it did. She stepped through the doorway against her better judgment because it put her within touching distance of this man. He was her Kryptonite. No—Superman avoided Kryptonite. She was a moth and he the flame that would consume her. Damn it. She shouldn't have come here.

He quietly closed the door behind them.

She dug for her anger and held tight. "My grandmother is none of your business. When I left the apartment yesterday, I believed you when you said you would respect whatever decision I made. Now you go behind my back to pay for my grandmother's care to guilt me into working for you."

He blinked rapidly and shook his head. "I didn't pay for your grandmother's care to guilt you into anything."

"Then why would you do that? It makes no sense. I never even told you about her."

He stepped closer and reached for her but dropped his hand before making contact. "She's obviously someone who's important to you. I wish you'd told me about her. I paid for her care not because I wanted to guilt you into anything, but because I want you free from the financial burden."

"Why?"

"Because I want you to choose to come back to us—*to me*—because you want to, not because you have to for the money."

"Why does it matter?"

He scrubbed a hand over his face and gave her a look like she was lost. At the moment, she was.

"Because I care about you. I don't want you to force yourself to work with me if you can't get past the way things started with us. I want you to be happy. If you choose to walk away, I'll learn to live with it. But know that everything I've done for the last week has been to show you I want you in my life. No ulterior motives."

Her heart raced. She wanted to believe him, but her brain kicked in, reminding her of every lesson Gram had ever given her. Once a liar, always a liar. How could she trust him?

"I know you're not there yet." He reached out and this time, he did take her hand. "You've been too angry, struggling with feeling betrayed. I never meant to hurt you, but I couldn't be disloyal to Mia. She's my family and best friend. If you need more time to think, take it. My feelings aren't going to change."

His declarations floored her. What the hell was she supposed to do with that? She'd come here for a fight and he took the steam right out of her. Her throat burned and her eyes filled.

When he tugged her into his arms, she let him.

For a minute. I can let him hold me for a minute until my world straightens.

AUDREY WAS IN his arms. She wasn't pulling away or fighting him. He wrapped his arms around her and held her to his chest. Of course he'd known she'd find out about his payment to the assisted living facility, but he hadn't been prepared for her to misread the entire situation.

He normally managed people and situations better. But she had a way of flipping his world around.

"Just because I'm letting you hug me doesn't mean you win. I still don't trust you," she mumbled against his chest.

At least she was being honest and not running away. That gave him the chance he'd been looking for. "I'd like to start over."

She snorted. "That only works in movies."

"We can try." He stepped back, holding her at arm's length. He flashed a smile. "Hi. I'm Jared Towers."

She narrowed her eyes. "Towers? Isn't that the guy who robbed a bunch of families of their life savings?"

She wasn't pulling any punches.

"Unfortunately, that's my father," he answered with a nod. "However, my cousin and I have a plan to alleviate some of the havoc our fathers caused. I'd very much like you to join us in our mission."

"Mission?"

"Yes. I happen to think you have the perfect skill set to help us."

The corner of her mouth lifted. "That's all you're looking for? My skill set?"

He stepped into her space again. "If all I can have access to is your skills, I'll settle for that. However, I want all of you."

Emotions flashed in her eyes so quickly, he couldn't decipher them all. He knew she had feelings for him. It didn't matter that they'd never labeled their relationship. She cared. If she hadn't, she never would've been so hurt by finding out his true identity. She would've reacted more like Nikki had.

Whether or not she would want to continue was completely up in the air and it was killing him. Why couldn't she be like the girl in the movie who would jump into his arms?

Because then she wouldn't be my Audrey.

"I have more thinking to do."

He wanted it all, but if this was the best he would get from her, he'd try to be understanding. At least she wasn't pissed off anymore.

"How much time do you think you'll need?" he asked, holding her hand, desperate for any connection.

"Mia said I could have two days. I guess I have twenty-four more hours."

"That's for the mission. There's no clock on us."

"Okay." She pulled away. Not angrily. Not hurt. Maybe confused.

"Is there anything else I can do to sway your decision?"

"You've already done plenty."

"I could get naked and remind you what you'd be missing."

She laughed, which was what he'd been going for.

He slapped a hand over his heart. "Hurtful. To laugh at a man who offers to reveal his physical imperfections to you."

Her smile was gentle. "Your physical imperfections are not the problem."

"What about a kiss?"

"What about it?"

"Can I give you one?"

She held up a hand. "That's definitely not a good idea."

"What I'm hearing is that not only can you *not* resist my naked body, you also can't resist my kisses."

"Good to see your self-esteem is still intact. Kissing you would only complicate things. I have to figure out if I can live with the way things started between us. I know you think I'm overreacting about it because we all have secrets and we're all criminals of some kind. But you're right. I felt betrayed. Not because you didn't tell me your name but because you wanted all of me even though you weren't willing to do the same. Then when I figured out who you are, you still didn't tell me everything. It took me leaving to get the truth."

"But—"

"No more buts. I know you had reasons. And maybe they were even valid reasons. I don't know if I can forget those feelings."

He hefted a sigh. Just once, he'd like something in his personal life to go as smoothly as it did in his professional life. "I'm not asking you to forget."

"Just get over it?"

"Understand. And forgive." Stepping away from her, he asked, "Do you need a ride home?"

She shook her head. "I'll be fine. Thanks."

"Will I see you tomorrow? Or is this one of those if I-don't-show-that's-my-answer things?"

"Maybe I'll just keep you guessing."

Then she turned and left, leaving him feeling hopeful yet worried.

TWENTY-SIX

AUDREY SPENT ANOTHER restless night in her crappy room. When she finally gave up on sleep, she had the sudden realization she no longer had to rent this cramped, miserable room from Misty. Since Jared had paid for Gram's care, she still had her entire take from the job. She could rent her own place. Maybe even buy something.

I must be delusional. I am not the kind of person who buys a cute little house and lives a normal life.

While she now had the means and freedom to live however she wanted, she had no idea where to start. She knew, though, that she would never be a punch-the-clock, regular job person. She'd lived in the gray for too many years.

She hadn't yet determined if she could move past everything that had happened with Jared, but a huge part of her wanted to. She sat on her bed, staring out the window at the streetlights illuminating the night.

Buzzing caught her attention and she reached for her phone. A text from Nikki.

I'm drunk and alone. Come rescue me from myself.

What am I supposed to do?

You're supposed to have an answer today, babe. Have you decided?

Idk.

You could come back and keep me out of trouble.

Idk.

For someone so smart, you say that a lot. I'm ordering breakfast. Am I ordering for one or two?

Without stressing, she answered, Two.

And as simple as that, her decision was made. She packed a bag and with the sun barely pink in the sky, she hopped a bus to the apartment.

When she arrived, she rang the bell, wondering if they'd ever give her a key. The door flung open and Nikki wrapped her arms around Audrey's neck in a giant hug. She really was drunk. Audrey had assumed she'd been joking.

"Have you slept at all?" she asked.

Nikki dragged her into the apartment. "Have you?"

"Touché." Inside, Audrey tossed her bag on her chair at the desk. It didn't look like anything had been moved. She glanced around the apartment while Nikki opened Styrofoam containers. "It's a little anti-climactic."

"What is?"

"I had this huge decision to make—stay on and work with you and for Jared and Mia or walk away. I wrestled with it for so long and now I'm here and…" She swept her arms out. "It feels like there should be more." Settling in at the table, she smelled the delicious breakfast.

Nikki laughed. "If you wanted some kind of grand entrance, maybe you shouldn't have answered my drunk texts and instead showed up later today when you know they're going to be here."

She shoved a forkful of pancakes into her mouth and pointed at the second tray. "Eat up. Then we can both crash and get some good sleep."

As it turned out, Nikki had known exactly what she needed. After they filled their bellies, they both crawled into their beds and passed out. She didn't really need a grand entrance. She was here for the money and adventure.

JARED CAUTIOUSLY WALKED into the apartment and announced himself before the door was even fully opened. He'd learned that was a smart move given Nikki's propensity for walking around in various states of undress. No one responded, so he went all the way in. Disappointment thudded in his chest. After last night, he was sure Audrey was going to come back. He'd had her in his freaking arms. He never should have let go.

Silence met him in the living room. On the table were two to-go containers of food. *Two. So help me God, if Nikki brought home some guy, we're going to have problems.* Then he took in the whole room. A big bag sat on the chair by the desk. He knew that bag.

"Audrey?" he called.

Nikki stumbled out of her room wearing a skimpy tank top and bikini underwear. Her long black hair was a tangled mess piled on top of her head. He'd discovered this was her typical hungover look. At least she wasn't coming from a cell this time.

"We talked about the need for you to wear clothes." He crossed his arms.

"I'm not naked. You'd see me in less if we were at the beach, so I'm dressed." Her voice was rough, verifying her drunk binge last night.

"I didn't expect you to be here," he said.

"I told you I'd stay out of trouble. Last night I was feeling like trouble."

"What did you do?" He rubbed his forehead. He didn't have the patience to deal with her crap today.

"I called your girl. Who said you shouldn't drink and text? I get luckier than most that way."

"What?"

She moved across the apartment to the kitchen and began making a pot of coffee. "Not lucky like that, you pervert. I meant lucky in that I get what I want. She's here. Asleep in the other room."

Whatever irritation he'd been feeling toward Nikki disappeared. Audrey was here. She came back.

He checked the urge to run into the next room and climb into bed with her. *Just because she's back here doesn't mean she's back for me.*

Reining in his hope, he asked, "Is she okay?"

"I guess," Nikki said with a wave of her hand as she stared at the coffeemaker bubbling and dripping.

Nothing in Nikki's words gave him a clue about whether Audrey was here for the job or more.

Moments later, the front door opened again and Mia came in carrying a brown shopping bag containing the forgery for the next job. London was working fast.

Nikki groaned. "Please don't tell me you're moving in here, too."

"Too?" Mia asked.

Nikki pointed at the bag. As if Mia would pack her personal belongings in a paper bag.

"Audrey's here," Jared answered.

Mia pulled out the paper-wrapped package from the bag. Her expression softened when she looked at him in question. He shrugged.

She continued moving through the apartment and set the package on the table. "Believe me when I say I have no desire to live here. This is our next job."

Turning back to him, she said, "Can you get the information up on the screen so we can develop a plan?"

"Ugh. I have to think this early in the morning?" Nikki complained halfheartedly.

"It's almost noon. And by the looks of things, you already had breakfast."

Nikki gulped her coffee. "Actually, that was a late night/early morning snack. I'll go get Audrey."

Jared picked up Audrey's bag and set it beside the desk. It was heavier than usual. Was she planning on moving in? Nikki implied she was. But this one bag couldn't be everything she owned. He booted up the computer and opened the file on their next target.

Voices from the other end of the apartment caught his attention, but he tried to tune them out. Nikki returned and said Audrey was getting dressed and would be ready soon.

Mia cleaned up the mess on the table and then returned to stand by him. "Have you spoken to her?" she asked quietly.

"She came to my place last night upset that I paid for her grandmother's care."

"You did what?" Her voice remained quiet, but it held a sharp edge.

"I used my money, not the cash from the job. Her grandmother is in an assisted living facility. Audrey has been paying for her care. I think that was the only reason she finished the last job with us."

"It was," Nikki interrupted. "I mean, besides the joy of working with me."

"She was pissed because she thought I was leveraging her to come back."

"Sounds that way to me," Mia said.

"I did it so she had a choice. If she came back, I wanted it to be because she wanted to be here. Once I explained, things were better, but I still have no idea where we stand."

"I think we stand as a team," Audrey called from the other side of the room. She stood near the kitchen wearing black stretchy pants and a tank top. Her hair was damp and hung in waves around her face.

They all stared at her while she got a cup of coffee. When she turned back she said, "What?"

Nikki leaned over from her perch on the couch. "I think they're looking for some kind of explanation."

With a roll of her eyes and a huff, Audrey added, "I don't like the way you started this. But after hearing the entire plan, I can respect what you're doing." She sipped her coffee. "We *do* have the whole story now, right?"

"Yes. No more secrets," Jared said.

Audrey pinned him with a look that said she didn't quite believe him.

Mia clapped once. "Let's get started, then, shall we?" She walked over to the TV and pointed at the pictures on the screen. "This is Elijah Davis. He owns a Caffrey sculpture we're going to take."

Jared flipped to the next screen with an image of the white blob of a statue.

"What the hell is that supposed to be?" Audrey asked, echoing his own thoughts.

"The title of the sculpture is *Bondage Number Six*."

"So there are at least five other of those things out in the world?"

"Actually, it is one of a series of ten." Mia pointed at the screen. "The photo doesn't really do it justice."

She crossed the room and unwrapped the brown paper. Without any further explanation, she moved the statue to the center of the table. Nikki and Audrey neared and lowered their faces to inspect it. It was small enough to fit in one of their hands, slightly wider than a palm, and maybe six inches in length.

"I get it. Those are hands." Nikki pointed to the bottom. "And this is the rope binding them together. Caffrey was getting his kink on."

Audrey glanced at Jared and blushed.

"The artist was known to be adventurous in the art world as well as in the privacy of his home. He had a string of mistresses. In fact, if one managed to sleep with Caffrey even once, you gained instant celebrity. However, some believe he had a revolving door of women because he couldn't have the one he truly wanted—his sister-in-law."

"Look at you knowing all the gossip," Nikki joked.

"Mia's an art curator with the Art Institute. All of her degrees are art-related," Jared told them.

"So that's why we're stealing art."

"Not exactly," Mia said. "Yes, art is easy for me to see the value in and know the market for resale. We're stealing art because all of these men went on an art buying spree after our fathers made them richer. Our fathers put them up to the purchases."

"Although money is quick to make disappear, it's noticed immediately," he added. "We want to be able to fly under the radar."

Nikki turned back to the TV. "What's the plan?"

"Unfortunately, since we're moving up my original timeline, I don't have all of the information. Last time I saw the sculpture, Elijah had it in his den. I have no idea what the security situation is, but as he's having a party this weekend, I'll be able to get what you need."

"Party?" Nikki asked. "How big?"

Mia pressed her lips together. "Not too big. Knowing Elijah, probably around fifty guests."

Audrey huffed. "That's your idea of not big?"

"Compared to the galas he usually hosts, this is small."

"Is it catered?" Nikki asked.

"Of course."

"Then let's go in during the party."

"What?" Audrey and Mia asked simultaneously.

"The house will be full of strangers milling around. We'll have full access." She pointed at the sculpture. "The statue is ready to go. Why complicate things?"

Audrey set her cup on the table. "Walking into a house full of people milling around does make it complicated."

"Not if you're the help. No one notices the help."

Jared saw where Nikki was going and it seemed like a decent plan—if they could get Audrey and Mia to agree.

TWENTY-SEVEN

AUDREY SAT ON a chair at the table and stared at Jared and Mia, who appeared to be seriously entertaining Nikki's crazy idea. "Have you all lost your minds? What happened to get in and out undetected?"

"I'm telling you, no one will notice me," Nikki protested.

Jared rubbed a hand on his jaw and she could almost feel the scrape of those whiskers. "You made three trips to the Scott house. I think if we can be in and out in one, it's a good idea."

"It would definitely help with the timeline, if we don't have to do a fact-finding mission… How do you think you could do this?" Mia asked.

"I'll go in as one of the caterers. Or a maid. Wait for a good time to sneak into the room and make the swap. Then I leave."

"There are so many holes in that plan," Audrey pointed out. "First, assuming you can make the swap, how are you going to get the sculpture in the room? It's small, but it won't fit in your jeans pocket. Second, what if there's an alarm on it? Third, if you're supposed to be working, I'm pretty sure you'll draw attention to yourself if you disappear."

"But I'll be gone."

"Audrey has a point," Mia said. "It would be suspicious."

It felt weird having Mia agree with her. Audrey was so used to being on the receiving end of the woman's snarky looks. This new amiable side to Mia was a little unnerving.

"I'm irritated you all have so little faith in my ability to pull this off. I've stolen items off people in the middle of a conversation with them. People see what they want to see. No one wants to see the help."

"What if there's an alarm on it?" Audrey didn't like this level of risk. Sure, they'd gone to the Scott house multiple times, but never with a crowd of witnesses.

"That's what you're for."

"I can't go in blind and hope I can figure out a way to disarm it."

"Then you better get cracking on what they have. Mia wants to bump the timeline up and this is the best bet."

Audrey looked to Mia and Jared for help. They didn't appear to be willing to contradict anything Nikki said. She was on the losing end of this battle. "Fine. What information *do* we have?"

Nikki clapped. "Yes."

"I can find out who's catering so you can look the part," Mia said to Nikki. Turning to Audrey, she said, "You'll have to go shopping to find something appropriate to wear."

"Uh, won't I be dressed like a waiter, too?"

"I assumed you'd be going as Jared's date."

"Why would you assume that?" The question came out harsher than she'd intended.

Mia's mouth slipped open and then she snapped it shut without responding. Speechless was a new look on the woman.

Jared stepped forward. "I think what Mia was going for was the fact that, as you pointed out, having someone disappear in the middle of the shift might be suspicious, but having two take off? That will definitely cause concern."

"And you don't think it'll be suspicious to show up with some strange woman none of your society friends have ever met before?"

He chuckled.

"You really don't know him that well. I'd have thought that once you started digging into our lives, you would have continued." Mia paused with a smile on her face. "I don't think he's ever had the same woman as a date at any two parties. People more or less expect him to have someone new on his arm."

"Oh." Audrey tried to keep the hurt from her voice, but she couldn't help but wonder how many other women there had been in the weeks they'd known each other.

The amusement left Jared's face and he stared at her. "Can we go in the other room and talk?"

"We are talking."

"I'd like some privacy."

Reluctantly, Audrey stood and walked toward the bedroom. She'd expected this, had tried to prepare for it, but her stomach was in knots. He was going to ask where they stood, what their relationship would be, and she still didn't have an answer. She did, however, know that she had no desire to be one of a string of *dates* he had on his social calendar.

In the bedroom, she continued to stand since the only place to sit was the bed and that way lay temptation.

As Jared closed the door, Nikki yelled from the other room, "I expect you to remain fully clothed. No monkey business!" followed quickly by a quiet admonishment from Mia.

He leaned against the door and held his hands up before she even thought to say anything. "I'm not here to pressure you. If you want to be nothing more than colleagues, I was serious when I said I'd suck it up and learn to live with it." He looked so defeated, but then he pushed off the door and closed in on her. Staring intently into her eyes, he continued, "But know that's not at all what I want. I want to explore what we have together—or what we could have. No secrets and no lies. My family was my biggest and only secret. You know what I do for a living, where I live, why I'm doing what I'm doing here. Is there anything else you want to know?"

"How many others are there?"

"Other what?"

"Women. Mia said you go to these things with a different woman each time. How many have you been with since we slept together?" She hated that she sounded needy and wanted reassurance.

"None. I had one dinner date with a woman who's nothing more than a friend. I haven't slept with anyone else. I might be a jerk, but I wouldn't do that. I do have some honor."

"So I'm supposed to go to this party as your date

and then what? Next time, I watch you go with some-one else?"

A sound came from his throat, something like a growl that he swallowed back. "If that's what you want. But I'd like you to always be the woman on my arm. If you're not ready or willing, I have a work-around for that. I can easily introduce you as my new head of IT."

"I'd have to pretend to be your employee?"

"Not pretend. I want you to come work for me full time."

"What?" The surprises didn't stop with this guy.

"If you work at my company, no one will suspect anything when we're together. Socially, I admit, we'd cause some raised eyebrows. We don't exactly come from similar backgrounds. The single socialites will want to question any newcomer. Fodder for the rumor mill. But for me to hire a techie as a full-time employee is what people would expect. I can have you do most of the jobs I normally hire out and we can continue to work on the thefts as well. We make a great team."

For a moment her head spun. He wanted her to be with him. Not just in bed here. Not just for some fling. But *always*.

Nothing in her life had ever lent itself to stability. *Always* never entered the equation. For the first time, *always* sounded pretty damn good. She tried to wrap her head around the concept and landed on an analogy.

"You want me to be your Huck like in *Scandal*."

He looked puzzled for a minute until her reference clicked. "Not exactly. In that scenario, I would be Ol-ivia Pope."

"You *are* a fixer. And your wardrobe is pretty damn fancy." She smiled at the thought.

"I'm pretty sure they never slept together." He narrowed his eyes. "You need a better metaphor."

She thought about a more accurate comparison. "How about Felicity Smoak to your Oliver Queen?"

"Huh?" He stepped closer.

"You know... Felicity is a hacker-IT chick who loves Oliver Queen and then finds out he's Arrow? Like the comic book *Green Arrow*? Rich dude by day, superhero by night." *They fall madly in love.*

"Don't know it. But I like that you think of me as a superhero." His left eyebrow quirked up with his smirk, as he took a few steps closer still.

She rolled her eyes at his arrogance. "We really need to work on your pop culture knowledge."

"Is that a yes to my proposition?"

"Which one?" She was feeling a little out of breath with his nearness.

"All of them." He was now in touching distance.

She swallowed hard. When they were like this, alone in their own bubble, it was so easy. Her heart knew him even if her brain didn't have all the details.

He reached for her hand. "I know you have reservations, but you don't hate me. Although I kept things from you, you understand my reasons for doing so. All I'm asking for is a chance."

"We barely know each other," she whispered.

"But sometimes, you just feel it. It's right." He tugged her until she was in his arms. "Nothing else feels as perfect as this."

She couldn't argue. She loved the feeling of his arms around her. Closing her eyes, she said, "Okay."

He jolted and said, "Okay? As in you're going to give us another chance."

"Yes. If we don't leave this room soon, Nikki and Mia will think we're in here messing around," she said.

"So?"

"We have a heist to plan."

"Work, work, work. Is that all you think about?"

"No. I'm thinking about getting naked with you later."

"That's the best plan I've heard in a while." Taking her hand, he led her from the room.

In the living room, Nikki sat on the back of the couch and said, "Well? Are we happy or do I have to maim him?"

"We're good. Thanks," Audrey answered. And she realized she really was good. "Let's crash a party."

TWENTY-EIGHT

Mia

MIA'S HEAD SPUN. The thought of pulling off a heist while in Elijah's house with him home, party in full swing, was both nauseating and exhilarating. Listening to Nikki's plan made Mia realize the woman was, in fact, the best person for the job. Jared had made an excellent choice. With both her and Audrey.

While Nikki and Audrey ran through how to switch the sculptures, Mia was a little jealous. She didn't have people she clicked with the way they had. They'd only known each other for a few short weeks, but they talked like they'd been friends for years. While she had college friends and family acquaintances, she didn't have anyone she could count on other than Jared.

Does he have the same problem?

He regularly had women in his bed, but nothing lasted. She didn't know if it was by choice or circumstance. Looking at their mothers, it wasn't surprising. They didn't have many real friends either. At least not anymore. But now, with Audrey, that might change for him.

"What do you think, Mia?" Jared asked.

"I'm sorry, what?"

"What kind of distraction would be enough to draw everyone's attention so Nikki can do the swap?"

"Everyone loves a good fight." She looked pointedly between Jared and Audrey.

"You expect me to start a fight with him and have everyone looking at me? What if Nikki needs my help?"

"Audrey's right. She might need to follow Nikki. How about you?" he asked.

"Me? I don't fight," Mia said. "I certainly don't start one."

"You don't need to start a brawl. You have a way with words," Audrey said. "I'm sure you could make a few well-placed comments and set someone off. Who's the most hotheaded female in the jet set?"

"Miranda Roberts," she answered without thinking.

"That was fast. Spill the tea," Nikki added, chin in hand.

"Miranda finds fault with everyone and everything. She also believes every available woman—and even some that aren't available—are after her boyfriend. As if."

"Is he uuuugly?" Nikki asked.

"He's passable. Not very bright. Nor ambitious."

"I guess you better practice flexing your flirting muscles," Audrey said from her station behind the computer.

"What?"

"Look, if Miranda is the jealous type, and she's hot-tempered, your best bet is to make a play for what's-his-name. Miranda gets pissed off. You have words. Cause a scene. Nikki and I get in and out. Easy-peasy."

A stab of panic drove through the center of Mia's

chest. She abhorred being the center of attention. Especially in a negative light. Everything her father had done had brought so much shame and embarrassment that even now, she felt like people looked at her as if she might be carrying some horrendous disease. She preferred to make connections personally, one-on-one. "Why can't Jared start a fight?"

"I'm pretty sure no one would believe I'm making a play for Tyler."

"You know what I mean. Flirt with some woman and make her husband jealous."

"That's a no-go, cousin. I'll be there with Audrey as my date. I wouldn't disrespect her like that. You don't have a date."

Mia huffed in irritation. She was the boss, the brains behind this entire operation. She should not have to cause a commotion to draw attention. But he was right. She didn't have a date. She never had a date. Everyone knew she was damaged goods, good money but no good name.

At least for now. When she brought her father back and had him arrested, she would clear her own name and show the world she was nothing like him.

"Fine." She had to be willing to do the unthinkable to win. And win she would.

TWENTY-NINE

SUDDENLY, AUDREY WAS thrilled at the idea of going to some fancy party. She never thought Mia would agree to start a fight. And while the ice queen hadn't been too enthusiastic about the plan, she did agree. That alone might make it worth getting all dressed up.

Dressed up.

What the hell was she supposed to do for clothes? She didn't have anything in her dresser that even remotely looked like something Mia would wear. Damn. She was going to have to use some of her money to shop. That meant going into a store and trying things on.

"I have to go shopping," she blurted out.

Everyone turned to look at her.

"Awesome!" Nikki said. "Let's go. I could use a soft pretzel. And a warm chocolate chip cookie."

"What about this plan?" Mia asked.

Nikki pointed at her. "I have little doubt you need to practice insulting people. That's the totality of your part."

"Nikki and I will brainstorm while we're at the mall," Audrey added so Mia wouldn't think they were slacking.

"Mall?" Mia looked as if she might actually vomit. "Please, do us all a favor and go down Michigan Avenue. Something from Target or Old Navy is not appropriate attire for this party."

"Oooh…if we're on the Mag Mile, Garrett's Popcorn," Nikki said with reverence. "Want us to bring some back for you?"

"No." Mia picked up her purse. "Get what you need. I'll expect to do a run-through the day after tomorrow. Call if you need something before then."

"Will do." Nikki offered a half-assed salute and then went to her room to get ready, and Mia waved and left.

Audrey spun in her chair. Jared came over and leaned against the edge of the desk. "Do me a favor?"

"What?"

"Don't get something too sexy for this party."

"Why not?"

"Because I don't want to be completely distracted, and I certainly don't want any other man to get ideas."

She blushed. "So, designer potato sack?"

"That might cause Mia heart failure. Maybe something conservative? Don't let Nikki pick it out."

She laughed and rose to stand between his outstretched legs. "You're kind of cute when you're jealous."

With his hands on her hips, he pulled her snug. "It's not cute. I don't like thinking about some other man putting his hands on you."

"What would you have done if I hadn't agreed to giving us a second chance?"

"I'd walk around in a near-constant state of depression knowing I would never get to sleep with you again. And if I saw you with other men, they might disappear. For good."

"That took a dark turn."

He half shrugged. "I'm not a good loser."

As they spoke, their bodies pressed together. He lowered his mouth and took her in a possessive kiss. They became lost in each other.

"Really? I can't leave you alone for two minutes," Nikki said from across the room.

They separated, but Jared held her hand. "Come to my place when you're done shopping. Plan to spend the night."

"Okay."

He kissed her temple and left.

As they headed out the door, Nikki asked, "Are you really okay with him?"

"Yeah," she answered honestly. "He made some good arguments for giving us a second chance. And I like him."

Nikki snorted.

"What?"

"You way more than *like* him. The two of you are scarily head over heels. It's weird. I don't think I could ever fall in love with a mark or a client."

Love? Is that what this is?

The questions should have brought thundering panic in her chest. She didn't do love. Her mother had shown her all the pitfalls of falling for guys. The woman had a habit of falling for a new guy every few weeks. None of them stuck. She'd grown up knowing that men were unreliable. It never stopped her mom from trying. Tina believed true love was out there. Audrey never bought it because she'd seen the aftereffects. But somehow, the thought of loving Jared didn't totally suck. It was only a little scary.

"My mom once said real love wasn't something you could plan for. It just smacks you when you least expect it." *I guess Mom was right about something.*

"It'll be interesting. I'll give you that."

"How about you? Ever been in love?"

"Once. A long time ago."

"What happened?"

"We wanted different things."

That was all Nikki said as they got to the El stop to hop a train to get to the Magnificent Mile. A month ago, she couldn't have even imagined a day like this—one where she planned to spend an obscene amount of money for ridiculous clothes while shopping with a girlfriend before going to her boyfriend's house to spend the night.

Her life was suddenly very full of people and it was a surprisingly good thing.

For as long as it seemed Jared and Mia had been plotting and planning this revenge-esque scheme, these past few days were flowing in fast forward. Audrey was back in his life in every facet. They worked together at the apartment and spent the nights together at his place so they could have privacy. He wanted her to move out of her apartment—which he recently found out was just a room—because she was never there anyway. Although she forgave him for his earlier deception, she wasn't quite ready to commit to moving in.

It was fast considering they hadn't known each other

for long, but as he'd told her, when it was right, you knew it.

And at this moment, it felt perfect. Audrey was leaning against him on his couch. She'd put on some TV show about thieves and con artists he had no chance of following even though she'd done a rundown of each person and their role on the team. While she continued with her running commentary, he scrolled on his phone checking messages from people who might be interested in the Caffrey.

At the commercial break, she hit pause and turned her head to look up at him. "Really? Can't world domination wait until tomorrow? We're supposed to be relaxing."

"I'm looking for our next buyer."

"You've spent enough time on the dark web that you should know the easiest way to handle this is an auction."

He had thought about it. "An auction opens the door to a lot of people knowing about the transaction. I don't think most of our targets have any clue what the dark web is or how to reach it, but I can't take that chance."

She pushed up to sitting and reached across him for her laptop on the table. "You can do an invitation-only auction. Kind of like a secret club. If they don't have the password—and you can create a unique one for each invite—they don't get in."

He mulled that over while she typed away on her computer. He hadn't considered such a process, simply because he liked to deal with individuals, but if an auction could speed things along...

Audrey clicked through pages and showed him a few different auctions, some of which were quite disturbing.

"How is this not monitored by the authorities?" he asked, even though he was aware of the answer.

"Make no mistake. They're there. Plenty of traps waiting to catch the bad guys, but they can't be every-where all the time. And really, are they going to bother with someone like me when they can go after the dudes who are in the process of auctioning off some young girl's virginity?"

"Probably not. It's still a risk, though."

"Everything we do is risky. That's what happens when you play in the shadows."

He stroked his fingers down her cheek. "Have you ever thought about what would happen to you if you were caught?"

She lifted a shoulder carelessly. "Not really. When I was younger and doing small jobs, I figured the stuff I did didn't matter. Then as I got better and took more chances, the thought occasionally crossed my mind. But it's all I have, all I know. Besides, no one would miss me if I disappeared."

His heart broke for her, not just because the state-ment itself was so sad, but because she truly believed it. "Your grandmother would miss you."

"Pretty soon she won't be able to remember me at all."

He wanted to tell her it would all be okay, but that was a lie. He also wanted to meet the woman who raised Audrey to be so amazing. "Then I guess it's a good thing we met because now you have me to miss you. I'll have to make sure you stay out of trouble."

She laughed at that. "I'm pretty good at keeping myself out of trouble and if I need some advice, I think Nikki would know what to do."

"That hurts. You think I couldn't get you out of a jam?"

She closed her computer and turned to climb into his lap. With a small sigh, she said, "I believe you would do everything in your power to help me, even if I was a lost cause." Lowering her lips to his, she kissed him softly. "I've never had that before. Someone willing to go the distance."

"We'll go the distance together." He pulled her snug against him and let his kiss show her how much he loved her.

When they separated, she remained close and rested her cheek on his shoulder. "What happens when all the heists are done?" she whispered.

"What do you mean?"

"The heists brought us together. They're our purpose. What happens to us when we don't have that purpose?"

"Look at me." He waited until she shifted to look him in the eye. "What we have is no longer just a financial work arrangement. I know you know that. When the jobs are done, we'll still be together. I just said we're going the distance."

She stared at him and he realized she had doubts about his feelings. As if he would toss her aside when the job was done. He reached up and held her face.

"I need you to pay attention and really listen to me."

"I am."

"I love you. What started as a playful flirtation with some woman I met in a chat room has become everything to me. I have to finish this with Mia, but after that, we can do whatever you want. You want to continue hacking and working with me, we'll do it. If you want to pick up and move somewhere to start a new life, my bags will be packed. I'm not going anywhere without you."

Her expression softened and went from caution and wariness to something more.

"You love me."

Although she said it, the question was implied, as if she needed to make sure she hadn't been mistaken.

"Yes, I love you. I'm in love with you. I want to spend my life with you."

"Whoa." She inched back.

He'd known the words would freak her out, which was why he hadn't said them yet, but she needed to hear them.

Tucking a lock of hair behind her ear, he said it again. "I love you."

She swallowed and licked her lips. "I think I love you, too."

He hadn't expected to hear it in return, but his heart swelled with her declaration.

"Now take me to bed," she said playfully. "Tomorrow we go back to hacker and fixer. Tonight, we can just be two people in love."

THIRTY

SATURDAY NIGHT, JARED was dressed for the party but his nerves were wrecked. As much as he'd wanted to bring Audrey as his date, part of him worried about pulling off the switch in the middle of a social function. Nikki was good, but they'd run into so many problems with the first theft, he feared they might face the same issues this time.

The women, however, were convinced they had everything under control. In truth, their trial run had gone smoothly. But that was without a crowd of people and prying eyes.

Instead of having a car drive them, as Mia was doing, Jared drove to the apartment to pick up Audrey. He'd wanted her to get ready at his place, where she'd been spending most nights, but she insisted she needed Nikki's help getting dressed.

What she probably meant was that she needed Nikki to talk her down. She'd been nothing short of a ball of nerves since they hatched this plan. He was pretty sure it was being his date, not the theft, causing her the most grief.

He smiled as he pulled into a parking spot near the apartment. She did her best to stay in the shadows, to go unnoticed, and the thought of being scrutinized because she was his date bothered her. But she could hold her own.

He let himself into the apartment. "Audrey?"

"Coming."

He waited in the living room and when she emerged from the hall, he lost the ability to think coherently. She wore a simple black dress with a skirt that flared out from her hips. The neckline plunged deep.

"What do you think?" she asked and he noticed her hands fidgeting.

"You're gorgeous." His gaze roamed her body and landed on her made-up face. She never wore much makeup, if any, so this look was different. It was a glamorous version of Audrey. Her eyes were smoky and her lips glossy red.

Pink rose in her cheeks. "Thank you. But the best part is this. Check it out." She thrust her hands at her sides. "It has pockets!"

"I had no idea pockets were so exciting." He chuckled.

"Spoken like a man. Women's clothes do not have real pockets. But with these, I can carry a scrambler."

He stepped close. "What was your plan if there were no pockets?"

"Strap it to my thigh."

Taking her hand, he led her outside. "Did Nikki get there on time?"

"Yes. Everything's going as planned. As long as Mia does her thing, and there's no alarm on the statue, we'll be all right."

In the car on the way to the party, he talked to her about a couple of jobs he had going that he wanted her help with. One of his semi-regular clients needed to get an audience with a congressman or two. A new client wanted him to dig up some dirt on his competition for the next election. The eighth ward alderman race looked to be a hot one this time around as the incumbent was finally retiring.

"You were serious about hiring me full time?"

"Why would you think I wasn't?"

"I'm pretty sure that breaks all of Mia's rules. When she hired me, she got all huffy about me working at the coffee shop."

"Don't worry about Mia."

"Plus, I don't know if I want to work for you. I kind of like being my own boss. I choose the clients I take on and the work I'm willing to do."

He hadn't considered she might decline his offer. He also hadn't thought about the ramifications for her as his employee. "So you decide."

"Huh?"

"If I ask you to work for a client you don't like or do a job that doesn't suit you, you can refuse."

She huffed a little laugh. "I don't think you fully understand what it means for someone to be your employee. By definition, I should do whatever you tell me to do."

"If only," he said with a wicked grin.

"You're awful."

"We can create our own definition of what we are and what we do. As long as you're with me, the rest doesn't matter."

He pulled into the gated driveway and Audrey's jaw dropped.

"Rich people are unbelievable."

"Stick with me and you'll be one of the rich people."

"Not so sure that will ever be me, regardless of how much money I've socked away."

He put the car in park and left the keys in the ignition. He met Audrey on the other side of the vehicle as a valet got behind the wheel.

Lowering his head, he whispered, "Generally, a woman waits for her date to open the door for her."

"As if I'm incapable of opening a door?" She snorted. "Like I said, I'll never belong."

He took her arm, looped it through his, and led her into the house. They barely made it through the foyer when Carolyn swept up to them.

"Jared. I'm so glad you're here." She air-kissed his cheek and added, "Mia said you were bringing someone new."

"Carolyn, this is my girlfriend, Audrey."

Carolyn's whole face brightened at the mention of girlfriend. Audrey, on the other hand, froze. Her hand tightened on his forearm.

Carolyn extended a hand. "It's so nice to meet you. What do you do for a living?"

"I'm in IT." She blinked rapidly. "In fact, I work for Jared. Head of his IT department."

"Oh," Carolyn said with a sigh. "A workplace romance."

"I guess," Audrey said.

"If you'll excuse us, Carolyn, I'd like to grab a drink and make the rounds."

"Save a spot for me at your table. I want to get to know you better," she said to Audrey.

After Carolyn left, Audrey gripped his arm. "I thought you were introducing me as your IT gal. Where the hell did that come from?"

"It's the truth. We agreed no more lies."

"That's between us. I'm totally okay lying to all these jerks," she muttered.

He turned and looked into her eyes. "What's the problem?"

"I don't belong with these people. They can smell it on me."

"You belong wherever I am. Come on." He took her hand and led her through the room, stopping to introduce her to everyone he knew by name and a few he didn't. There was no way he was going to let this brilliant woman feel inadequate in his presence. With every introduction, he proudly announced their relationship status.

By the fifth handshake, she seemed to accept he wasn't changing his tune.

AUDREY WAS OVERWHELMED. She hadn't expected Jared to tell everyone they were a couple. He acted as if these people had no choice but to accept their relationship, like if they rejected her, he would force them to reconsider. It sent relief through her entire body.

The only other person she could remember accepting her unconditionally like that was Gram.

She waited for the comments or the snickers behind her back, but they didn't come. When Jared stepped away to get them drinks, she scoped out the room. She looked for cameras and motion sensors. So far, cameras all appeared to be external. They had some not-so-discreet security keeping guests from roaming the entire property.

With this many people in attendance, it didn't appear as though the alarm was set, especially with security on site. If it weren't for the security, Audrey would've assumed they'd simply bypassed part of the house and left the alarm armed for the rest.

"What are you looking at?" Nikki's voice sounded in her ear.

Audrey raised her glass as if to drink and muttered, "Don't talk to me. It's distracting. I'm looking for cameras and motion sensors."

"People have opened and closed every door in the place, so I don't think sensors are an issue. One camera in the hall outside the office."

Suddenly, a tray was thrust at her. With a smile, Nikki asked, "Hors d'oeuvre?"

"Thank you." Audrey picked up a cracker with something on it she had no intention of eating.

"The only problem we might encounter is if there's a trip on the statue."

Audrey nodded.

"Have you seen Mia?" Nikki asked.

"No, but I haven't been looking for her."

"I'll make my rounds and find her, make sure she's ready to brawl."

Audrey nearly choked on her laugh. Mia was far from a brawler. Audrey couldn't imagine her breaking a nail much less throwing a punch. Although she found it easier to picture the punch than say, hair pulling. Something about Mia made Audrey think the woman would fight dirty. Nikki winked and moved through the room offering food to guests.

Jared returned to her side and Audrey handed him the cracker.

He popped it in his mouth and she cringed.

"What was that?" she asked.

He shrugged.

"You just eat things without knowing what it is?" She barely repressed a shudder.

"I'm hungry." With a quick glance over his shoulder, he said, "Everything ready?"

"Nikki said she can get into the room. She won't know until she gets there if the alarm is rigged to the statue. She's going to look for Mia now."

"Have I told you yet how sexy you are?"

Heat crept over her face. In her ear, Nikki said, "I don't need to be a voyeur tonight. Remind him I can hear what he's saying."

"I can hear you, too, Nikki. I just don't care if I have privacy."

Audrey rolled her eyes. "I care. So stop it."

"Mia says she's ready to go," Nikki said from across the room.

Jared took Audrey's hand and kissed her cheek. Whispering in her ear, he said, "I guess it's time for you to go powder your nose to be close to Nikki. In and out. Something's not right, bail."

"Yes, Dad," Nikki responded.

But they all knew Nikki had no intention of bailing on anything. If something went wrong, it would make it more exciting for her and she'd forge ahead.

Jared gave Audrey's hand a quick squeeze and she

was amazed at how much comfort the small gesture gave her. She moved slowly through the room. From the corner of her eye, Audrey saw Mia talking to some dude, then throw her head back in a ridiculous, over-the-top flirtatious laugh.

Hmm... I never would have thought Mia would be so good at this. Audrey hadn't given the woman enough credit.

Audrey stopped in the hall near the washroom, two doors down from Davis's office. An older woman left the bathroom and nodded to her to acknowledge it was free. Instead, Audrey continued to study the paintings and photographs on the walls. What held her attention most was the camera up in the corner.

"I'm at the camera in the hall," she said into her comm.

"And?" Nikki asked.

Audrey rolled her eyes even though no one could see her. "I'll need a few minutes to hack in and put it on a loop."

She felt the tension shift in the room behind her before she heard anything. It was as if anger sucked the oxygen from the area.

She had to move fast to get the camera under control. Moving to the corner below the camera, which would be a convenient blind spot, she pulled out her phone. She had her jammer, but if she scrambled the signal and the cameras were actually being monitored, they wouldn't have any time to make the swap. A loop was their best bet.

A moment later, she heard a barely restrained voice. "I'm sorry you can't get a man of your own, Mia, but to stoop to flirting with mine is sad."

It was said loud enough obviously for others to hear and Audrey had no doubt it was intentional. She couldn't hear Mia's response, but from the corner of her eye, she saw the crowd shift, probably to get a better view. Audrey typed furiously, desperate to get the loop in place so Nikki could take full advantage of the distraction in the other room. Without the loop, their risk increased at least twofold.

THIRTY-ONE

Mia

MIA GRITTED HER TEETH. Flirting with a dullard like Tyler had nauseated her, but having Miranda accuse her of not being able to get a man was infuriating. Partially because it hit close to home, but mostly because it had come from Miranda.

She leaned closer to Miranda. The woman's cloying perfume filled her nose. Lowering her voice, she said, "If I wanted to take Tyler from you, we both know I could. It wouldn't even be all that difficult."

"What's that supposed to mean?" Miranda asked.

"Look at what you have to offer." She wagged her fingers at Miranda's designer dress as if it had come from a thrift store. "And what I bring to the table."

Miranda's face flushed and a small crowd not only gathered but began to close in on them. Damn vultures. Every last one.

Mia's stomach flipped. The scene was reminiscent of everything that had happened after their fathers fled. The flying accusations, the hushed tones, the dirty looks. The difference this time was that Mia could defend herself. She was stronger than they gave her credit for.

After a deep inhale and pulling herself up to her

full height, which was easily five or six inches taller than Mia, Miranda spoke clearly. "We both have family money and education. We grew up in the same circles. The difference between us is that I still have a good name and the respect of my peers. Respect you'll never have."

Mia clenched her fists to prevent herself from slapping Miranda. The words were bad enough but the fact that she spoke loudly to enable everyone to hear just to embarrass her was unforgivable.

"This is a party. A simple social function. I have no idea why you insist on slinging these slurs," Mia added, instead of hurling more insults of her own. The crowd around them was growing and she hated this negative attention. Despite what Miranda said, Mia had worked hard to regain the trust and respect of her peers.

"If you're so interested in *socializing*, find a single man. I'm sure there are some around here." The woman looked around as if searching, but Mia knew she was really playing up for the audience.

"Insecurity does not look good on you. Tyler asked about my work—you know, my *career* as museum curator—" Mia knew that little dig would bother Miranda because she longed to be seen as more than a socialite, even though that was exactly who she was "—and after I answered his question, he made a joke. It would have been rude not to laugh."

"I am more than aware of how funny and entertaining my boyfriend can be. However, when I see the ice queen laughing like a giddy schoolgirl, I know she's up to something."

"I'm just trying to enjoy my evening. Why don't you do the same?" Mia hoped Nikki and Audrey were almost finished. She had no idea how much longer she could extend this charade. Never in her life had she fought over a man, much less a boy like Tyler.

A passing waiter held a tray of champagne and Mia grabbed a fresh drink. Her skin was warm from being the center of attention and her throat was dry. After taking a quick sip, she accepted the altercation with Miranda was finished and she turned to walk away. Save what dignity she had left.

"Where do you think you're going?" Miranda gasped. "Running from the consequences of your actions like your father?"

Without thinking, Mia spun and tossed the bubbly, gold liquid from her flute, splashing it into Miranda's face. Her muscles locked with anger. "I don't run, Miranda. Nor am I anything like my father. I simply do not feel the need to waste my time and breath on anything so inconsequential."

"You bitch!" Miranda yelped.

A warm hand gripped her elbow and as she was about to yank away, she realized Jared held her arm. His free hand thrust forward and gave Miranda some napkins. A waiter followed with more and offered to escort her to the washroom to freshen up.

Jared led Mia away from the pack of onlookers. "Good job, cousin. I think every pair of available eyes was on you."

She didn't respond. Her stomach was in knots and

anger flooded her system. Of course, that was the exact moment their esteemed host, Elijah, decided to join them.

"Is everything all right?" he asked.

"Everything is fine," Jared answered. "Mia and Miranda had words."

"It looks like more than just words to me."

"I'm sorry, Elijah. Miranda said some upsetting things and I reacted poorly. It won't happen again."

"Maybe you two should head out. I'm sure you've given the gossip hounds enough to chatter about already." Elijah leaned forward, squeezed Mia's hand and brushed a kiss on her cheek. "I know things have been hard."

What was that supposed to mean? She supposed the acknowledgment was meant to convey sympathy, but he failed. As if his words could soften the effects of her father's crimes.

Just as she was about to let Elijah know exactly what he could do with his feigned concern, Jared said, "Thank you for your understanding. I'll go find my date and we'll be on our way."

He pressed a hand to Mia's back to move her along, and it took all of her willpower to not stand her ground. *The plan. Think of the plan. They had too many more men to go after to allow this one to ruin it.*

"I'm fine," she muttered as they walked away. "I'll wait by the door."

"You, my dear, are more than fine. Your performance was stellar," he whispered before taking off to find Audrey.

Her blood was still running hot. She didn't know how

much of that was performance. Miranda's words had struck a chord and she'd reacted. She'd wanted to lash out at every last one of them for the way they'd treated her for years. Closing her eyes, she centered herself.

Once I make this right, they'll all see.

THIRTY-TWO

CARRYING AN EMPTY TRAY, Nikki walked past the corridor where Audrey was working. Audrey held up a single finger to signal her progress. Audrey tapped the last couple of keys to offer an image of an empty hallway for anyone who might be sitting in front of a security monitor as Miranda raised her voice to yelling. *Yep, Mia pissed her off. She's definitely good at that.*

Nikki hastened back toward her and they snuck into the office. Nikki set her tray on the desk and turned on a small flashlight. She swept the light across the room. The beam caught on the white blob on the bookshelf behind the desk.

They walked around the desk and checked for wires or triggers around the sculpture. To be safe, Audrey turned on the scrambler, so that if they did trip the alarm, they would have a few extra minutes to get out.

Nikki pulled the counterfeit from inside her pants.

"How the hell did you fit that in there?"

With a snicker, Nikki said, "I had it in my bag. I tucked it in here on my last pass through the kitchen. As long as I have a tray in front of me, no one notices the bulge." She made the swap seamlessly.

"See? You didn't even need me," Audrey said.

"Wrong. You have the camera on loop so no one will know I was here. That's priceless."

In their ears, Jared said, "Move it along, ladies. Mia is going to be escorted out."

They headed back out into the hall. As soon as Nikki pulled the door closed behind them, a security guard was headed their way. Audrey froze. Damn it. They were caught. Nikki held the tray protectively in front of her.

Audrey doubled over and moaned.

The man asked, "What are you doing here?"

Audrey waved a hand. "I'm sorry. I'm not feeling well. Must've been something in the food."

Without missing a beat, Nikki said, "When I saw her going into this room, I went to check. She missed the bathroom. I'm helping her get there."

With an arm around Audrey's shoulder, Nikki guided her down the hall to the bathroom as the guard opened the office door and stuck his head in. Audrey keyed in the information to stop the loop of the camera. Hopefully, no one would notice. The man backed away without any comment.

"Is there anything else I can help with, ma'am?" Nikki asked sweetly and a little too loudly.

"I'm fine. Thanks." She moved to close the door, but Nikki slapped her palm against the wood. Reaching in her pants, she removed the statue. "Take this."

"What? What am I supposed to do with that? I don't even have a purse."

"I don't know. Dude's suspicious now. He'll probably search me on the way out." She pointed to Audrey's skirt. "You have enough room. Tape it to your leg."

Audrey sighed and closed the door. After engaging the lock, she opened the drawers below the sink. A supply of feminine products, extra toilet paper, cleaning supplies. "Tape it to my leg. With what? What kind of stupid idea is that?"

"Everything okay?" Jared asked quietly in her ear.

"Oh, just swell. Nikki shoved me in the bathroom with this thing and told me to hide it. As if I know anything about hiding evidence."

"Take a breath. You're creative. You got this."

She inhaled deeply. He was right. She could handle this. She opened the medicine cabinet and found a first aid kit. Bingo. A small roll of medical tape sat in the little metal box. After she wrapped the statue in a layer of toilet paper, she ran tape around her entire thigh. Twice.

She let her skirt fall back into place and twirled. "Damn if she wasn't right," she muttered.

A knock at the door startled her. "Honey, are you all right?"

Jared had come to rescue her.

"I'm fine. Not feeling quite myself. I'd like to leave." She opened the door.

He smiled and held out a hand. As they made their way to the front door, Jared made excuses for them and nodded toward Mia. No one would question why they were leaving.

Audrey's blood raced and her heart thundered in her ears. Adrenaline pumped through every muscle. It took all she had not to start running. Her skin felt clammy and she wondered if Jared noticed.

The valet brought the car to the bottom of the steps and held the doors open for Mia and Audrey. Audrey almost went to the back seat and realized she should be in front with Jared.

Once the doors were closed and Jared put the car in gear, Mia said, "I certainly hope you made the switch because that was mortifying."

Audrey lifted her skirt and Jared swerved on the road.

"Mind out of the gutter. I'm not flashing you." She yanked the tape from her skin, leaving red stripes in its wake, and passed the wrapped figure to Mia.

"Why do you have it?"

"Nikki and I were interrupted on our way out of the office. She thought it would be better if I took it."

"Looks like she was right," Jared said.

AUDREY SAT IN the passenger seat tempting him all the way back to the apartment. She hadn't readjusted her skirt, so he saw the fleshy part of her thighs. He wanted to reach out and caress her skin, especially the abraded section from the tape, but he refrained.

He parked in front of the apartment building. Mia tucked the sculpture under her arm and eased from the back seat. When he came around the car, Audrey was still sitting with the door closed. He opened it for her.

"See? I can follow directions. Still seems incredibly dumb for me to sit there and wait on you when I could be hustling up the sidewalk like Mia, but whatever."

He couldn't help but smile at her snarkiness. He lowered his mouth to hers and kissed her.

She shivered.

"Is my kiss that good, or are you cold?"

"Your kiss is definitely that good, but I think I'm coming down from the adrenaline rush."

He wrapped his arm over her shoulder and followed

Mia up the walk. Inside the apartment, Nikki said, "About time."

"How the hell did you get here so fast?" he asked.

"I bugged out as soon as Audrey had the statue." She held up a hand. "Don't worry. I didn't just disappear. I screwed up and got fired."

"Why would you do that?" Audrey asked.

"Security escorted me out. Searched me before letting me go."

Jared smiled at the simple brilliance.

"Poor Amy Van Cleis, though, will never work in catering again," Nikki added, referring to the alias she'd used to get the job.

"That was some fast thinking." With a nod to Audrey, he added, "Both of you."

But Audrey zoned out on the couch. She rubbed her arms. The adrenaline crash was hitting her hard.

"Let's get you home." He removed his suit jacket and draped it over her shoulders.

She burrowed into it. "I don't want to go home."

"I meant my home."

"Oh," she said, her eyes going soft. "Don't we have to debrief or something?"

"It'll keep until tomorrow. We're going to leave," he said to Mia and Nikki, who were inspecting the sculpture.

"What about food?" Nikki asked. "I'm starving."

"You're always starving," Audrey said.

"She has a point," he said. "We left before dinner was served. Food might help you feel better."

"I'm fine," Audrey said.

"Pasta," Nikki said emphatically. "We can all use a good carb overload."

Before anyone else offered a different suggestion, Nikki had her phone out and was ordering with the Italian place a block down. Then she went to the fridge and brought out drinks. Handing Audrey a beer, she said, "You were amazing tonight. You distracted that guard so fast, I almost didn't even know what you were doing. With a little practice, you would be an excellent grifter."

Jared sat beside Audrey.

"Thanks. I think," Audrey replied sleepily. She clinked bottles with Nikki. "I don't think I would've been that brave if it hadn't been for you. You're calm and cool no matter what's going on." She sipped her beer. "But you can keep the thieving. I'll stick behind my computer where I can hide from everyone."

She sank down and nestled against him and Jared thought it was one of the best feelings in the world.

The two women began to recap how things had happened in the office. Then they wanted to know what Mia had done to Miranda. Mia didn't like the way Jared relayed the story, so she jumped in to correct him and tell her version.

When the food arrived and he carried in the bags, he took in the sight before him. These three women were fast becoming the most important people in his life. They'd become a team and he liked everything about that.

And when Audrey tilted her face and smiled up at him, he knew it didn't matter how successful they were at art heists, no treasure would top having her in his life.

He set the food on the table, took her hand, and whispered in her ear, "I'm glad you're back."

"I'm glad I'm back, too."

He kissed her again to let her know he loved her, even though he didn't say the words. Saying it might freak her out—again—but he could let her feel it.

When they broke the kiss, he leaned his forehead against hers.

"Stop the making out," Nikki said as she shoved a forkful of pasta in her mouth. "We have a crap ton of heists to plan. Who's next?"

THIRTY-THREE

Mia

MIA LOOKED AT her cousin sitting on a couch with two women who normally would never have come into their lives. But something about them made Mia want to trust them. Maybe it was because they'd come through. Maybe it was the ease with which they worked together. They'd become quick friends and Mia still felt like an outsider. It should have bothered her more than it did, but this was the norm for her.

She might not be friends with them, but she believed she had their loyalty. And that was without manipulation. Maybe her father wasn't right after all.

"Taylor Rivers will be our next. It's party season and we have functions most weeks." She used the remote to pull up a picture of the metal sculpture she wanted.

Nikki and Jared began to develop a plan. While they plotted, she tapped Audrey on the shoulder. The woman appeared utterly exhausted, but Mia beckoned her to the other side of the room.

As Nikki and Jared bantered like siblings, Audrey followed her to the desk. "What did you need?" she asked.

"How difficult would it be for you to set up a proxy

server so I could make anonymous payments and not be detected?"

"Not long at all since I have one running for this computer."

"I need you to set up a shell to handle the extra finances." She scribbled on the notepad beside Audrey. "The Stokes family has twins who got into Northwestern, but financial aid isn't covering what they need. I want a direct full-ride scholarship for both of them."

A wicked little grin danced across Audrey's mouth. "Let's do this."

And just like that, for at least a brief moment, Mia felt like she was part of a team.

Audrey did her thing and Mia watched with a smile. This made the stress and anxiety worth it.

When it was out in the world, she and Audrey joined Jared and Nikki again, who had moved on from talking about the next heist and on to whether they thought Mia could've taken Miranda in a physical altercation.

"I don't know," Nikki said. "Miranda was a lot of bluster."

Audrey nodded. "Mia could've handled her, though."

Mia raised her glass. "Damn right I would have."

MONDAY MORNING, MIA stared at the list of twelve names, loving being able to cross them off one by one. Soon Taylor Rivers would also be marked.

After the first heist at Randall Scott's house, which had been nothing short of a caper worthy of the Muppets, their band of criminals had come together to function as a team. Once they gave Nikki and Audrey all the information, the women were running point on planning and they found a rhythm that allowed them to plan multiple heists at once, enabling them to move faster. In between planning the heists, Audrey had been searching for all of the victims.

And now the information in her file had grown. For every theft they completed, she would add to the list of people who benefitted.

The Stokes twins had their full-ride scholarships.

The Longs' mortgage would be paid off by a Good Samaritan.

The Chens' medical bills would be taken care of, so they could focus on spending time with their father who was recovering from his battle with cancer.

She tucked the list of names behind the painting above her fireplace mantel. Soon, they will have taken millions from her father's friends, and with any luck, effectively forced her father and Jared's father out of hiding. According to the last report from the detective they'd hired, their fathers were still in Montenegro, but in her gut, she believed they were readying to move again, surely to another country with no extradition treaty. The only way to stop them would be to cut off all of their finances.

Without money, how much longer could they run?

Her phone rang and her heart stuttered when she saw the name on the screen: Randall Scott. It was as if her thoughts had conjured him.

"Hello?" she asked, keeping her voice smooth and calm.

"Mia?"

"Yes."

"It's Randall Scott. I need a favor."

"What kind of favor could I do for you?" The man had to be desperate to come to her.

"I need your expertise in art. I have a Mathis painting that I planned to sell."

"The one that used to hang above the stairs?"

"Yes. Anyway, as usual, the insurance company requires an inspection. Their appraiser is trying to tell me that my painting is a forgery."

"Oh my goodness. I'm sorry to hear it. What can I do?" Giddiness rose in her chest. This was what she'd wanted. Randall Scott in a panic, knowing he'd been had. The only thing that could make this moment better was if she could divulge that she was behind the forgery. She wanted to make sure he would no longer funnel cash to her father.

"It can't be. I bought the painting with complete papers. It has to be a mistake. Can you come over and take a look? Explain how they're wrong."

Bile rose at the thought of actually helping this despicable man. "I can do that. I mean, modern art isn't my area of expertise, but I am familiar with the artist and his body of work." She had done extensive homework on every piece of art they planned to steal.

"Thank you. I appreciate it. Your father always said what a good girl you are."

The muscle in her jaw twitched as she tried to rein in her temper. "Don't thank me just yet, Mr. Scott. If it turns out to be a forgery, I can't lie."

"It's the real deal. They hired someone incompetent. I just need to create enough doubt to make them reassess."

"When would you like me to come over?"

"Do you have time today? I already have a buyer in place, and if word gets out that the deal fell through because of suspicion of counterfeit, my reputation will be shot."

And I should care about his reputation? No one cared about mine after my father fled the country. "I can be there within a couple hours."

She disconnected and a rush of pleasure raced through her. She grabbed her things and headed to the north suburbs to witness the beginning of the end for her father.

* * * * *

ACKNOWLEDGMENTS

THE IDEA FOR this series has been nothing more than a scribbled note in a book for years because I really wanted to write it, but I was afraid I wouldn't be able to pull it off. Thanks to my pals from the Sunday night Panera supper club, I decided to go for it. And it has been a blast. My writer friends were there to brainstorm and offer advice and read early drafts and poke and prod me to get it done. These books wouldn't exist without their encouragement.

And thank you to my editor, Deb Nemeth, who fell in love with my crew of criminals who take a stab at being heroes. I'm so happy Carina was willing to take a chance on this slightly unconventional series.

ABOUT THE AUTHOR

SLOANE STEELE IS the pen name for Shannyn Schroeder. Shannyn is a part-time English teacher, part-time curriculum editor, and full-time mom, even though her kids are pretty self-sufficient teens. In her downtime, she bakes cookies, reads romance, and watches far too much TV.

If you want to connect with Sloane (and Shannyn):
www.SloaneSteele.com.

Sign up for her newsletter here:
https://www.subscribepage.com/sloanesteele.

https://twitter.com/SSchroeder_

https://www.facebook.com/shannyn.schroeder/

Get 4 FREE REWARDS!

We'll send you 2 FREE Books plus 2 FREE Mystery Gifts.

Harlequin Intrigue books are action-packed stories that will keep you on the edge of your seat. Solve the crime and deliver justice at all costs.

FREE Value Over $20

Visit
ReaderService.com
Today!

As a valued member of the Harlequin Reader Service, you'll find these benefits and more at ReaderService.com:

- Try 2 free books from any series
- Access risk-free special offers
- View your account history & manage payments
- Browse the latest Bonus Bucks catalog

Don't miss out!

If you want to stay up-to-date on the latest at the Harlequin Reader Service and enjoy more content, make sure you've signed up for our monthly News & Notes email newsletter. Sign up online at ReaderService.com or by calling Customer Service at 1-800-873-8635.

RS20